PARADOX
LAKE

PARADOX LAKE

A THRILLER

VINCENT ZANDRI

OCEANVIEW ◖ PUBLISHING
SARASOTA, FLORIDA

ISBN 978-1-60809-498-1

Published in the United States of America by Oceanview Publishing

Sarasota, Florida

www.oceanviewpub.com

10 9 8 7 6 5 4 3 2

PRINTED IN THE UNITED STATES OF AMERICA

"She did not know that the wolf was a wicked sort of animal, and she was not afraid of him."
—LITTLE RED RIDING HOOD

"Monsters are real, and ghosts are real too. They live inside us, and sometimes, they win."
—STEPHEN KING

PROLOGUE

THE STOCKY MAN drops to his knees before the prison chaplain.

"Do you believe in the Lord and savior, Jesus Christ, Theodore?" Father Sean O'Connor asks. "Do you repent all your sins? Do you seek Christ's forgiveness for what you did to that little girl all those years ago?"

The short, stocky, bald man brings his hands together like he's about to pray. He might be focusing his blue eyes up at the concrete ceiling, but it's more like he's gazing upon heaven itself.

What big eyes you have.
The better to see you with.
What big hands you have.
The better to grab you with.
What big teeth you have.
The better to eat you with.

Theodore smiles.

"You know how sorry I am, Father," he says, in his high-pitched voice. "I was just a boy then. A confused little boy. I've paid for my sins and I believe the good Lord above has forgiven me. Those people on the TV news, they called me the Wolf because of the things I did to Sarah Anne Moore. But I'm not the Wolf anymore.

I'm just a man who is sorry for his sins. I'm ready to begin again and live in the likeness of our Lord and savior, Jesus Christ."

"Are you truly ready to become a healthy, productive member of society, Theodore? A respected man?"

"Just said I was, Father," Theodore says. "The parole board believes it too. I'm ready to leave this place."

"It's a different world out there now, Theodore," O'Connor goes on. "It's not like it was back in 1986. You might not recognize what you see. It might frighten you."

"The Lord will protect me, Father."

"I believe he will, Theodore, so long as you follow the straight and narrow."

The light from the newly risen sun shines into the prison chapel through the stained-glass windows. The red, yellow, and blue beam reflects off the concrete floor. It washes over Theodore "The Wolf" Peasley's body, making it appear as if he's glowing in the grace of God.

Maybe he's right, O'Connor thinks. *Maybe this man has paid for his sins these past thirty-three years. Maybe he is ready to be free.*

Theodore turns to the chaplain, looks up into his eyes.

"Will you pray with me, Father?"

"Yes, my son," the priest says while gently lowering himself to his knees.

Both men make the sign of the cross and begin to recite the Lord's Prayer. When they are finished, they both make the sign of the cross once more, and slowly stand. The chaplain glances into the small mirror mounted to the concrete block wall above the tabernacle. He locks onto his own tired eyes.

But then he finds himself looking into the reflection of Theodore's face. It's a round face, covered in salt and pepper scruff. His nose is long and slightly crooked, like it's been broken more than once. He can't help but make out the tattoo on the right-hand side of the middle-aged man's tree-trunk thick neck. It's a wolf, its jaws opened wide, like it's about to bury its fangs into something or someone. Just as Theodore did back in 1986, when he raped and murdered the twelve-year-old Sarah Anne Moore on the shoreline of Paradox Lake. A girl he bit more than one hundred times before tossing her body into the cold water.

The chaplain's folded hands are trembling. He thinks, *Are we doing the right thing? The compassionate thing? Is Theodore truly ready to be released into civilization? Is the Wolf truly ready to be released back into the wild?*

The chaplain finds himself staring into the Wolf's eyes and he swears he sees the whites turning red, not like the devil has just entered into his body and soul. More like the devil never left. Or perhaps it's just the effect of the sunlight shining through the stained glass, and the way it reflects against Theodore's eyes.

Just then, a knock on the door.

"Yes," Father O'Connor says. "What is it?"

The guard sergeant opens the door, sticks his head in.

"We're ready to go, Father," he says.

The chaplain nods, places his hand on the Wolf's thick, tight shoulder.

"The time has come, my son," he says, in a voice that sounds like God himself.

The Wolf turns to the chaplain he has known since he was first incarcerated inside the Matteawan State Hospital for the Criminally Insane back in late 1986. He gazes into the chaplain's eyes, and he smiles a mouthful of crooked, gray, sharp teeth. Big teeth.

All the better to eat you with . . .

"Thank you for all your help, Father," the Wolf says. "You've been like a dad to me."

Gradually leaning into the chaplain, the Wolf kisses him on the cheek. It's a tender, loving kiss. The kiss of a son to his father. Until the kiss becomes something else when Theodore runs his long, pale tongue up and down O'Connor's scruffy cheek . . . does it quickly, like a snake. It's enough to cause a frigid chill to shoot up the chaplain's backbone.

"Be seeing you, Father," the Wolf says as he slowly makes his way to the guard sergeant and, for the first time in thirty-three years, his freedom. "Maybe someday we can grab a bite to eat together."

As the Wolf disappears back into the bowels of the old concrete prison, Father O'Connor feels a painful pit growing in his gut. His brow breaks out in beads of cold sweat.

"You will kill again, Theodore," he whispers to himself. "Like a rabid wolf, you will kill again. That much God and I can be sure of."

BOOK I
THE CALM

CHAPTER 1

Two Years Later

"YOU'RE LEAVING, JUST like that. Don't I get a say in the matter?"

"Don't be so dramatic, Tony," I say as I strap the last of the bags to the roof of my red Mini Cooper. "We're only going for the semester so I can finally get some sculpting done in peace."

"Oh, now that hurts," my boyfriend of more than a half dozen years says, while pulling his hip flask from the top pocket on his worn bush jacket.

The jacket is one of the things he wears night and day so that, in his overly dramatic mind at least, people recognize him as a world-famous novelist and adventuring freelance journalist— "Hemingway wore a bush jacket," he often points out. So what if most months he can barely make the rent? It's the image that counts. But mostly I think the bush jacket just makes him look silly. He steals a quick sip from the flask.

"I can write from anywhere," he says. "Why don't I come with?"

I turn to him and gently place my hand on his shoulder.

"Because this is a chance for Anna and me to get to know one another better," I say, turning to my daughter who is presently seated on the Mini's rear bumper staring at her iPhone and sulking. "Isn't that right, Anna?"

I can't really see the tall, thin, dark-haired girl since I'm standing next to my boyfriend at the front of the car. But I know damn well she's rolling her eyes and saying something nasty about me in a text to her friends, now that I'm making her spend the semester with me up at Paradox Lake. Or what she lovingly refers to as "the jungle."

"Tone can go in my place, Mother," she says, pronouncing mother like *mu-ther*. "I'm good with that. I can spend the semester at Nicole's house, and I won't have to be homeschooled like the short bus kids."

Tony steals another sip from his hip flask and smiles.

"She's got a point, Rose," he says. "What do you know about homeschooling? It's been like a half century since you attended the eighth grade."

I grab hold of his hip flask and steal a sip of his Irish whiskey. It burns going down, but it tastes so damn good. Handing him back the flask, I look him up and down. I guess it would be wrong to say I'm not going to miss him. He might wear that infernal jacket everywhere but he also looks kind of hot for a middle-aged guy in his tight Levis, brown cowboy boots, and denim work shirt, unbuttoned enough that his bench-press-carved pecs are more than visible.

I guess you can say that I'm more or less the middle-aged female version of him. Meaning I, too, love my Levis. I also love my cowboy boots. Instead of a bush jacket, however, I prefer t-shirts, like the red one I have on right now that's advertising my favorite hot chili sauce, Sriracha. Listen, I'm a sculptor and the clay gets everywhere. So jeans and t-shirts work for me. As for the rest of me, well, I've got the height just like my daughter, and her dark hair, but at my age, unless I dye it every few months, it would be as gray as Tony's mood is right now.

He returns the flask to his chest pocket.

"What about I come up this weekend, Rose?" he says. He forces a smile when he says it, like that's going to somehow change my mind.

"We already talked about visits," I say, coming around the front of the Mini to the driver's-side door. "Give us a little time to get acclimated to the place. Then, we'll talk about visits."

Okay, now Tony looks like he's about to break out in tears. I hate to hurt him like this, but even though I love him, lately that love has been getting, well, for lack of a better term, old.

"Well that sucks," he moans.

Taking him into my arms, I hug him tightly.

"Come on, honey," I say. "Turn that frown upside down and look on the bright side."

"What bright side?" he asks.

"Yeah, what bright side?" Anna chimes in.

"Put a sock in it, you," I say over my shoulder. Then, turning back to Tony, "Just think of the freedom you'll have now, Tone. You can belly up to the bar whenever you want. Eat what you want without my bitching about your high blood pressure. You can come and go as you please." Leaning into him, and whispering in his ear. "Enjoy it now, because if we were ever to get married, it's ball and chain time, honey."

"Ball and chain," he says. He's got his smile back.

"That's Mom all right," Anna says. "The ball and chain, forcing me to live in the jungle."

I offer Tony a peck on the lips, and for a brief, but what's becoming a rarer and rarer sweet moment, we hold one another tight. I feel his scruff on my face, and for the first time since I arranged for this sabbatical, I'm beginning to realize I am going to miss him. But just how much remains to be seen. In any case, the things one must do for one's art.

We separate and already I'm feeling that much freer. I plant a smile on my face.

"Let's go, Anna," I say, opening the car door and slipping inside. "Our adventure in the great green north awaits."

"Great green jungle," Anna says, her sarcasm as palpable as the hot sun.

"Wait just a minute," Tony says.

As my daughter goes to the passenger-side door, he takes her in his arms and kisses her cheek. Even after all these years, she is a little hesitant when my old boyfriend shows her some affection. It surprises me, because she never knew her father, he having died by suicide months before she was born, and less than a full year after we lost our first child, Allison, to leukemia. Tony came into my life when Anna was still just a toddler and he is the only man she has ever known in terms of a father figure.

He releases her.

"Now, Anna," he says, "you have my cell phone number. You need me for anything, don't hesitate to call or text or both. You got it?"

"Yes, T," she says, opening the door. "You da man."

"And don't forget it, little lady."

She throws herself in the passenger seat and immediately crosses her arms angrily over her chest.

"I hate it when he calls me that," she says. "Little lady. I'm like a foot taller than him."

Out the corner of my eye, I can see her tight, ticked-off face. What's the word for it? Her bitch-face. Hey, she's my daughter. It's my job to call her out on it.

Starting the car, I throw the tranny in reverse.

"Say goodbye to Albany for a few months, honey."

"Just drive already, Rosie," Anna says. "The jungle awaits."

Tapping the gas, I back out of the drive.

"Are we having fun yet?" I say.

CHAPTER 2

THE WOLF SWEEPS the floor of Paradox Lake's Ferguson General Store. The store's owner, a salt-and-pepper-bearded man named Tim, is the only business owner who would hire him when he returned to his hometown after more than thirty years locked up in a maximum-security prison for the criminally insane. That kind of thing does not look good on a resume. Neither does the fact that the law required him to register as a sex offender. His minimum wage paying job might be a crappy one, but he's lucky to have it.

The short, stocky man stocks the shelves, cleans the toilets, and sweeps the aisles. He keeps to himself, avoiding eye contact with customers, some of whom are repulsed at his presence. Since life in the present tense no longer exists for him, he lives mostly in the past, inside himself with his memories. All too often, something will trigger his memory into reliving that hot, sunny day back in August of 1986. In this case, it's a rare edition of *Little Red Riding Hood* that his boss is selling on the book rack not far from the checkout counter. The book is so rare, it's stored in a one-gallon plastic freezer bag.

He stares at the colorful cover and its illustration of the Big Bad Wolf hovering over Little Red Riding Hood who is carrying a wicker basket on her arm. He focuses on the wolf, at his black fur, massive claws, dark round eyes, and big teeth. He sees himself in the Big Bad Wolf. When he looks at Little Red Riding Hood, he sees Sarah Anne Moore.

But right now, right this very moment, he sees himself back in August of 1986. He's following Sarah along the trail in the woods. The trail leads to the lake. The twelve-year-old Sarah likes to swim there in the hot afternoons. Her mother doesn't mind that she goes alone. She's twelve now. She's old enough to look after herself. She's old enough to watch out for strangers. She's not a little girl anymore. She's become a young woman in every sense of the word. The Wolf smells her scent.

What big eyes you have.
The better to see you.
What a big nose you have.
The better to smell you.
What big teeth you have.
The better to eat you.

Sarah walks, whistling a song by Madonna. "Like a Virgin". The Wolf laughs on the inside. He can already taste his virgin.

"Something wrong, Ed?" Tim says from behind the counter, his bearded face stern, his blue eyes wide. "That broom isn't gonna sweep the floor on its own."

The Wolf shakes his head.

"No, boss," he says. "Sorry, boss."

"Some boxes need to be unpacked in the back," Tim says. "Get to it."

"Yes, boss," the Wolf says, about-facing and heading towards the back of the store.

In his head, he sees Sarah alive again—his Little Red Riding Hood. He sees her undressing before plunging her naked body into the lake. What would become of the Wolf, if not for his precious memories?

CHAPTER 3

WE DRIVE FOR an hour in tortuous silence. Correction, it's not entirely a tortuous silence since it's so gorgeous up here and the smell of the pine-covered mountains fills the car. Anna has been doing her best to ignore me by burying her face in her iPhone, her thumbs going a mile a second while she texts her friends. I can only imagine what she's texting them. Probably something like, *OMG my mom has kidnapped me.* Oh the pleasantries of parenthood.

But something happens once we pass Lake George and head deeper into the Adirondack Park.

"You've got to be kidding me," Anna barks. "I don't have a connection."

Here it comes . . .

"Internet and phone service is a little spotty up here, honey," I say. "It comes and goes."

I steal a glance at her. She's gazing at me wide-eyed and panicked.

"What am I going to do with myself?" she begs.

Glancing at her once more, I don't see the impatient, blue-jean-wearing, red t-shirted—The Doors, not that she's got a clue about Jim Morrison—long-black-haired preteen she's become. I still see the sweet little kindergartner, dressed in her little pink dress, her hair pulled back in a ponytail, and white Mary Janes on her feet. I recall hitting up the Red Robin at least once per week for her cheese and macaroni fix. I recall hours and hours spent on the couch under a thick comforter, watching Nickelodeon reruns and eating bowls of buttered popcorn.

In the wake of my husband's suicide and Allison's passing, it was just the two of us. Anna was my world and I was hers and nothing could interfere with it. Nothing could threaten it. Nothing could break our impenetrable bond. Nothing, that is, except the pubescent years, I should say. But then, I was a preteen once too, so I guess I should have seen all this coming.

She tries to text again and again, but it's fruitless. She slaps the phone down in her lap. For a few minutes, I gaze out the window onto the lush forest that flanks us and the rugged mountains that loom directly ahead. I gently set my hand on her thigh.

"Tell me a story, Anna," I say. "What's on your mind other than hating me right now?"

She clams up for a long beat or two. But then she finally exhales a long, deep breath.

"Nicky is like so freaking happy now." Her tone is more than sarcastic. It's positively toxic.

"I don't get it," I say. "Isn't Nicole still your best friend?"

You might think as a good, if not overly doting, parent I would be well aware of just who my only child's best friend is. But trust me when I say, at her age, the best friend tends to change with the weather.

"Does a best friend steal your boyfriend when you're not around?" she asks.

OMG boys!

Anna is only twelve years old. Is she already into boys? How is that possible? I try to recall the first time I actually looked at the opposite sex as anything other than an annoyance. I guess I must have been in junior high. Anna is in junior high. So I guess therein lies the answer to my question.

"What boyfriend?" I ask, one eye on the road, the other on my, let's call her, perturbed daughter.

"Jake Walls," she says.

"Little Jake Walls?" I say. "He's even shorter than Tony, Anna."

I can't help but laugh, but I quickly get the hint that this is no laughing matter.

"I'm tall for my age," she says. "Boys sprout later on."

"You don't say," I say, like my daughter is telling me something I don't already know. "How long have you been in . . . ummm . . . like with Jake?"

Stealing a glance at her, I can see that she can't help but smile and blush.

"I don't know," she says, cocking her head over her shoulder. "Maybe like two or three weeks. A long time anyway." She turns to me. "Long enough that he should be paws off with Nicole, that bitch."

I bring my hand to my mouth, like I'm shocked at her choice of adjective.

"Such language for a nice young lady," I say. "Where ever did I go wrong in my child-rearing abilities?"

"Cut the crap, Rosie," Anna says. "We all know you swear like a truck driver."

She's back to calling me Rosie again . . . We're making progress.

Just then, a fire-engine-red Mustang blows by us in the right lane. It scares the daylights out of me. How did I not see him in the rearview?

"Passing in the slow lane," I say, punching the horn. "That shit will get you killed."

"I rest my case, Rosie," Anna says.

"Fucking A," I say.

*   *   *

Forty-five minutes later, we're pulling into the sleepy town of Paradox Lake. It's not much of a town. Just a small main street that's got a sheriff's headquarters with a small jail attached to it. There's a white clapboard church, a library, and a bar called Bunny's. Next to that is a combination general store/diner/gas station. The long sign that's attached to the exterior of the two-story wood building reads FERGUSON GENERAL STORE in green lettering. Since the Mini Cooper needs a fill-up, I pull up to one of the pumps, kill the engine, and get out. Anna does the same.

I hand her a ten-dollar bill.

"You hungry, honey?" I say. "Why don't you grab us a couple hot dogs and Diet Cokes."

"What if I feel like a cheeseburger?" she says, brushing her hair back over her ear.

She's got her round sunglasses on, and taken along with her tight shorts and Doors t-shirt, I'm sure she's feeling very much the city glam girl around the country folk who inhabit these parts.

"Then get a cheeseburger," I say with a roll of my eyes.

"Be right back, Rosie," she says. "Unless, of course, I decide to walk back home."

"Very funny," I say. "You have your dad's sense of humor."

"Dad killed himself," she says. "How funny could he have been?"

Her words are like a small jab in the gut.

"He was a funny guy once upon a time. And a talented architect. I wish you could have known him, honey."

"Me too," she says. Then, pursing her lips, "I shouldn't have said that about him. Sorry I'm being such a jerk, Rosie."

We are indeed making progress.

"Apology accepted," I say.

After Anna heads into the store, I start on filling up the tank. When the job is done, I grab my receipt, stuff it into my jeans pocket. Where the hell is Anna already? How long can it take to grab something to eat? Getting back in the Cooper, I start it up and pull into a parking space in front of the diner/general store. Shutting off the engine once more, I get out and enter into the store. To my right is the diner portion of the place, and to the left is the grocery. That's when I spot Anna. She's holding a paper bag that's no doubt got our lunch stored inside it. She's also staring at a metal rack filled with books. Paperbacks mostly, from what I can see. I approach her.

"Something strike your fancy?" I ask.

She turns quick.

"Oh hey, Mom," she says. "They sell these really cool old editions of all those old nursey rhyme books you used to read to me when I was a child."

"Oh," I say, "way back then, huh?"

In her free hand, she's holding a copy of *Little Red Riding Hood*. The edition is so old it's protected in a plastic freezer bag. The cover art is terrific—take it from a visual artist. It's a lush depiction of Little Red Riding Hood walking in the woods in her red cape and hood. She's carrying a basket of food to her grandmother's house. The woods are dark and foreboding. Stalking her from behind is the Big Bad Wolf, with his big bad eyes, sharp teeth, and thick black fur. He's walking on his hind legs, the claws on his two forelegs poised like he's about to dig them into the sweet little girl's neck.

"God, Mom," Anna says, after a time. "You remember how much this story used to frighten me?"

"I do," I say. "But that didn't stop you from insisting I read it to you every night, now did it?"

People are coming and going from the store. Locals I can only assume. Maybe some late-season vacationers too. I see a young family checking out their purchases at the counter. A little boy and a little girl in bathing suits are annoying one another.

"He's touching me," the little girl keeps whining. "Make him stop." But of course, her complaints only egg him on all the more. The sight of them brings back memories of me and my big brother annoying the crap out of one another during our weeklong summer vacations in Cape Cod back in the seventies and eighties. An entire lifetime ago.

The young mother and father are also wearing bathing suits and flip-flops. Sunglasses cover their eyes. The husband wears a red New England Patriots baseball cap and the wife has her long hair pulled back in a ponytail. They're buying beer, snacks, and assorted junk for the kids. They seem to be having a great time and it makes me sad.

There was a time my family was whole. A time when we consisted of a mom, a dad, a daughter, and one in the oven, so to speak. But leukemia took our Allison from us before she made it to the second grade, and in his grief, my husband shot himself in the head only weeks before Anna was born. If only he could have coped with the loss.

I try my best not to dwell on the past and the situations the good Lord had in store for me, for us. How does the tired old saying go? The Lord only dishes out what we can handle. In my husband's case, he most definitely could not handle it. It shattered him. Now I am mother and father to Anna, and a huge part of me doesn't want to see her grow up. An even bigger part of me wants to see her stay a child who I can protect and fuss over for the rest of my days. But then, that's an impossible dream.

What do you think, Allison? You're eighteen now.
Am I being overprotective of Anna?

You can never be too overprotective, Rosie. Anna's all you got now. She's a great kid. Twelve is a tough time, not that I ever got to see it. She's becoming a young woman. Stay close to her. It's a dangerous world out there. Even more dangerous than when I was living there. Don't let her out of your sight.

Thanks, Allison. I love you.

Love you too, Rosie. Hang in there.

I see the man out of the corner of my eye. He's so quiet, his sudden presence startles me. He's a short, but very thickset guy. He's bald, his scalp covered in scars, like someone took a knife to it. His round face is covered in stubble. His blue eyes are wide. They don't see us so much as glare at us. He's wearing an apron like a butcher would wear. The apron is stained. He's holding a push broom with both his thick hands. Hands covered in black hair. Anna must notice him too because she takes a step back, pressing herself into me.

"Mom," she whispers, "why is that creepy man staring at us?"

I try and do the polite thing. Work up a nice, friendly smile. But he's just staring at us, his granite, scarred face expressionless, emotionless. But when another man appears, this one tall and good looking, Creepy Man is suddenly broken out of his trance.

"Ed," the salt-and-pepper-bearded tall man says, "I need you to get started on unpacking those boxes in back. We've got shelves that need to be filled."

Creepy Man/Ed nods and makes a sound that's best described as a grunt.

"Okay, Mr. Ferguson," he says in a surprisingly high-pitched voice.

He's about to walk away when he locks eyes on Anna and me once more. But this time, instead of issuing us an emotionless expression, he works up a smile. I smile back while Anna presses herself tighter into me. I find myself wrapping my arms around her. When Creepy Ed turns and heads for the back of the store, Mr. Ferguson offers up a friendly face while approaching us.

"I hope my employee didn't frighten you kind folks," he says while fingering the bottom of his full beard with the tips of his fingers. "He's getting on in years and he's also a little bit slow, if you know what I mean. But he's harmless."

Now I feel foolish and sort of bad for the poor man. I kind of agreed with Anna when she called him creepy. But then, I guess it's human nature to prejudge people.

"No worries," I say. "No harm done, isn't that right, Anna?"

"Yeah," she says. "No harm, I guess."

Mr. Ferguson is the general store owner, no doubt. He crosses his arms over his chest. His Levi's jeans are clean. His denim work shirt looks like it's been professionally cleaned and pressed. His brown cowboy boots are polished. He's a man who takes pride in his appearance and pride in his family business. Or so it seems, anyway.

"Are you a fan of rare editions?" he asks Anna.

At first, she's not sure how to respond, because it's the kind of question that's never been posed to her before.

"Use your words, Anna," I say.

She's still holding the plastic-encased edition of *Little Red Riding Hood*.

"Oh," she says. "I was just showing this to my mom. We used to read it every night a long time ago."

"Back when she was just a kid," I say, along with a wink.

Mr. Ferguson gets it and he returns my wink.

"I see," he says. "Would you like to buy it? Introducing rare editions to the store was one of the better ideas I've come up with in recent years. The tourists love them. The ones who appreciate books anyway."

Anna immediately replaces it on the rack.

"Oh no," she says. "I'm over *Little Red Riding Hood* these days."

"It's a fine collector's item," he pushes. "You're never too old for that. Tell you what, I'll knock a couple bucks off."

"Maybe next time," I say.

He smiles and looks not at me, but into me, in a good way.

"Jeez," he says, "where are my manners?" Holding out his hand. "I'm Tim Ferguson. I own and operate the general store. It was my dad's before me, and my grandpa's before that. Back when you could hitch your horse to the place."

I try to imagine a time when horses were the main mode of transport in the little lakeside town of Paradox. It must have been a far simpler time. Imagine no smartphones, no internet, no texting, no YouTube, no Facebook or Twitter. People must have actually had no choice but to talk real sentences to one another.

"I'm Rose Conley," I say. "This is my daughter, Anna. We're staying on the lake for a few months. I'm on sabbatical from my college in Albany."

He smiles broadly. "You don't say. Which house did you rent?"

I'm suddenly speechless.

"Good question," I say, pulling out my phone and checking my saved emails.

When I see the one I want from Airbnb, I click on it. A photo of a two-story country bungalow nestled among the pines comes up along with an address. I show it to Tim Ferguson.

"This ring a bell?" I say.

He nods.

"Most definitely," he says. "That's the old Moore place. It's been a year-round rental for more than three decades since the family moved away. You'll be happy there. It's secluded and it's on the lake. It's even got its own dock." He pauses for a second and picks at his beard again, like it helps him to think. No, that's not right. More like it helps him to remember something. "If you like, I can show you how to get there. GPS can be a bit funky up here, and you need to navigate more than one back road to get there."

I glance at Anna and she glances back at me. We don't need to speak to one another to know what we're both thinking. Can Tim Ferguson be trusted? Is he leading us into a trap? But that's nonsense. I'm just being paranoid as usual. He seems like the nicest guy. A sweet general store owner who's willing to help out a couple of out-of-towners. I guess we must be city folk to him.

"That would be great, Tim," I say. "I've just got to gather a couple of supplies and we'll head out to the Moore place. Does that work for you?"

He smiles warmly and makes his way over to the wine rack.

"Let me guess," he says. "Are these the kind of supplies you're talking about, Rose?"

I can't help but laugh.

"Tim," I say, "I think this is the beginning of a wonderful friendship."

CHAPTER 4

THE WOLF UNCRATES the boxes. The arrival of the little girl and her mother has sparked something inside him. The girl, with her long dark hair and her tall build . . . it's amazing how much she resembles Sarah Anne. And her mother . . . it's amazing how much she resembles Mrs. Moore. Could it be that Sarah Anne and her mother have returned from the dead? Has his Little Red Riding Hood returned to Paradox?

He smiles and dives deep into his memory bank.

He follows Sarah along the trail until she arrives at a small, secluded section of beach. He doesn't expose himself quite yet. Instead, the Wolf hides himself in the bush, his big eyes watching her every move, his big ears listening to her gentle humming and breathing, his big nose smelling her sweet lavender scent, his big teeth gnashing in his mouth.

He wets his lips with his tongue.

The wolf is carnivore incarnate are the words he recalls from the rare edition of *Little Red Riding Hood* that rests on the store's book rack, *and he's as cunning as he is ferocious; once he's had a taste of flesh then nothing else will do.*

He watches Sarah Anne Moore as she pulls off her t-shirt exposing her red bra and the small, pale, peach-shaped breasts that fill it. He feels his heart pounding against his rib cage, and the blood that rushes to all the right parts of his body.

"What big teeth I have," he whispers. "The better to eat you with, Sarah."

CHAPTER 5

"YOU'RE SURE THIS is a good idea, Rosie?" Anna asks while we drive the curvy lakeside road towards what will be our home in the woods for the next three months. "Mr. Ferguson seems awfully friendly. Maybe he's just trying to hook up."

I shoot her a wide-eyed look.

"Are you kidding me, young lady?"

Giggling, her face is covered in what can only be described as a shit eating grin. Or so my husband, Charlie, would put it, back in his better days.

"Hey," she says, "I'm just being honest. And I do have to say, he's not all that bad looking for an old dude."

"That old dude isn't much older than me, kiddo," I say. "And what about my boyfriend, Tony? Remember him?"

"Tony's a tool, Mom," she says, "and you know it."

I focus on the road and the green Ford F-150 directly ahead of me. Both the driver's-side and passenger's-side doors bear the name "Ferguson General Store" in big white letters. From behind the wheel of the Mini Cooper, I can see Tim's baseball-hat-covered head. I have to admit, it's a pleasant sight.

"Okay, I'll admit, Tony gets on my nerves from time to time. But he's been good to us. And he means well. He's been like a dad to you."

"Nothing will ever replace Charlie, Mom."

"You never knew Charlie, sweetie. But that's nice of you to say."

She presses her fist against her chest. "Maybe not, but I feel like I know him and he knows me. Like he's watching out for us, you know?"

I feel the oxygen suddenly exit my lungs, because it's precisely the way I also feel about my late husband. I guess you could say I'm haunted by ghosts. But they're friendly ghosts. Ghosts I love with all my heart. My eyes fill with tears, but I do my best to swallow them. That's when I see the red brakes lights on Tim's pickup engage and his right directional go on.

"This looks like our turn," I say.

The truck turns onto a two-track that's flanked by thick, tall pines, white birch trees, and scrub brush. I follow, feeling the Mini Cooper buck and bounce along the uneven road.

"We should have a Jeep, Mom," Anna points out, her right hand gripping the handlebar mounted above the passenger-side window. "Tony's Jeep."

"Had I known it was going to be this rough," I say, "I would have asked him to switch up. Not that he would ever give up his precious Jeep."

We continue on for about a half mile, until Tim hooks a right onto a gravel drive that is a whole lot smoother than the two-track. Thank the good Lord. The smell is pure pine and the air fresh. Soon we can see the small wood clapboard house and beyond it, Paradox Lake. My heart is beating, because I haven't been this excited in a long time. When you work on a college campus there's almost never any alone time, other than when you lock yourself in your studio at night, and even then the night owl students are always knocking on your door, asking if you wouldn't mind taking a quick look at their sculptures, drawings, or paintings. Not that I mind. It's my job after all. But students never produce anything of quality. They are graded on the promise they display, the dedication to their art, and their potential to become a worthwhile artist. But I digress.

Tim pulls up to the front of the little house and gets out. I pull up beside him and kill the engine.

Turning to Anna. "Ready to do this, honey? Ready to start our new adventure?"

"Do I have a choice, Rosie?" she says. "I've been kidnapped and dragged to the jungle by my own mother."

I smile, give her thigh a pinch.

"I promise it will be fun," I say.

She pulls out her smartphone, searches for a signal.

"You know something?" she says, "I think my phone works."

"There must be a tower nearby," I point out.

"Thank God!"

She opens the door and gets out, dare I say it, enthusiastically.

"Thank God is right," I whisper.

*   *   *

Opening the door, I slip out from behind the wheel and give the humble house a good look. It's simple but it's also quaint, if not perfect. Tim approaches me. Recalling the instructions emailed to me by the Airbnb owner, the keys to the place are supposed to be stored in the mailbox, which is mounted to the wall beside the front door. Climbing the porch steps, I go to the front door and stick my hand in the mailbox. I pull out a small white envelope. Inside it are two identical keys. No note, no further directions, nothing.

"Some welcome party," I say, with a scrunched brow. "Just a set of keys and that's it."

"I guess the owner is into his minimalism," Tim says.

"Or maybe he just wants to keep me guessing about how things work around here."

"How about I give you folks a hand unpacking?"

"You're too kind, Tim," I say, opening the screen door and unlocking the front, wood door. "But if it's not too early, there will be a beer or two in it for you."

He shakes his head.

"Quit the stuff fifteen years ago," he says. "Best move I ever made. I actually get up with the dawn now. Every day is a gift."

"Wow," I say, pocketing the keys, "good for you. I'm afraid I wouldn't be able to survive without a cold beer or a glass of wine at the end of the day."

"Nothing wrong with that cither," he says. Then, "Pop the hatchback and I'll grab some stuff."

"Anna can help too." I look over both shoulders for her, but she's nowhere to be seen.

"Anna?" I call out.

"Don't worry about her," he says. "She's just getting acquainted with the place and the lake. We got this, you and me, Rose."

"You sure?"

"Never more so," he says with a smile.

As he grabs two overfilled duffels from out of the back of the Mini Cooper, he locks his eyes on mine. I feel something then. Something in my stomach. It's more than a friendly smile. It's the kind of smile that tells me this man is developing a crush. I have to be honest here, I am too. Oh no, poor Tony. I'm not away from him for a half day and already I have my sights set on someone else. Oh well, what's the old saying? All's fair in love and war.

It takes maybe three trips back and forth from the front porch to the car to unpack everything. That's when I get to take a tour of the house. I've already mentioned the front porch. It's got a swing that hangs from four ceiling-mounted chains. Some potted plants hang from the porch eaves and the wood slat floor has recently been stained along with the house's wood siding. Whoever owns the place certainly takes care of it, even if they don't live here anymore.

Unlocking the front door, I step inside. I'm immediately hit with cool, sweet-smelling air. There's also a hint of burning wood, like a fire was recently roaring in the massive stone fireplace that's located on the opposite side of the living room. Pressed up against the wall immediately facing us is an upright piano.

"You play?" Tim says as he enters, two duffel bags gripped in his hands.

He sets the bags onto the floor.

"Not a lick," I say. "Sculpture and painting are my thing."

"Thus all the bags of clay powder," he says. "You nearly broke my back."

He laughs.

"I'm sorry," I say, setting my hand on his arm, "but you asked for it."

I feel more of that wonderful tingling in my stomach when I touch him. I wonder if he does too, because for a long beat we seem frozen in time. But then he heads over to the piano, sits down. He takes a moment to position his hands over the keys. Then he starts in on a clunky version of "Love Is a Many Splendored Thing."

When he's through with a few bars, he stands back up and takes a bow. I can't help but clap.

"I heard someone playing piano," Anna says as she enters into the living room through the open front door.

Much to my surprise, she's carrying her own duffel bag.

"Our new friend, Tim, is multi-talented," I say.

"Aw shucks," he says, in a mock hillbilly voice. "I used to play a lot, but not anymore."

"You're invited to play for us anytime," I say.

Anna rolls her eyes.

"Where's my bedroom?" she inquires.

"Upstairs," I say, gesturing with my hand to the staircase that's directly in front of me. "Why don't you head up and claim your space."

"Sounds like a plan," she says, trudging up the wood steps.

"Let's give the rest of the place a look," Tim says.

I follow him into the kitchen. It's large enough to eat in. There's a kitchen table set by a big window that looks out onto the lake, and plenty of cooking and counter space. The appliances are relatively new, and the stove is powered by natural gas, which is a plus. At the other end of the long kitchen is a pantry with a counter and a couple of stools set under it for a quaint breakfast nook. Next to the kitchen is a dining room that contains a long harvest table. A sunroom sports a heavy wood table along with a couple wicker chairs. It will make the perfect art studio once I get rid of the chairs.

Tim looks into my eyes.

"I only just met you, Rose," he says. "But if I didn't know any better, I'd say you are one happy camper right about now."

"You have no idea," I say. "And I haven't even seen the lake yet."

"Shall we?" he says.

"Yes, we shall."

*　　*　　*

Together, Tim and I head out back by way of the two kitchen doors, one of them wood with glass panes embedded in it, the other a screen door. A path leads down to a dock. The rocky shore contains a few massive pine trees that provide excellent shade and there's a firepit that's been used recently, judging by the burnt logs inside it. Two hunter-green Adirondack chairs have been placed before the pit. Placed a few feet away from the pit is a charcoal cooker and a picnic table. A few feet behind the picnic table is a long pile of stacked firewood that's covered in clear plastic.

"I have a feeling we'll be spending a lot of time out here," I say.

"Break out the wine," Tim says.

Once again, I find myself gently touching his forearm.

"I'll buy some Pepsis for you," I say.

"I like me some Mountain Dew," he says. "Was a time I loved my Jack Daniel's."

"Done," I say, getting his drift. "Mountain Dew it is."

Heading down to the dock, I gaze out onto the pristine lake. The view is gorgeous and the lake is so still and clear it looks like glass.

"Why do they call it Paradox Lake, Tim?" I ask.

He's making his way towards the woodpile when he stops and faces me.

"Paradox refers to an old Iroquois Indian adage," he says. "In this case, when translated, it means water flowing backwards."

"Really," I say. "Not sure I understand."

"In the spring, when the mountain runoff occurs, the lake gets really high. The resulting runoff flows into the nearby Schroon River. But because the Schroon River gets really high and is located at a higher elevation than Paradox, the river water actually reverses course and flows back into our lake. The fish love it because along with the backflow comes a whole lot of food. Big fat juicy worms."

"Big fat juicy fish," I say.

"You betcha," he says. "Best in the Adirondack Park, you ask me. We'll have to catch a whole bunch of perch and have a fish fry some weekend."

"Hi, Mom," comes the booming sound of my daughter's voice.

Startled, I turn around to see her standing inside her open bedroom window.

"I have the best room in the house," she says, not without a smile.

"Great, honey," I say. "It's all yours."

"And the cell phone connection is great," she adds, before disappearing.

I turn back around, face the lake once more. Could it be that Anna's attitude over our little Adirondack Mountain adventure is adjusting for the better? We'll have to wait and see. Now if only little Jake Walls will stay true to her. Now that would be a bonus.

"What do you think, Tim?" I ask. "Maybe my daughter really is liking it here, after all."

He doesn't respond.

"Tim?"

Turning around, I spot something strange. Tim is standing over the wood pile, his back to me. He's staring into the woods behind the pile. It's like he sees something I don't see.

"Tim," I call out, "are you okay?"

But again, he doesn't answer. He's standing there, stone stiff, just gazing into the forest as if he's mesmerized by a spell that's been cast upon him by a ghost or a goblin.

"Tim!" I bark.

He then shakes his head, as if breaking himself out of the spell. He slowly about-faces.

"Sorry," he says, his face suddenly pale, his nice smile no longer painting his face. "I sort of drifted away for a second." Then, doing his best to make a happy face, "You said something?"

I'm not sure how to react to his little bit of, how shall I put it? Leave taking? Probably the best reaction is no reaction at all. Could be he was simply thinking about something he had to do or something he'd forgotten about and only just remembered. Could be he was remembering someone close to him who died at some point. Someone he never quite got over, like a wife or a child. Hell, maybe he was watching the squirrels.

"I said, I think Anna is going to be very happy here," I say.

He nods.

"This is a very happy place," he says. "Especially for you girls."

Especially for you girls . . .

Interesting choice of words. But I'm guessing he's just being genuine.

"Tell you what," he says, "I'll bring in some firewood for you. Even in late summer the nights get pretty chilly. I'll also turn the water on and check the breaker box in the basement."

"Let me help you with the wood," I say. "I'm glad you're taking care of the basement. I can't imagine it's pleasant down there."

"The basement is a bit dark and spooky," he says as he pushes away the plastic and begins to gather up wood in his arms. "By the way, when you grab the wood, watch out for spiders."

I feel a chill run up my backbone.

"I hate spiders, Tim," I say.

"You do, huh?" he says, making his way towards the kitchen door with a load of wood cradled in his long arms. "Then you're gonna love Paradox Lake. Get it?"

CHAPTER 6

It only takes a few minutes to fill up the firewood rack inside the house. Tim cleans out the used embers and then prepares the fireplace with newspaper, some dry pine kindling wood, and a couple of starter logs. He also makes double sure the chimney flu is open so we don't smoke ourselves out whenever we decide to light the fire.

I make sure Anna comes back downstairs to say goodbye and to thank Tim for all his kindness and hard work. She doesn't hop down the stairs, but instead trudges down them, like each of her feet have suddenly put on fifty pounds apiece since we arrived.

Oh my God, teenagers and their ever-changing moods . . .

I want to ask her what's the matter, but I want to wait until Tim is gone first before the tears and the anger start flying. He bids us both a smiley so long. But before he goes, he reaches into his pocket and pulls out a business card. It's got his name, cell number, and the Ferguson General Store vintage green pickup truck logo printed on it.

"Call me," he says. "Call me if you need anything. You understand, Rose? Anything at all."

I slip the card into my jeans pocket.

"I will," I say. "You've been very kind, Tim."

He turns, starts down the porch steps. That's when the thought comes to me.

"Hey, Tim," I say. "Would you like to come for dinner tomorrow night? Nothing fancy. Maybe just burgers on the grill."

He faces me and smiles, ear to ear.

"I'd love that," he says. "I'll bring some wine for the campfire, that is, if it doesn't rain. For your enjoyment only, of course. And some Mountain Dew for me and Anna."

"Terrific," my PO'd daughter whispers under her breath.

Turning back around once more, Tim hops in his truck and takes off. For the first time since we arrived here, I feel very much alone with my daughter. It's both an exhilarating and scary feeling at the same time. I gaze into her angry eyes.

"I'm sure glad your love life has picked up since we got here, Rosie," she says, the sarcasm drooling from her lips.

I could haul off and slap the brat, but I'm a twenty-first-century mom. Meaning, I give in to my child's every whim.

"Okay," I say, crossing my arms over my chest. "What's happened now?"

"Nicole," she says.

It's all she has to say for me to know things are not kosher with the best friend after all.

"Jake," I say.

"Nicole asked him to take her to the fall mixer since, get this, I won't be around."

Her face is so tight it's like the skin is about to split down the center. I can also tell she's about to cry, but she's trying her best to hold back the tears. Not because she's afraid to cry in front of me, but because she doesn't want to give Nicole the satisfaction, even though Nicole would have no idea.

Taking her in my arms, I hug her tightly. She might be taller than my five feet four now, but she's still my baby girl. She starts to cry and I shush her, just like I used to do when she was a toddler and fell flat on her face trying to race from the dining room into the kitchen to grab a chocolate chip cookie fresh from the oven. Once, she split her lip after tripping on the sidewalk outside our house. We raced to the ER in Tony's Jeep where they stopped the bleeding with four stitches to the underside of her lower lip. The tiny scar is still there.

"I hate this place," she says through her tears.

"Oh, honey," I say, "I know it's hard right now. But give it a chance. It's really so beautiful, I'm sure you'll learn to love it."

She releases me and wipes her tears from her face with the backs of her hands.

"You really think so, Mom?"

"I know so," I say. "You've been given a special gift. You don't have to go to a real school for a full semester. Instead, you can do all your learning in one of the most beautiful places on earth. Nicole is just jealous. That's what this is all about."

Her face lights up a little. "You really think so?"

I place my hand on her shoulder.

"Trust me, kiddo," I say. "I know so."

She smiles and gives me another tight hug.

"Thanks, Mom," she says. "I'll do my best to be happy."

She yawns then. A long, deep yawn.

"Easy with that," I say. "It might be contagious."

"I didn't sleep at all last night thinking about this trip," she says.

"Why don't you lie down," I say, checking my watch. "Dinner isn't for a while. It'll make you feel better."

"Okay," she says, "I could use a little nap."

Turning, she heads for the stairs.

"And Anna?" I say.

"Yes, Rosie," she says, looking at me over her shoulder.

"Maybe give the texting a rest."

She nods.

"Okay," she says. "I get it."

She climbs the stairs to her new bedroom overlooking Paradox Lake.

"Glad someone gets it," I whisper.

CHAPTER 7

BY THE TIME I've carted all my pottery equipment—bags of powdered clay mix, whole blocks of clay, sculpture table, and stool—into the sunroom, I'm ready for a cold one. What did my dad used to call it? Miller time.

"What the hell," I whisper to myself. "It's got to be five o'clock in Europe, anyway."

I go to the kitchen, grab a bottle of beer from the GE refrigerator, and pop the top on—get this—a wall-mounted, solid metal bottle opener that's got the words *Coca Cola* embossed in it. I grab a sip of the cold beer while I head for the back door. Now that I'm covered in sweat and pottery dust, the beer tastes especially good, not to mention refreshing.

Taking the beer out onto the back property with me, I steal a moment to gaze out onto the still lake. A fish breaks the calm when it jumps out of the water, snatching an insect in its mouth, and immediately splashing back down into the very same hole it made in the lake surface. It's an amazing thing to behold. I wonder what kind of fish it was. Trout. Perch. Bass. My outdoorsmen dad and brothers would know.

Another long, refreshing sip of beer. I wipe my mouth with the back of my hand and breathe in the fresh mountain air. Is there anything better in life? Then, something vibrating in my back pocket. My cell phone. Pulling it out, the digital screen reads, *Tony*. He's already calling. I guess I can't blame him. He must miss his girlfriend. Do I miss him too? Admittedly, not as much. That's not to say I don't love Tony. But I like to think of myself as more independent than he is. He's a writer, and a sensitive one at that, and he wears his heart on his sleeve. Although he'll try and tell you how tough he is and how he really doesn't even need a woman in his life, he can't go more than a few nights alone before he gets as lonely as an abandoned puppy dog.

My eyes lock on the phone. I want to answer the call, but I don't want to answer it at the same time. What's my gut tell me to do? Ignore it, let him leave a message. Better Tony learn now that I'm not going to be available to him 24/7 for a while like I am back in Albany. This sabbatical is as much about my art as it is about my independence and my time with my only surviving daughter. The phone stops ringing. I can breathe again. Setting the phone back into my jeans pocket, I make my way to the picnic table.

Can you blame me for keeping Tony at a distance, Allison? At least for now?

Do what your heart and soul are telling you to do, Rosie. Tony is wicked needy, you ask me. Nice, but needy.

Thanks for that sweetheart. I love you.

Right back 'atcha, Rosie.

But I don't take a seat atop the table right away. Instead, I find myself strangely attracted to something beyond the woodpile. It's not something I might have noticed had the late afternoon sun not been shining on it. It's an old, rectangular tin trail marker that's nailed into an old pine tree. It's so old I can barely make out the words, "Paradox Lake Trail." Although I strain my eyes to make out a path hewn through the woods, it's impossible to see anything other than the thick vegetation. That doesn't mean a trail didn't exist at one time, however. Is this what Tim was staring at earlier when, for a few brief moments, he seemed to be caught up in a trance?

Curiosity gets the best of me. Coming around the woodpile with the beer bottle in hand, I make my way to the marker. I'm wondering if this is indeed the trailhead, or if there are many more markers like this one scattered along the perimeter of the lake. One thing is for sure, the trail is no longer being maintained and hasn't been maintained in many, many years. That is, judging from the overgrown vegetation on both sides of the long, winding path.

The trail has become so narrow over the years it almost looks like a deer trail. My curiosity is further piqued. Show me a trailhead, I want to see where it leads. Welcome to Rose Conley's world.

Pushing back some of the brush, I step onto the trail. Naturally, that's when my phone vibrates again. Pulling it out of my jeans pocket, I see that once again it's Tony. I press the *ignore* icon while making a silent promise that I will call him back as soon as I am done exploring. Returning the phone to my pocket, I make my way deeper into the woods, following the narrow path through thick foliage and trees so old, so tall, and so large, they block out the late afternoon sun almost entirely.

The deeper I go, the more I feel blanketed by the cold. It's summertime still. It's hot out, even if it is late summer. But these woods are so thick, the temperature drop inside them makes them more than cool. They are downright cold. It's a bone-deep cold. A lonely cold made all the lonelier by the shadowy darkness. Still, I feel the need to move on.

Soon, my beer is gone, and I'm holding onto an empty bottle. I'm not sure how long it takes . . . ten minutes or a half hour . . . but I eventually come upon a clearing that abuts a small, sandy beach. I make my way over the clearing and step onto the beach. It's lit up in the late-day sun, which warms my body. Under the thick canopy of trees and brush, I felt cold and lonely, but now I feel warm and happy. By the looks of it, I've discovered my own little oasis. A private beach in the middle of nowhere.

A thought enters my head. A somewhat naughty thought.

"Go for it," I whisper to myself, a smile painting my face.

Pulling my t-shirt over my head, I then reach around my back, unclasp my bra, set them both onto a log that's fallen on the edge of the beach. Seating myself on the log, I then remove my boots, socks, and jeans. Then I remove my panties. With everything I own now set on the log, I go to the water's edge, and dip my foot into the clear, cold water. Walking into the water, I am surprised to find that the bottom quickly drops off, so that before I know it, I'm bathing up to my breasts in the lake. That's when I go for it completely, ducking my head under the water and swimming farther out towards the open lake.

Rolling onto my back and gazing back onto the shore, I can actually make out my little rustic house maybe three- or four-hundred feet to my left. It looks like a nice peaceful little slice of heaven. If only my little girl were happier.

"We'll make her happy," I whisper while treading water.

I take in the clear sky, the thick woods I've just hiked, and the little piece of secluded beach and I truly feel like I've never been happier.

"Don't forget to call Tony," I say aloud, as if this simple act will help me remember.

That's when I shift myself forward and start swimming for shore. As soon as I can stand, I wade my way to the little beach and allow the still hot sun to dry me off. Getting redressed, I grab my empty beer bottle and head back onto the trail. I make my way back home through the cold, dark forest.

CHAPTER 8

HE WATCHES HER through the trees, the same way he watched Sarah all those years ago. It was a day just like this one. Hot and bright. A day for a beautiful woman to take all her clothes off and swim into the cold, clear water.

What big eyes you have.

The better to watch you.

Having followed her through the thick woods, maintaining a far enough distance behind her, he ducked down when she came to the little patch of hidden beach. He then watched her undress. He savored every bit of clothing she removed, every piece of red satiny underwear. When she was fully naked, he thought he might pass out from lack of oxygen. If this woman is that attractive, imagine how beautiful her daughter must be underneath her clothing and underpants.

The Wolf so badly wished he could snatch her up with his big hands.

What big claws you have.

The better to tear you to shreds.

He wished he could sink his teeth into her, like he did to Sarah Anne Moore.

What big teeth you have.

The better to devour you, my love.

When it's time for her to get dressed again, he makes sure he doesn't make a sound, doesn't make a move. There's no need to make his move quite yet. The Big Bad Wolf must be patient. The Wolf must wait until he is entirely famished before he feasts.

CHAPTER 9

As the sun goes down on Paradox Lake, I open another beer and start a fire in the outdoor firepit. I also fire up the charcoal cooker. I cook some boneless chicken breasts, which I serve with a salad and some ears of fresh corn. Anna is quiet through most of our first dinner on Paradox Lake, even though I do manage to get her to laugh a few times over some silly jokes. I also tell her all about the trail that starts at our backyard and that leads to a small private beach.

"Maybe you can help me clear the trail tomorrow," I say. "Give you something constructive to focus on. Then we can have a little picnic lunch on our very own private beach and do a little swimming. Whaddya say?"

She nods half-heartedly and cocks her head over her shoulder.

"Sure, Mom," she says. "If it will make you happy."

Kids . . . the great mystery.

When we're done, we each pitch in to clean up. That's when Anna goes back upstairs—to look at her phone again and stew, no doubt—and I retire to the firepit, this time with a mug of Chianti—I couldn't find a wineglass. It's then I remember I haven't called Tony back. He's got to be absolutely apoplectic by now.

Going to my contacts, I speed-dial his number. Curiously, as the phone is ringing, I can't help but picture Tim Ferguson. His gray-black beard, his musky smell, and his muscular and agile body. His gentle smile and selflessness. Holy crap, what am I doing? I've only known the man for maybe a couple hours and already I've asked him on a dinner date—if that's what you wanna call it—and he's officially taking up space in my brain.

"Hello," Tony says.

Already I can tell he's angry. I can't say I blame him.

"Hi, Tim," I say, my spell suddenly broken. But then, realizing what I just said, panic sets in.

"Hi, Tony, I mean," I add, correcting myself.

My face feels like it's suddenly on fire. I'm blushing that much. *Stupid, stupid, stupid . . .*

"Who the hell is Tim?" Tony asks, his tone toxic.

How exactly do I answer this? When in doubt tell the truth. Rather, tell a version thereof.

"Oh my God," I say, "I'm sorry, honey. It's been such a long, tiring day. The house we rented by the lake took a lot more preparation than I thought. A fellow by the name of Tim helped Anna and I get set up. Nice man."

"Tim," he repeats. "Tim who?"

I can tell he's fishing. Listen, he's not fishing because I'm a notorious flirt or anything like that. I've never cheated on Tony, nor have I ever wanted to—it's hard enough trying to keep one man happy. If he's fishing, it's because he's the possessive type and that's all.

"Tim Ferguson," I say. "He owns the general store in town. He showed us where to find the house and he helped us with the firewood. He even turned on the water for us. Stuff like that. He's lived here his entire life."

"Why didn't you answer when I called?" he pushes. "I called a couple of times."

"I was walking a trail, honey," I say. "It leads to a little beach so I decided to take a swim. Then, by the time I got back, it was dinner hour. So Anna and I made dinner and sat down to eat."

He exhales a long, drawn-out breath.

"How is Anna doing?" he says. "She still moping?"

I hear people talking and laughing in Tony's background. Glasses are clinking and some music is going on the jukebox. He's hanging at Lanies, his favorite bar where he holds court every afternoon after putting in his daily word count. He'll be sitting in the corner in what he considers his personal stool, and he'll be wearing his standard uniform of ratty bush jacket, worn Levi's jeans, cowboy boots, and Ray Ban Aviator sunglasses. The fact that he likes to think of himself as a local celebrity is no secret.

"She's been up and down all day," I say. "It seems her best friend, Nicole, is making a move on Anna's shrimp of a boyfriend."

"Anna's boyfriend," he says like he's shocked. "Since when does she have a boyfriend?"

"Jake Walls. It's just a boy she likes from a distance. You know how kids are."

"Give me a shot of Jameson, babe," he says to what I assume is a female bartender. Then, "Sorry, just making a drink order, Rosie. And no, I don't know how kids are these days. When you and I were young, we might sit next to one another at lunch and maybe hold hands on occasion. That was being boyfriend and girlfriend pre-internet. But today they have cell phones and Snapchat, and WhatsApp video. Who knows what they're doing behind closed doors."

I feel my pulse elevating because my boyfriend has a point. But didn't Anna and I come up here for a while, in part, to escape that kind of anxiety? Suddenly, I just want to get off the phone.

"I'll just have to keep a close eye on her for a while, Tone," I say, my eyes staring into the fire. "Look, I'm gonna have to go now and check on Anna. It's getting dark and this is our first night."

"Okay," he says. "You be careful up there. Lock all the doors, you hear me?"

"Yes, boss," I say. "I'll make sure the hatches are battened down."

He hesitates for a few beats.

"Love you," he says after a while.

"Love you too," I say.

"Tim Ferguson, huh?" he adds.

"Just an acquaintance, Tone," I say. "Goodnight and don't drink too much."

I'm waiting for a goodnight in return, but all I get is a hang-up.

* * *

For a time, I sit there, staring into the fire, feeling the good warmth of the heat against the cool breeze that comes off the lake in the night. The moon is just about full, and I can see its long white reflection on the water. It's so beautiful and so peaceful it almost takes my breath away. For certain it makes me wonder why anyone would ever move away from such a gorgeous place. Sipping wine, I suddenly get the urge to inquire about buying the place so we can live here full-time. But then, this is only our first night, so best not to get ahead of my skis.

"Mom," I hear suddenly.

I look up towards Anna's bedroom. Grabbing hold of the flashlight I pulled out of the kitchen junk drawer, I shine it on her face, which is framed inside the open window.

"Jeez, Mom," she says, squinting her eyes in the bright white light.

"Oops," I say, shifting the flashlight. "Sorry, honey. What is it?"

"I'm going to bed," she says. "Are you coming up soon?"

It's a reasonable question. But I know what she's really asking me is this: Are you coming up to sleep with me tonight? Because I'm too scared to sleep alone.

"Come to think of it, honey," I say, "I'm really tired. I'll be right up."

"Good," she says. "Don't forget to come in and say goodnight, Rosie."

"Would you like me to read *Little Red Riding Hood* to you?" I ask.

"Oh God, Mom," she says. "I'm not a child anymore."

"Oh," I say. "I forgot. Yes, I'll be in to say goodnight. Just let me finish my wine."

"Whatever," she says, disappearing from view.

Disappointment taints her voice, like I'm putting wine ahead of my daughter. Okay, maybe I am putting off my daughter just a tad while I relax in front of the fire. But this is as peaceful I've felt in quite a long time, and I intend to enjoy it, damnit. Just me, the lake, the cool breeze, the warm fire, and this constant vision of Tim Ferguson running through my brain.

When the shadow of a figure scoots behind the woodpile and onto the Paradox Lake Trail, I nearly drop my wine mug.

CHAPTER 10

CORRECTION. I DO indeed drop my mug. Here's what else I do: I don't head for the back door off the kitchen. I sprint for it. Heart beating in my neck, I stare out the screen door at the trailhead. I don't see a thing in the moonlit night. Reluctantly, I shine the flashlight on the area just beyond the woodpile. The hand I hold the flashlight in is trembling. My mouth has gone so dry, it hurts to swallow.

"Who's out there?" I whisper.

It's useless to whisper, of course, but I don't want to shout because I don't want to alarm Anna unnecessarily. What if I was merely seeing things? What if I'm just not used to the shadows that are created in the moonlit woods? I mean, even a tree branch moving in the breeze can cast a strange shadow. Let's face it, I'm a suburbanite. I'm not used to things that go bump in the woods at night.

I eye the campfire through the screen door. I'll be damned if I left my wine mug out there.

"Come on, Rose," I whisper to myself. "Don't tell me you're too afraid to go out there and get it. Be real."

Sucking in a deep breath, I slowly open the door and step back out onto the first of the three descending wood steps. Why does it feel like I'm stepping down into hell on earth? But this is crazy. Just moments ago, I was basking in the beauty of Paradox Lake, feeling the cool breeze and the warmth of the open fire and the calming effects of a good bottle of red. Now, just because I happen to make out a moving shadow, I'm scared to death. Clearly, I've got to get out more.

Inhaling and exhaling a breath, I descend the final two steps and quickly make my way to the firepit. Bending, I take hold of the mug. The wine has spilled out of it, but there's more in the house. My eyes can't help but gravitate towards the trailhead. In the moonlight, I can barely make out the opening. My mouth goes dry again and my pulse elevates. Peeling my eyes away from the trailhead, I start walking back to the house. I'm not halfway when I hear the howl. It's a high-pitched howl that seems to be echoing across the lake surface. It stops me cold in my tracks.

How do I describe it for you? It's a long, lonely, high-pitched drawn-out noise like something a cat might make. *Saaaaaarrrrr-rrrrr . . . Saaaaaarrrrrrrrrrr . . . Saaaaaarrrrrrrrrrr . . .* It's the craziest thing. Spooky, but sad at the same time. I'm not sure what to make of it other than to remind myself that the forest surrounding Paradox Lake must be filled with all sorts of wild animals. What the hell do I know about animals other than your garden variety dog or cat? I'm just an art professor from Albany who barely leaves her studio when she isn't teaching a whole bunch of rich kids how to paint, draw, or make clay sculptures (they are always particularly bad at the latter).

Saaaaaarrrrrrrrrrr . . .

"Mama," Anna suddenly calls out through her open window.

"Yes, dolly?"

"What's that noise?"

I try and paint a smile on my face since she can no doubt see it in the moonglow along with the flashlight.

"Oh, it's nothing," I say. "Probably just a bird. Maybe an owl, if I had to guess."

I'm making this shit up, but it's not exactly a bad guess.

"It's spooky, Mama," she says, crossing her arms tightly around her chest. "Are you coming up soon?"

"Yes, honey," I say. "I'll be up in a few minutes. I'm going to lock up now."

"Okay," she says. "Don't take too long."

I head into the house to the sound of Anna closing her window and locking it.

*   *   *

First things first. Turn off the flashlight, store it on the counter beside the sink, and pour a fresh mug of wine. Second thing. Pull out Tim's business card. I can't get the image out of my mind of that shadowy thing moving through the woods behind the woodpile and then entering onto the trail only to disappear in the thick foliage. A huge part of me wants to call or text him, explain what I saw. But then another part of me knows he'll just think I'm being a scaredy cat. A frightened grown woman who's afraid not of her own shadow necessarily but the shadow of some tree branch or something silly like that.

In the end, I decide to shove the card back into my pocket. I'm about ready to turn out the lights, but there is one thing I want to do first. My laptop is set out on the kitchen table. I sit down in front of it, open the lid, and boot it up. I sip my wine until the Google search engine appears. That's when I type in "Paradox Lake Trail."

The first few hits I get are sponsored by the Paradox Lake Association. I peruse the site but don't see anything in particular about the Paradox Lake Trail. I decide to switch to images. In one of the first photos that comes up, I spot what looks to be the very trailhead that's located behind the woodpile. It's a black-and-white picture that looks like it was taken many years ago.

I click on the photo. It belongs to an old newspaper story that came out in 1986. My eyes are perusing the headline when Anna shouts out for me once more.

"Mama, you promised you were coming up!" she barks.

"Crap," I whisper to myself.

No choice but to leave my detecting until morning. But that doesn't mean I don't catch the headline to the story first. "Local Girl Goes Missing on Paradox Lake Trail." The fine hairs on the back of my neck stand up. In a big way, I don't want to read anymore. Not tonight. Not when I've just seen a shadowy figure enter onto the trailhead behind the woodpile. Not when some animal is howling in the night, its high-pitched voice reverberating desperately across the lake. Not when I'm already spooked beyond words.

Getting up, I lock the kitchen door and apply the dead bolt. I also head into the living room and lock the front door and also apply the dead bolt. The windows are already closed and locked since I never bothered to open them in the first place. As for the light that's still on in the kitchen, I'll feel better if it stays that way, damn the wasted energy. The Big Bad Wolf might think twice about entering into a house that's well lit.

Heading up the wood stairs, I go into Anna's bedroom. Just as I expected, she's sitting in bed, the covers tucked up under her chin, both her hands gripping her phone.

"It's about time, Rosie," she says.

What happened to mama?

"I trust you're reading your Kindle app," I say. "Something good like *Wuthering Heights* or *To Kill a Mockingbird*?"

"Yuck," she says. "I'm playing *Minesweeper.*"

"At least you're not texting," I say, going to the window and opening it just enough to provide some fresh air.

I come around the bed, kiss her on top of her head. I recall a time when I would have held her in my arms and rocked her to sleep. The memory of my Charlie and Allison would have been fresh and it was all I could do to never let go of Anna. But of course, you have to let go eventually. What's the old saying? If you love someone, set them free. But, boy oh boy, is it a hard thing to do or what?

"Goodnight, my love," I say.

Coming from outside the window, *Saaaaaarrrrrrrrrr . . . Saaaaaarrrrrrrrrr . . .*

"What the heck is that, Mom?" Anna begs. "It's soooo spooky."

"If I had to guess," I say, feeling a chill run up my spine, "it's an owl. Or maybe another kind of bird." I finger-comb her thick dark hair. "We're not in the Albany suburbs anymore."

"Yeah," she says, in her deadpan voice. "The jungle."

I guess I stepped into that one.

"Like I said, don't worry about it. Only friendly animals in this particular jungle."

"Good to know," she says.

"Get some sleep," I say. "Tomorrow we'll do a little trail clearing, have a picnic on our little private oasis, and do some swimming. But come day after Labor Day, we're gonna dig into your studies."

"You're just chuck full of good news these days, Rosie."

Turning, I head for the open door.

Saaaaarrrrr . . . Saaaaarrrrr . . .

"Mama," Anna says, as I reach the doorway.

She doesn't have to say a word for me to know what she's about to ask. Slowly I turn. My daughter is gazing at me with the biggest wide puppy dog eyes you ever did see. I can't help but gaze at the room, the mostly bare pine wood walls, the bare wood floor, and a bed that must be older than me. It probably won't be the most comfortable accommodations, but like the great Warren Zevon once said, *I'll sleep when I'm dead.*

What do you think, Allison? She's twelve years old.
Am I spoiling her?

She's only twelve once, Rosie.

"Okay, kiddo," I say, "but just this one time. You're getting too old to have your old ma sleeping in the same bed."

She paints a bright smile on her pretty face. A face that screams of Charlie and Allison. Undressing down to my undies, I slip under the covers and fight my daughter for at least a small piece of pillow.

"Goodnight, Anna," I say, hugging her slim arm.

"Night, Mama," she says.

Saaaaaarrrrrrrrrrr . . .

"Night, Mr. Owl," Anna adds. "I hope you go to sleep soon too."

* * *

I'm standing at the trailhead, my eyes focused on the battered old tin trail marker. Paradox Lake Trail. Although the trailhead is overgrown with brush and tree limbs, there is a bright light coming from deep inside the trail. I'm attracted to the light. Pushing aside the brush, I step onto the trail and follow the light. Soon, I see two ghostly figures reflected inside the brightness. A tall figure and a shorter figure. They are coming for me. It doesn't take me long to make out their faces.

It's Charlie and Allison.

"Rosie, baby," Charlie says, a happy ear-to-ear smile on his handsome, scruffy face, "I thought you'd never get here."

"Took you long enough, Rosie mama," Allison says, fingering her lush, sandy-blond hair. My first daughter has grown into a beautiful young woman. She gives me a kiss on the cheek while Charlie takes me into his arms.

"Where am I?" I ask.

They both look at me with wide eyes and scrunched brows, like it should be obvious where I am.

"You're home," they say.

CHAPTER 11

THE BIG BAD WOLF stands below the open bedroom window, listening to the women sleeping in the bed. He doesn't have to see them to know what they look like. He sees the girl in her long Lady Gaga t-shirt and pink underpants, sleeping on her side in a curled-up, fetal position. He sees her mother, sleeping on her side, facing her daughter, dressed only in her red bra and matching silky panties. The two are snoring gently. So gently, they barely make a sound.

Closing his eyes, he breathes in through his nose.

What a big nose you have.

The better to smell your bodies with.

He chomps down repeatedly with his upper and lower jaw.

What big teeth you have.

The better to eat you both.

He slips his tongue in and out of his mouth, like a snake.

What a big tongue you have.

The better to lap up your blood.

About-facing, the Big Bad Wolf gallops across the backyard, past the woodpile and onto the dark Paradox Lake trailhead.

Saaaaaarrrrrrrrrrr, he howls into the moonlit sky.

CHAPTER 12

WAKING UP WITH the sun, I head down to the sunroom studio and over a freshly brewed cup of coffee, start in on a brand-spankin'-new project. I'm not one to plan what I'm about to create. Like a mystery writer who writes his novels by the seat of his pants—Tony works this way when he's writing fiction—I just go with my gut. This morning, I find myself starting on a bust. I'm not even sure if what I'm creating is a man or a woman yet, or a boy or a girl. All I know is I'm shaping the heavy block of clay so that it resembles the ovular structure of a human head. This process alone eats up the time it takes to drink a full cup of coffee.

Getting up from my stool, I head back into the kitchen and make another cup. That's when I spot my computer. My coffee in hand, I sit down in front of it, and once more peruse the article that I brought up prior to heading to bed last night.

"Local Girl Goes Missing on Paradox Lake Trail."

Setting my coffee mug beside the computer, I feel a pit form in my gut. The Paradox Lake Trail begins in my backyard. Could the little girl mentioned in the article have begun her hike just a few feet away from where I'm sitting? As much as I don't want to read the article, I can't help but get started on it. It's the same sensation

I get when I pass by a bad car wreck. You don't want to look at it, but you can't help but look at it. It's human nature.

The article is about a twelve-year-old girl named Sarah Anne Moore who was said to have told her mother she was heading out for a hike on a Friday afternoon in the summer of 1986. According to the report, the tall-for-her-age, long-brunette-haired, brown-eyed girl packed a sandwich and a Diet Coke into a knapsack and began her hike on the trail at its trailhead, which was located behind her family home.

Her family home . . .

That's when I stop reading.

The kitchen I'm sitting in right this very second belonged to the Moore family. The reality of this is enough to make me break out in goose bumps. Right now, I'm sitting in Sarah Anne's kitchen. I continue reading. Sarah was gone four hours when her mother got worried enough to call the sheriff. While Sarah had been known to hike the trail at least once a week during the summer months, she always returned within a couple of hours. What her mother feared the most is that she might have decided to take a swim and, in fact, drowned. But when local sheriff's deputies examined the trail, there was no sign of Sarah. There was also no sign of her clothing or backpack. It was like she just disappeared into thin air. The article then goes on to say that authorities teamed up with state police to scour not only the trail but all of Paradox Lake.

I go back to the Google page and scroll down to the next story. I click on it. It's from the same paper and the date is a couple of days after that of the first article. The headline that goes with it is enough to break my heart, even more than thirty years after the fact.

"Moore Girl's Remains Discovered Off Hiking Trail."

Here's how I react: tears immediately fill my eyes and my breathing grows shallow. My hands begin to tremble while I continue to read about how she was apparently abducted and raped while walking the heavily forested trail. Her assailant, a local Paradox Lake young man by the name of Theodore Peasley, was arrested not long after her body was discovered once it had been established that the bite marks on her body matched those of his dental records. Even more amazingly, his own parents warned the police over and over again that one day he would do something bad to some innocent child. It wasn't a matter of *if* it ever happened, it was a matter of when and how. The *when* occurred in the summer of 1986 and the *how* was rape, strangulation, and mutilation of the flesh by over one hundred severe bite marks.

I sit back and try to breathe.

"That poor, poor girl," I whisper to myself. "I hope the bastard Theodore rots in prison for all his days."

It feels good to say it. It dawns on me that I have no idea how long the Paradox Lake trail runs. Clicking on the trail's Google Map, I see that it runs almost the entire perimeter of the big lake. If Sarah was gone for four hours, she might have been murdered miles into her hike. This might sound crazy, but a big part of me suddenly feels the need to see where it happened. Maybe it has something to do with sitting inside what used to be her kitchen, but I can't help but feel like I've become a part of her life now. Or maybe I'm just being dramatic. How many families have rented this house in the thirty-three years since Sarah died? Hundreds I'm guessing. Anna and I are just another pair of guests who will come and go.

The knock at the door startles me so much that I spill my coffee. I bound up.

"Shit, shit," I say, going for the roll of paper towels set out on the counter. Ripping off four or five of them, I place a couple on the spill that's formed on the table not far from my computer. The rest

I place over the puddle on the floor. I then make my way across the living room to the front door.

"Mom, who's there?" Anna calls down from the top of the stairs.

"Hang on, Anna," I say. "I have no idea."

"It's a little early for visitors," she says. "I hope it's not Tony."

She's got a point. If it is, in fact, Tony, I'm going to be more than a little pissed off. But then, if it is him, I'm sure he has nothing but good intentions. Gazing out the small rectangular pane of glass embedded in the door, I don't see anything but an empty porch and semi-overgrown front lawn. If someone is standing on the other side of the door, they're doing so out of sight.

"You're not gonna just open the door, are you?" Anna asks.

"Relax," I say. "We're up in the woods, not the hood."

But then I think about the murder that happened here all those years ago and I realize even a place as beautiful and seemingly serene as Paradox Lake can be dangerous. Mortally dangerous.

"Hello," I say into the small pane of glass. "Who's there?"

Silence.

"Try again," Anna says nervously.

"Go into the master bedroom, Anna," I say. "Look out the window and tell me if you see anything."

"Roger that," she says, heading into the master bedroom, which is located at the front of the small bungalow. I wait for a beat. Then, "Nothing, Mom. Not a thing."

No choice but to open the door. Heart beating against my ribs, I unlock the dead bolt, then unlock the big wood door. Stepping out onto the porch, I see immediately that no one other than myself occupies it. I shift my focus to the gravel drive. Just my Mini Cooper parked by the unattached garage.

"Well, that's bizarre," I whisper aloud.

"Anyone there?" Anna asks, poking her head out the open door.

I turn quick.

"No one," I say. "Not a soul. Maybe I imagined the knocking."

"That means we both did, Rosie," Anna says, not without attitude.

"Good point," I say.

For another few seconds, I just gaze out onto the empty lawn and the trees that flank the front property.

"Hey, look," Anna says, after a time. "Somebody left us a package."

I shift my focus to her as she pulls a plastic grocery bag off the doorknob. The bag has the Ferguson General Store green pickup truck logo printed on it. Before I can protest, Anna opens the bag.

"Oh my God," she says, her face lighting up like a bulb.

She pulls something out of the bag. It's a book. A book that's protected in a plastic freezer bag. More goose bumps.

"Is that what I think it is?" I ask.

"*Little Red Riding Hood*," Anna says, her face filled more with wonder than actual joy. "The rare edition we saw yesterday in Tim's store."

"That would be the one," I say.

Once again, I gaze out onto the front lawn. Tim must have pulled up, dropped the book off as a surprise, knocked on the door, and took off before we could thank him. Could he be any more thoughtful? I feel my insides warm up, like I'm stepping into a soothing hot bath. Could it be that I'm falling for the general store owner before I even get to know him?

Poor Tony . . . I never intended to come up here and fall for anyone . . .

"Do you think Tim dropped this off, Mom?" Anna asks.

"No other explanation for it, sweetheart," I say. "I'd ask you to call him and thank him, but he'll be over later tonight for dinner. You can thank him then."

She nods and clutches the book to her chest.

"My first rare edition," she says. "You think it's worth some cash?"

"You're not planning on selling it, are you?"

She smiles slyly.

"EBay never crossed my mind," she says.

"Go get some breakfast, lady," I say. "We have some trail clearing to do."

CHAPTER 13

By MIDMORNING WE'RE both standing at the trailhead, a pair of manual hedge trimmers gripped in my hands, while Anna insists on using a hatchet. We found the tools in the small unattached garage located beside the house at the top of the driveway.

"Be careful with that thing," I say. "You bury it in your leg, we're a dozen miles away from the nearest hospital."

She's awkwardly chopping away at an overgrown branch, working up a sweat. If I get a half hour of manual labor out of her, I'll be lucky. But the truth of the matter is that it's just plain fun to work on a project together that doesn't involve the use of a computer or some other digital twenty-first-century tool. I busy myself with chopping away at the overgrown scrub and twigs, clearing the trailhead opening so that it looks like a trailhead.

Soon we're well inside the forest, snipping here, chopping there, cutting away anything that's in the way of the trail. The occasional felled tree trunk blocks the path, but there's not much we can do about that since we don't have a chainsaw. We simply walk over the obstacle. After maybe twenty minutes go by, the small, isolated beach appears for us on our right-hand side.

"This is it, Anna," I say. "Time for lunch."

"Great," she says, the hatchet still in hand. "I'm starving. All this work really makes me hungry."

Walking out onto the isolated beach, I open up my pack and spread out a small picnic lunch of ham and cheese sandwiches and potato chips. I brought along a cold Pepsi for Anna and for me a cold beer. Hey, why not indulge a little? For a while, we sit on the felled log and eat without saying much of anything. The woods and the lake are just so peaceful and alive with the birds flying overhead and fish jumping. Each and every one of our senses seems to be occupied.

After a time, Anna says, "How about a swim, Rosie?"

"Did you bring your suit?"

"Wearing it under my jean shorts."

She pulls her shorts and top off revealing her navy-blue Speedo one-piece I purchased for her at the beginning of the summer. Without waiting for me, she goes to the water and dives right in. It makes my heart beat with joy to see her one hundred times happier today than she was yesterday. Pulling off my boots, jeans, and t-shirt, I consider hopping in the lake in my underwear. But since I don't feel like walking back home in soggy underclothes, I decide to dress down to my birthday suit.

"Haha," Anna barks, "Rosie is naked!"

"Don't tell anyone!" I say, before diving in.

The water is not only crystal clear, it is still cold and refreshing this late in the summer. I swim towards Anna and splash water in her face. She splashes water back at me. It's the most fun we've had in a long, long time, and I never want this moment to end. It's almost surreal how happy I am. We're treading water, soaking in the midday sun, when I notice that Anna has her eyes focused on something back on the beach.

"What is it, honey?" I ask.

"Something in the sand," she says.

Before I can ask her to explain, she's swimming for the lake-shore. I follow her. Standing on the sand, she goes to the far edge of the beach, and begins to dig with her hands.

"I spotted something reflecting the sun," she says. "Something yellow. Like gold or something."

"Gold," I say, slipping back into my clothing after drying myself with a towel I stored in the backpack. "We struck gold? Now that would be unbelievable luck, young lady. Just make sure you share your good fortune with your poor old mom."

"Rats," she says, after a time, pulling up some very old yellow plastic ribbon. "It's not gold, after all. It's just trash."

My eyes focus on the ribbon. It's so old, parts of it have lost its yellow coloring and faded to white. But the words printed on the tape are still plainly visible.

CRIME SCENE: DO NOT CROSS

"Why does it say crime scene, Mom?" Anna asks.

My heart shoots up into my throat. Here's what my gut is telling me: I've discovered the exact spot where Sarah Anne Moore was raped and murdered. Here's what else my gut is saying: If I reveal the truth to Anna that a girl her exact age was brutally killed here thirty-three years ago and that she lived with her family inside the house we are now living in, she's liable to freak out. No—correction—she would most definitely freak out. And who could blame her?

"It's probably just some garbage left over from a party or something like that," I say, offering up a weak lie, but a lie nonetheless. "You know, some kids drinking and messing around. Give it to me and I'll add it to the trash."

She hands me the approximately foot-long length of plastic ribbon.

"You sure are dedicated to cleaning up Paradox Lake, Mom," Anna says, not without a giggle.

"Least we can do," I say.

Then, before she has the chance to dig up anything else that might be left over from Sarah Anne Moore's murder, I tell her to pack it up. Time for me to get some work done on my new sculpture project, or so I offer up as an excuse.

"No more trail clearing," my daughter says like a question.

"I'm giving you the rest of the day off," I say, with a smile. "How's that sound?"

"Awesome," she says.

Together, we head back into the woods, following the very same trail Sarah walked before she was abducted by a madman.

*   *   *

As soon as we come to the trailhead and the woodpile, Anna shoots for the back door and heads inside. I know precisely where she's going. Up into her bedroom for a chat session either with Nicole and/or Jake Walls. May the day's drama begin. But on the bright side of things, I did manage to get her out for half a day in the fresh air and sunshine. Thank the Lord for small victories.

As I'm heading over the backyard towards the house, my phone vibrates. Pulling it out, I see that it's a text from Tony.

Thumbing the text icon, I read: *Can you at least give me your address up there in case of emergency?*

He's right. He should at least have our address. I guess I avoided giving it to him so that he didn't have one too many Jameson shots at Lanies Bar and decide to drive up here to surprise us. The last thing I need is a Tony DWI on my conscience.

Sorry, I text with my thumbs—not with the speed and accuracy that Anna can accomplish, but not bad for a woman of my years. *22 Paradox Lake Road*

Thank you Rose, he responds.

You're welcome Gonna get some work done now Talk later XO

If I don't add the X and O, I'm going to get an earful about it later on. Tony doesn't just wear his heart on his sleeve, he holds the pulsing organ in his two hands for all the world to see. He's an artist, and an overly sensitive one at that. Maybe that's why I fell in love him all those years ago.

Heading inside, I make a mug of tea and take it with me back into my studio. I dig into my jeans pocket, pull out the crime scene ribbon, and set it on the small worktable pushed up against the far wall. For a while I just stare at it. Until I sit down at my clay bust and, taking hold of the sculpting knife, begin to work on the face, cutting away a little here and slicing off a little there. I spin the bust around and start forming the head and the hair by slicing fine, thin lines into the clay. Thick, lush, long hair, like a woman would have. A young woman. Or perhaps even younger.

I find myself working frantically, my creative left brain constructing something my cognitive right brain has no idea about. I call it sculpting in the dark. My hands and the sculpting tools they hold are nothing more than conduits for whatever it is my brain wishes to construct. It's a miraculous process for which I have little or even no control.

By the time I've completed what amounts to a half hour session of sculpting, my forehead is covered in sweat and my upper back is aching. Setting the sculpting knife down, I wipe my forehead with the back of my hand, and take a good look at the face I'm creating. It most definitely belongs not to a mature woman, but instead, a girl.

A girl very much like Anna or Sarah.

CHAPTER 14

BACK IN THE kitchen, I pour a tall glass of cold water and drink it all down at once. I'm parched—the dusty clay literally coats your mouth and tongue. That was the most intense sculpting session I've had in a long while. My self-imposed exile in the mountains is working its spooky magic. My mind is spinning. I look around the empty kitchen, at the appliances, the wood counters, and the kitchen table. The crucifix that hangs on the wall above the window over the sink must be as old as the house itself. My guess is that it's the same cross Sarah Anne Moore looked at day in and day out when she lived here. The very same cross she gazed at before she decided to go hiking on the Paradox Lake Trail all those decades ago.

Stealing a quick glance at my watch, I find that it's going on two in the afternoon. It suddenly dawns on me that Tim Ferguson is coming for dinner and I don't have anything to feed him. It means a trip to his general store, which might be kind of awkward since I'll be shopping for him. Therefore, he'll feel funny about charging me for it. There's a Price Chopper supermarket in the nearby town of Schroon, which is located just a few miles past the town of Paradox. I'll have to go there to stock up.

I go to the staircase and stand at the bottom.

"Anna," I call out.

I wait for a few beats until she appears at the top of the stairs.

"Yes, Rosie, what is it?" she asks, her phone gripped in her hand. At this point, I'm surprised it hasn't become spontaneously biologically attached.

"Listen, honey, I'm heading into Schroon to buy some dinner for tonight. Would you like to come with me?"

"Any chance I can stay here?" she asks. "I'm not afraid or anything like that during the day."

She seems chipper. A little too chipper.

"Let me guess," I say. "Little Jake Walls."

She smiles, her cheeks turning a distinct shade of red.

"How'd you guess?"

"Sounds like things are working out after all."

"He thinks Nicole is a drip," she says.

"Okay," I say. "Go ahead and do whatever it is you kids do. I'll be back within the hour."

"Take your time, Rosie."

When a preteen tells a parent to take their time, you most definitely want to do the opposite. I grab my keys and exit the house by the front door.

* * *

Pulling out of the gravel drive, I make my way over the packed gravel road until I come to the two-track that accesses the Paradox Lake Road. Hooking a left, I drive the winding, pine tree-lined road all the way into Paradox. When I pass the general store, I can't help but crane my neck to see if Tim might be hanging around outside.

Sadly, he's not.

However, I do spot the creepy, stocky man who smiled at Anna and me in the store yesterday when we were looking at the books. What's his name? Ed. He's wearing a pair of ratty farmer overalls over a green t-shirt and work boots. He's opening the door of what I take to be his old, run-down pickup truck, the color best described as a combination brown and rust.

He catches sight of me as I slowly pass, not like he can see me, but like he senses my presence. Maybe they don't see a lot of Mini Coopers up here. What's strange is the way he stares at me. He also offers a smile. His unblinking eyes remain locked on my eyes until I pass. It's all I can do to peel my eyes away from his. When the car directly ahead of me hits the brakes and turns into the general store parking lot, I have no choice but to slam on the brakes or rear end it.

"Watch where you're going, lady!" an older, crazy-gray-haired man shouts out his open driver's-side window.

I'd offer up an apology if only I weren't already down the road from the store. As I drive out of town, I can't help but see Creepy Ed's round face and bald, scarred head. In my brain, I see his blue eyes. Chills fill my veins. But then, Tim said he was harmless. Maybe I'm just a spooked woman—a stranger in a strange land. A land where an innocent preteen girl was murdered thirty-three years ago. Now, I'm living in her house, while Anna is sleeping in her old bedroom.

Maybe the old murder is hitting too close to home.

*   *   *

It takes me fifteen minutes to get to the town of Schroon. It feels a little odd, because back home, it takes me no more than four or five minutes to drive to my local mega-mart. But this is the country, and out here, nothing is close by. I will say this, however—compared to Paradox, Schroon is a bustling metropolis. The main street is lined with small mom-and-pop shops along with a Subway, a McDonald's, a couple of banks, an old red brick church, a Death Wish coffee shop, and a Stewart's bread and butter shop. When I come to the Price Chopper, I pull into the lot and park the Mini Cooper.

Heading into the store, I buy some fresh hamburger, a block of sharp cheddar cheese, three Idaho potatoes for homemade French fries, a head of lettuce, a couple of vine tomatoes, and finally, a half-dozen ears of corn. Talk about serendipity, but I was just about to buy a blueberry pie when I receive a text from who else but Tim. I don't remember giving him my number. Or did I? Oh well, whatever the case, he's able to text me.

Hey it's Tim . . . Don't bother with dessert . . . I'm bringing a freshly baked apple pie . . . some wine and Mountain Dew

He follows up with a yellow smile-face emoji.

Great Thanks Tim

I add a yellow smile-face emoji to go along with his.

Looking forward Rose

I feel a wave of excitement shoot up my spine. My stomach goes a little tight, and my brain buzzes with adrenaline. What's happening to me? I'm supposed to be in love with Tony. I'm feeling both elated and guilty at the same time. But then, I'm not married to Tony. And yet, I'm fooling myself if I refuse to believe he hasn't become a sort of surrogate husband to me since I lost Charlie. He has certainly been like a father to Anna, even if she does give him a hard time on occasion.

I shake my head and make the decision right there and then in the supermarket bakery section not to get ahead of myself with Tim. But I also tell myself that you only go around once. Life is short. Charlie and Allison are evidence of that. If I like Tim, it doesn't hurt to spend some quality time with him.

Isn't that right, Allison?

Tony is a cool, creative guy, Rosie. A bit unhinged at times, I gotta say. But a real good guy. A creative guy. On the other hand, you're not married either. You don't even live together. It doesn't hurt to hang out with Tim a little. Get to know him a bit. It's not like you're gonna jump right in the sack with him.

You're making me blush, young lady.

What are daughters for, Rosie?

Okay, maybe it seems strange to speak with my dead daughter, but I'll let you in on a little secret. I truly believe she can hear me, and I can hear her. Sometimes I talk to Charlie, too. It's the strangest thing, but even if their physical bodies are gone now, their souls are able to communicate with mine. We are biologically attached, after all. We are blood. And the blood, she runs thick. Their spirits are constantly on my mind and ever present. And nothing can ever change that.

Before checking out, I make sure to buy another twelve-pack of Stella beer in cans. What the hell? Better to have more than less booze hanging around the house on the lake.

Back in the Mini Cooper, I get another text from Tony.

Miss you.

I'm picturing him bellied up to Lanies Bar a little earlier than usual, since he's fighting loneliness. As I've already intuited, Tony is one of those guys who can't stand being alone. I guess it never dawned on me until now that he might find himself a new girl-friend while I'm gone. Admittedly, the thought makes me sad. But what's good for the goose . . .

Miss you too Tony.

But I'm not sure I mean it and I pray he doesn't read anything into my response. Just to make sure we don't get into anything, I put the phone on silent. But then realizing Anna is all alone in the lake house, I decide against the move and put the sound back on. Oh the never-ending responsibilities of parenting.

Starting the car, I pull out of the lot and head back in the direction of Paradox, hoping that I get a quick glance at Tim when I pass by the store.

CHAPTER 15

THE WOLF DOESN'T walk along the Paradox Lake trail. He sprints on all fours, shooting and scooting along the path like a man—an animal—far younger in years and physical condition. A full mile separates his old family house in the deep forest from the Moore house, but he's able to cover the ground in a hair less than twelve minutes. By the time he arrives at the Moore trailhead, he's dripping with sweat, the green t-shirt under his overalls soaked to the skin.

He slips on past the woodpile to the back door of the house. Pausing for a moment, he hears the beating of his pulse in his temples. He also hears the voice of a girl. She's talking on the phone. She keeps saying the name Jake and then giggling afterwards. He even hears her say, "Jake, I love you." It makes the Big Bad Wolf smile to know a girl Anna's age can actually love a boy.

What big ears you have.

The better to hear you having phone sex with your boyfriend.

He wonders if they're talking on the phone or if they're WhatsApping, looking at one another's smooth naked bodies. That's what all the kids do now. They don't wait until they're older like the kids used to do before he was sent up to prison. Now they use electronics to satisfy their young animal desires. Father

O'Connor was right when he warned the Wolf the world was far different than it was in 1986.

Slowly, he opens the screen door off the kitchen. He tiptoes across the kitchen floor and into the living room. He goes to the staircase and stands there looking up onto the second-floor landing. He breathes in deeply, and breathes in Anna's scent.

What a big nose you have.

The better to smell every bit of you.

He feels himself getting aroused, and for a quick beat, he's tempted to pull his sex out. But he refrains. For now, he's happy with playing this little game of catch as catch can. Only, Anna is not about to catch him since she's so absorbed in her conversation with Jake. The Wolf wonders if she loved the gift he left for her this morning. He wonders if she's perused the pages, stared at the brilliant drawings of the Big Bad Wolf. He loved giving her the gift, just as he loved giving Sarah Anne all her gifts way back when—he also gifted her a copy of *Little Red Riding Hood*, which the police later confiscated as evidence.

Then, the sound of a car pulling up outside the front door. That would be Rose. Turning, the Wolf scoots on all fours back across the living room floor, past the piano, through the kitchen, and out the back door. He skitters across the backyard and the woodpile, heading back onto the Paradox Lake Trail. Soon the time will come when the real Big Bad Wolf will take what is his. It will be a beautiful thing.

What big hands you have.

What big claws.

The better to snatch you up and tear into your flesh.

CHAPTER 16

As soon as I arrive home, I call out for Anna while carting the groceries into the kitchen. She answers with a "Hi, Rosie." She sounds happy. We're on a roll here and it warms the heart. However, a couple hours hanging out in bed and texting—or talking—on the phone is much too much.

Making my way back to the stairs, I bark, "Come help me with dinner, honey!"

"Oh, really, like now?" she says.

"Really," I say. Then, clapping my hands. "Chop, chop."

"Chop, chop," she repeats. "What does that mean, Rosie?"

"It means get your little butt down here now and let's have some fun. It's mom and daughter time."

"Okay, give me a minute, Rosie."

Back in the kitchen, I pull out the hamburger and start making the patties. I add plenty of salt and pepper for flavor. When Anna comes in, I ask her to start on peeling the potatoes.

"Boring," she says.

"Hey," I say, "all chefs gotta start somewhere."

Anna peels the potatoes over the sink and I flatten the hamburger patties with all the care and precision I put into my sculptures. I notice her iPhone is set on the kitchen table. When the screen lights up with a WhatsApp call from little Jake Walls, I nearly burst out laughing.

"Ummm, phone call, Anna," I say.

She turns quick, her face turning beet red.

"Aren't you gonna get it?" I press.

"He can wait," she says, continuing with her peeling.

I finish up the last patty.

"So you guys are WhatsApping now," I say. "You just talk, right?"

She doesn't look at me. Rather, I can tell she's refusing to look at me, like I might find the answers I'm looking for in her expression.

"Of course, Mom," she says, a little too defensively for my tastes. "What else do you think we do?"

I start on shucking the corn over the garbage pail.

"I was young once, Anna," I say. "I know what it's like to have needs. You're growing up into a very attractive young lady. You're going to be desirable to lots of boys, some of them older and far more experienced than you. Not all of them will be like innocent little Jake Walls."

She finishes peeling the last potato and sets it on a paper towel beside the other two.

"Oh my God," she says, "are we like having, the *talk*?"

Now it's me who's blushing.

"What talk?" I say, stupidly.

"You know, Mom," she says, "like, *the* talk."

Without answering her, I go to the fridge, pull out a can of Stella. I pop the top, steal a deep swig of the cold beer.

"Snagged," I say as soon as I come up for air.

Anna bends over in laughter. I, too, laugh. What the hell else is there to do?

"The funniest thing about this," I say, "is you probably know more about sex than I do."

"I'll let you know when I finally have it," she says.

"Which, my still very maturing, yet still adolescent young lady, will not be for quite some time. Are we in agreement?"

"We're in agreement, Rosie," she says. "Just the thought of doing it makes me a little nauseous."

"Good," I say. "Let's keep it that way."

*   *   *

With all the food prepped, there's only one last thing to do. Clean up and dress into something a little more presentable. I take a quick shower, dry my hair, and slip into a brown, summer-weight, shoulder-strap dress. Since I'm in a funky mood, I choose a pair of brown cowboy boots to go with it. I slip some silver bracelets on along with some matching necklaces. Gazing at myself in the big mirror attached to the dresser of drawers in the upstairs master bedroom, I realize I don't look half bad for a woman who will never see forty again.

Heading out of the bedroom, I make a check on Anna. I'm surprised to see that she too has decided to dress up a little. By that, I mean she's put on a pair of clean, high-waisted blue jeans, a pair of clean white Ked sneakers, and a black t-shirt that says "The Beatles" in big white letters. Her hair is pulled back neatly in a ponytail.

"Do you even know who the Beatles were?" I ask. "I hardly even remember them myself."

"Paul is my fave," she says. Then, singing, "I love you, Paul, oh yes I do. When you're not with me, I'm blue . . ."

Oh the power of YouTube.

The sound of a truck pulling up outside makes my pulse pick up speed. My stomach goes a little bit tight and my mouth goes dry.

"Looks like your date is here, Rosie," Anna says with a sly smile. "Do we need to talk about anything?"

"Haha," I say. "Very funny."

The truck door opens and slams shut. Then, footsteps up onto the porch and a solid knock on the front wood door.

"Showtime," I say, heading down the stairs.

"Just be yourself, Rosie," Anna says.

"That's what worries me," I say, coming to the door, seeing Tim's handsome bearded face on the opposite side of it.

I unlock the door and open it.

"How silly of me," I say. "I should have left it open for you, Tim."

He's holding a wine bottle in one hand and a Ferguson General Store bag in the other. A bouquet of wildflowers is sticking out of the bag. Like yesterday, he's wearing Levi's jeans, cowboy boots, and a denim work shirt unbuttoned just enough to reveal a hint of his muscular pecs.

"Hey, safety first," he says.

"Well, come on in," I say, opening the screen door for him.

Anna comes down the stairs. She smiles kindly.

"Hello, Mr. Ferguson," she says.

"Oh please," he says. "Call me Tim, Anna. Mr. Ferguson was my dad."

I can tell my daughter is thrilled about this since it will make her feel like more of an adult. Why is it kids want to grow up so fast?

"Sure thing, Tim," she says.

"Anna," I say, "do you have something you want to say to Tim?"

"Oh yeah," she says, "thanks so much for the book."

Tim looks dumbfounded.

"What book?" he asks.

"*Little Red Riding Hood,*" Anna says. "The rare edition you pointed out yesterday at the store. You left it on the door for me. Thanks so much."

His eyes go wide.

"Oh yes," he says, laughing. "Slipped my mind. I must be having a senior moment. Glad you like it." Then, refocusing on me, "Where shall I put the goods?"

"Oh my," I say, "bring them right into the kitchen."

He does as I suggest. Meanwhile, I'm a little confused as to how he can't remember dropping the book off this morning. But then, maybe he's been having a super busy day. He is pretty much Paradox's only means for food, gas, booze, and Lotto Quickdraw, after all. He pulls out the flowers and hands them to me as I enter into the kitchen.

"Wildflowers," I say. "My favorite."

I find an old vase in the cabinet over the sink, add some tap water to it, and then place the flowers inside. Setting them on the table, I pull out the wine and a six-pack of Mountain Dew.

"I'd love one of those," he says, gesturing towards the soda.

"I'll take one, too," Anna says, "if that's cool."

"I'm gonna crack the wine if no one minds," I say.

"No one minds," Tim says while pulling the tab open on a can of Mountain Dew and handing it to Anna. Then, "Hey, Anna, you want to help me start a fire in the firepit?"

"Sure," she says.

"You two can start the grill too," I say.

"We're on it," Tim says, grabbing a can of soda for himself. "Come on, Anna."

She gladly goes with him. I've never seen her so chipper and eager to please around an adult. It's really something to see. Just two days ago she was miserable at the prospect of having to spend three months in the woods. Now all she does is smile. Who would have *thunk* it?

How am I doing, Allison?

Just fine, Rosie.

Charlie, you there?

Keep it up, babe. You deserve to be loved. But if you fall too hard, you're gonna have an issue with Tony. Just saying.

I'll try and not to get too excited.

But as I watch Tim and Anna gather up some firewood, my happiness knows no bounds.

CHAPTER 17

WE COOK AND then feast on the burgers, homemade French fries, and corn. When we're through, we have coffee and share a homemade apple pie that is to die for. I drink half the bottle of wine and by the time everything is cleaned up and the sun is setting, I'm feeling pretty good. I'm not sure if she truly feels like it, or if she's purposely giving Tim and me some privacy, but Anna excuses herself and heads back up to her room.

"Goodnight, Anna," Tim says.

That's when she does something nothing short of miraculous. She wraps her arms around Tim, gives him a bear hug. Tim gazes at me, offers me a wink, then pats her back gently.

"Sweet dreams, Anna," he says.

She turns to me, gives me a hug.

"Good luck," she whispers in my ear.

With that, she heads back inside to reconvene with her iPhone and her friends.

"Guess it's just you and me, Tim," I say.

"How about a little friendly fireside chat," he suggests.

"Don't mind if I do," I say.

Taking hold of the wine bottle on the table, I fill my mug and seat myself on one of the Adirondack chairs that surrounds the firepit. If this isn't heaven on earth, I don't know what is. Tim sits beside me, his coffee cup in hand. For a time, we just stare into the bright red-orange flames, listening to the good sound of the dry pine wood popping and snapping. Leaning forward, Tim adds another small log, then sits back.

"I know about the girl," I say after a time.

"Excuse me?" he says.

"The girl who was murdered back in 1986. Sarah Anne Moore. I know she lived in this house. They sort of skipped that bit of info in the Airbnb description."

He nods slowly, both his hands wrapped around the coffee mug.

"That was a terrible time for all of Paradox," he says. "I was barely out of college then, working for my dad in the store. The Moores were terrific people. Terrific customers. He, the father, was friends with my dad. They used to play seniors pickup basketball at the high school gym on Monday nights. He and Mrs. Moore attended my wedding. I remember when she was pregnant with Sarah back when I was in grade school." Shaking his head once more. "Just a terrible tragedy."

"Whatever happened to the Moores?"

Cocking his head over his shoulder, like he's about to say something along the lines of, *what the hell ever happens to two heartbroken people whose only child was murdered in cold blood?*

"He died in his sleep maybe five years after Sarah passed," he says, somewhat under his breath. "An ice fisherman found Mary Moore's body floating faceup in the lake as the ice was receding the next spring." He looks at me, the firelight reflected in his eyes. "She was still dressed in her nightgown. She must have gotten up one morning, walked out onto the dock, and jumped into the water that doesn't freeze around the dock. She'd been in the lake for so long, she was almost unrecognizable to the coroner. If not for the ice, there wouldn't have been much of anything left."

I sip some of the wine. It's not doing much for numbing the sadness that's building in my heart. In my head, I can't help but picture the crucifix that hangs on the wall in the kitchen.

"What about the man who did it? Theodore, I believe the newspapers called him. Did he go to prison forever?"

He nods again, sips his coffee, his eyes now refocused on the fire.

"They sent him to a maximum-security psychiatric prison in upstate western New York, due to the very violent nature of the murder. He used his teeth on Sarah, just like a rabid animal. Bit her hundreds of times." Glancing at me. "He tried to bite her face off, Rose."

"Oh dear God," I say, suddenly feeling slightly sick to my stomach. "I'm not sure I want to hear any more."

"I'm sorry," he says. "I didn't mean to disturb you."

Acting on instinct, I take hold of his hand, squeeze it.

"It's okay," I say. "I just can't imagine a human being doing something like that to another human being."

I go to remove my hand, but he squeezes my fingers. When I don't let go, neither does he. My heart goes from sad and somewhat sickened to happy and content in three seconds flat. That's when I hear the howling again.

Saaaaaarrrrrrrrrrr . . .

I sit up straight.

"You hear that, Tim?" I say.

"Hear what?" he asks.

Saaaaaarrrrrrrrrr . . .

"That," I say. "That noise. That howling. What the heck is that?"

He grins.

"Oh that's just a loon," he says. "They like to call out for their mates at night. They only have one mate in their lifetime, and they are forever in love. It's as instinctual as breathing. They don't know any other way."

I squeeze his hand once more.

"That just might be the most romantic thing anyone has ever told me," I say.

Then, coming from upstairs in the house.

"Mom," Anna calls out. "Did you hear the noise again?"

"It's just a loon, dolly," I say. "That's what Tim says anyway."

"Oh good," she says. "Because I thought it might be the Big Bad Wolf."

Once more I'm reminded of the rare edition that was left on our doorstep. Could it be that Tim left it for us, but is too embarrassed to admit it? Rather, that's why he said it slipped his mind? Some men try really hard at first and then pull back a little in fear of being too needy. In any case, it was a beautiful gesture.

"Can I ask you a personal question, Tim?" I say.

He nods. "Shoot."

"Whatever happened to you and your wife?"

He purses his lips and releases my hand. Crap, if I knew he was going to do that, I wouldn't have posed the question in the first place.

"We had two children, early on. Two boys. Tim Junior and Jason. They're grown adults now living down in the city building video games."

"Wow, good for them," I say.

"Will be when they start making some money," he says, not without a wry laugh. "But as for their mother, we drifted apart years ago. One day in the early two-thousands I came back from the store after I locked it up for the night, and she was gone, along with most of the furniture, plus our bank account and any cash we had in the safe in the bedroom closet."

"Oh God, I'm sorry I brought it up."

He smiles sadly. "No worries. Like I said, we'd been drifting apart terribly, and I could always make more money. We're actually on better terms now. You know, for the sake of the boys. She's remarried, happily I assume, to a stockbroker. They live in Westchester, which is nice because she gets to see the boys a lot."

"That's a good thing, right?"

"It is," he says. Then, dumping what's left of his coffee, and standing. "Well, I've got an early one. I'd best be getting back. I had a wonderful time with you and Anna, Rose. Truly, I did."

I set my mug on the chair's armrest and stand. I face him, the firelight reflecting off his handsome face. He takes both my hands in his. He leans into me, and I lean into him, and for the first time, we kiss. Is there anything in this world like that first kiss? It's magical, no matter what age you happen to be when it comes calling for you.

When we release, we hug one another tightly.

"I had a terrific time, too," I say, feeling my heart pounding inside my ribs. "Perhaps we'll do it again in a couple of days?"

"I'd like that," he says, taking hold of my left hand while together we make our way slowly toward the house. "You know what? This might sound silly, but I have a gift certificate to a really good Italian restaurant in Schroon that I've been dying to use. Would you be interested in an early dinner Saturday night, Rose?"

I'm walking, but my feet don't feel like they're touching the ground.

"I'd absolutely love to, Tim," I say. "If it's early enough, Anna can stay here by herself."

Just then, a vibration in my back pocket. It tells me someone is texting me. I can bet who that someone is. Tony. It's like a subconscious alarm has just gone off inside his head.

We head back into the house and I see Tim to the front door. He nods in the direction of the fireplace.

"You still haven't lit the fire I built you," he observes.

"There's been no need," I say. "The nights thus far have been beautiful."

"It starts getting cooler in September. Tomorrow is the first, so give it a few days and you'll be using it all the time. I guarantee it."

"Well, I'm sure with you having prepped it, the fire will burn instantly."

"That's a beautiful old stone fireplace," he says. "You almost never see them anymore. Most people nowadays stick to wood stoves since they are so much more efficient."

For a beat or two, we both stare at the beautiful stone fireplace.

"I can picture them in my head, Tim," I say, after a long beat. "The Moores sitting by the fire, enjoying the night." Turning towards the piano. "Maybe Sarah learned to play that very piano."

In my head, I picture the long-dark-haired girl seated on the round stool, the slender gentle fingers on her hands tickling the keys.

"Simpler times," he says. "The Moores were very much alive and very happy. Trust me when I say they had no idea the fate that awaited them."

"A fate worse than hell on earth," I say, shaking my head as if to break myself out of my spell. "Now I'm beginning to sound like a drama queen. You'll have to forgive me."

"No worries," he says.

He opens the screen door, steps out onto the porch. I follow. The yellow porch light gives off a wonderful glow. It also doesn't attract insects the way a bright white light would. For the first time that night, I notice that the temperature is indeed beginning to drop now that fall is around the corner. Great sleeping weather is upon us.

Tim turns to me once more. We lock eyes and before I know it, we're wrapped in one another's arms. Our mouths connect, and we kiss for what seems like hours. When we come up for air, we're both smiling like happy teenagers.

"I'll call you tomorrow, Rose," he says, "unless I see you at the store."

"I might come in for coffee before work," I say.

"That would be nice," he says. "See you then, maybe."

I watch him cross over the lawn to the driveway. He gets in his truck, fires it up, and backs out. Before he takes off along the country road, he hits the horn. I offer him a wave.

"Oh crap," I whisper as he disappears into the night, "I think I've gone and fallen in love."

CHAPTER 18

Entering back into the house, I close the big wood door behind me and lock it.

"Anna," I yell up the stairs, "you still up?"

"Yup. You coming up soon, Rosie?"

"In a minute, hon. Just locking up."

Entering into the brightly lit kitchen, I once more find myself attracted to the crucifix that hangs on the wall over the stove. I'm not the religious type, but I find myself doing something that is so not like me. I make the sign of the cross.

"God bless you and keep you, Sarah," I whisper.

A cool wind blows in through the open back door then. The lonely loon cries, *Saaaaaarrrrrrrrrr*. Goose bumps rise up on my skin. The sad noise gives me pause. It also makes me want to indulge in one more small drink of wine. Looking around for my wine mug, I realize I once again left it outside.

Heading back out through the rear screen door, I skip on down to the firepit. Out on the water, I see a pleasure boat making its way across the lake in the night, its green and red running board lights lit up against the dark of night. Makes me want to invest in a boat. Maybe a second- or thirdhand outboard that Anna can manage on her own if she so chooses. Something to look into tomorrow.

The fire is dying out, which is a good thing. Locating my mug on the Adirondack chair armrest, I grab hold of it, and turn back for the house. My eyes are drawn to the Paradox Lake trailhead. The shadow appears. My blood runs cold, pulse skyrockets. It's the shadow of a man. Or is it? It appears to be poised on four legs, like a deer or maybe a bear. Whatever it is, it shoots and scoots from behind the woodpile to the trailhead and then disappears inside the woods.

Heart be fucking still . . .

I keep telling myself that it's just a deer. The deer come out at night, right? But why does the shadow seem like it could belong to a man? And what kind of man gets around on all four limbs? I'm standing stone stiff by the light of the dying fire. It's like my feet are buried up to my shins in curing concrete. *Saaaaaarrrrrr-rrrr*, cries the loon. Where's Tim when I need him? More vibration coming from the cell phone in my pocket.

Swallowing something dry and bitter, I run for the back screen door and nearly plow through it. Slipping inside, I close the wood door and lock it. I press my back up against it, feel my heart pounding in my throat.

"What the hell is that thing out there?" I whisper to myself.

Inhaling and exhaling a few deep breaths, I tell myself, "It's just a deer, Rose. Nothing more."

But why do I not believe that?

Tomorrow morning, I'll go to the Ferguson General Store and I'll tell Tim about the shadow. That I've spotted it two nights in a row. Hopefully he won't think I'm a crazy lady. Hopefully he will have a logical explanation for it, just as he did the cry of the loon. The woods . . . it could be I'm just not used to them.

I set the empty mug on the counter and realize I didn't bring the wine bottle back in with me. No way I'm going back out there now. Best to call it a night. Staring up at the crucifix, I decide to leave the light on yet again. I head upstairs, and rather than sleep in my own bed tonight, I go straight to Anna's room.

* * *

But before I get in bed, I brush my teeth and put on a long t-shirt. Then I get in bed beside my daughter who, naturally, is texting with someone.

"Everything okay, Rosie?" she asks.

In my head, I'm seeing the shadow going from behind the woodpile to the trailhead. No way I'm telling Anna about it. It will only freak her out unnecessarily since the more I think about it, the more I'm convinced it's got to be a deer—or a black bear or a wolf. Yikes!

"Of course, kiddo," I say. "Why would anything be wrong?"

"Because you don't usually volunteer to have a sleepover with me unless you've had a fight with Tony."

"Oh crap," I say, "I almost forgot. Tony texted me and I haven't answered yet."

My phone is set on the small table beside the bed. I take hold of it, gaze at the screen. Sure enough, he's left me two texts.

"Are we feeling just a little guilty, Rose?" Anna says, matter-of-factly, if not maturely, like our roles have suddenly reversed.

I open the first text.

Where are you?

Typical Tony. Not, *Hey, just thinking of you*, or, *Hope you guys are having fun*. But like the worrywart he is, he needs to know where we are and what we're doing precisely when he wants to know it.

Next text.

Haven't heard from you in a while.

Okay, shift the onus onto me. I see what he's doing.

"You haven't answered my question, Rosie," Anna presses, while typing something into her iPhone.

In my head I see Tony seated at Lanies Bar. All his friends will be gone by now, and the bartender will be asking him about calling an Uber on his behalf, because no way is he driving tonight. Or who knows, maybe he's safe and sound at home in his North Albany bottom-floor apartment, a stack of paperback and hardcover books by his side.

"Oh crap, Anna," I say, "am I a bad person for liking Tim?"

"What's this?" she says. "You're actually asking me my opinion?"

"Sure," I say. "I'd like to know."

"Well, listen, I like Tony. I really do. Deep down inside, I probably have love for him. He's helped me out a lot. But I have to admit, Rosie, there's something about Tim that's very attractive. I can see why you like him."

I exhale while staring at Tony's texts. Or should I say sigh? Because, as I said before, I do love Tony. But also, as Anna just said, there's something very attractive if not alluring about Tim.

"I do feel guilty," I say. "But then, I do like Tim. No doubt about it." Then, turning to her and smiling. "He invited me to an Italian restaurant this weekend in Schroon."

"Really," she says. "You accepted, I hope."

Me, back to staring at Tony's texts. I have to respond with something.

All good here, I text. Then, *Sweet dreams XO.*

This is the part where I feel like a total cheat and a cad. But what am I gonna do? I swear on my mom's grave that I would never openly cheat on Tony if we were married. I would honor our commitment. But, and this is a big but, not only are we not married, but I've caught Albany's favorite writer in compromising positions with some of his more adoring fans on more than one occasion—Anna has no idea about this BTW. And in each instance, he's begged for my forgiveness and promised to be good from thereon in. I always took him back, sucker that I am. That's not to say what's going on with Tim is revenge. It's not. What's going on with him are real feelings. Feelings I haven't experienced in a long, long time.

Saaaaaarrrrrrrrrrr, howls the loon outside the window. *Saaaaaarrrrrrrrrr . . .*

"There she goes again," I say, putting my phone back on vibrate and setting it on the bedside table. "Did you know that when loons mate, they mate for life, Anna, and that they are always in love with their mate?"

"Oh my God," Anna says, her eyes wide. "That means I'd be with Jake Walls for the rest of my life."

I can't help but laugh at the possibility.

"I thought you were like in love with little Jake Walls," I say.

"Not that in love," she says. "There's a lot of guys out there."

I pat her thigh.

"Now you're cooking with Wesson, honey," I say.

"Wesson," she says with a furrowed brow. "I don't get it."

"Never mind."

Saaaaaarrrrrrrrrrr . . . Saaaaaarrrrrrrrrrr . . .

Both of us fall asleep to the sound of a lonely loon on Paradox Lake.

CHAPTER 19

THE NEXT MORNING I'm up at seven, feeling a bit rusty from all that wine. But otherwise, feeling happy about my dinner date with Tim and about the work in progress going in the studio. Instead of making my coffee, I decide to head into town to grab a coffee and breakfast sandwich for me, and an apple fritter and a hot chocolate for Anna. And yes, I have every intention of seeing Tim. That is, if he's there that early in the morning.

As luck would have it, Tim is in the house, as they say. He's behind the counter, checking out the early morning risers and working folk who are grabbing their coffee and daily Lotto tickets and scratch-offs. He spots me as soon as I come through the front wood and glass door. His face goes immediately into smile mode, which makes me smile. I offer a wave and then gesture towards the coffee bar with my right hand. He nods and winks while ringing someone out.

Heading to the coffee bar, I pour a large Green Mountain Roast and add some two-percent milk to it, no sugar. Capping it off, I make a small hot chocolate for Anna. Placing both beverages in a cardboard holder, I shift on down to the donuts and the pre-made—but homemade—breakfast sandwiches that keep warm under a long heat lamp. Egg, bacon, and cheese, or egg, ham, and cheese. Decisions, decisions. I choose the ham version, then grab an apple fritter for Anna. Placing everything on the tray, I await my turn in line at the counter.

Peering over my right shoulder, I see him sweeping the floor. Creepy Ed. He's wearing what I now recognize as his usual uniform of overalls, work boots, and t-shirt. He looks at me with his striking blue eyes and grins. I notice something on his neck. It's a tattoo. A black tattoo of an animal. A cat maybe, or a dog. The more I look at it, I begin to realize it's a wolf. I never noticed it till now, but then, I guess I tried not to pay all that much attention to him.

I try and work up a grin for him, but it's entirely forced. Maybe Tim claims him to be entirely harmless and slow, yet there's something about him that doesn't sit well with me. Or maybe I'm just being paranoid. Maybe he's the sweetest man in the world, with a tattoo of a wolf on his thick neck.

The door opens again and a cute, middle-aged, auburn-haired woman enters. Like Tim, she's wearing the forest green Ferguson General Store pickup truck logo t-shirt.

"Kathy," Tim says, as I take my place at the counter. "Just in time."

Kathy comes around and stands beside Tim. They kind of resemble one another in that they possess the same eyes. Having rung me out, Tim hands me my change.

"Kathy, this is my friend Rose," he says. "She's staying in Paradox for a few months with her daughter, working on a new art project or projects."

His sister. I didn't know he had a sister.

"Nice meeting you, Kathy," I say, holding out my hand over the counter.

She smiles warmly and takes my hand in hers.

"I'm going to reveal a secret," she says, even with her brother standing right beside her. "You're all Tim has been talking about for the past couple of days."

Tim's face turns a noticeable shade of red, even with half of it covered by a beard.

"Thanks for that, Sis," he says. Then, his eyes on me. "I'm taking a quick break, if you want to join me, Rose."

"Sure," I say. "I'll bring my coffee."

He comes around the counter and goes for the door.

"Let's head outside, Rose," he says. "It's a beautiful Adirondack morning."

"Absolutely, Tim," I say. Then, eyeing Kathy, "Nice meeting you."

"Don't be a stranger," she says. "Sometimes the girls get together for happy hour on Fridays. We head over to Bunny's Bar a few doors down and play darts and pool. We stink at pool, but it's fun."

"I'd love to."

"It's a date," she says.

I head out the door behind Tim, laughing on the inside at the notion of dating both Tim and his sister.

*   *   *

I set my tray on the passenger seat of my Mini Cooper, but grab hold of my coffee and carry it to the picnic table set on the far side of the general store. Tim is already there, seated on top of the table. Surprise of surprises, he's smoking a cigarette.

"Didn't take you for a smoker," I say, as I climb up onto the table and set myself beside him.

Uncapping the plastic coffee lid, I steal a sip. It's hot, rich, and delicious. I can't wait to dig into my sandwich. Everything is so homemade up here, and because of it, it tastes so much better than the everyday Dunkin' Donuts fare I'm force-fed down in the Albany suburbs.

"Sadly," Tim says, exhaling a cloud of blue smoke. "But when I stopped drinking, I needed something to replace it."

"I used to smoke," I say. "Gave it up on Christmas day almost fourteen years ago now. My daughter Allison had been diagnosed with leukemia and I needed something positive in my life. So I quit, cold turkey."

"Just like that, huh?" he says.

"Just like that."

I sip more coffee.

"The drinking," I say. "Was it a problem? Or am I out of bounds, Tim?"

He sets his hand on my thigh.

"You're not out of bounds at all," he says. "It's not so much that it was a problem. It's just that I liked it too much. My personality changed when I drank. Don't get me wrong, I didn't become mean or anything like that. I was just . . . I don't know . . . kind of wild, I guess. So, I thought it best to give it a rest."

I try to picture a wild Tim Ferguson in my head, whatever that means. Maybe it means he used to have a few beers and then get up on the bar and be the life of the party. If that's the case, I can see why he quit. Tony, on the other hand, is the type to stew the more he drinks. He starts in on his, *"No one realizes what a terrific talent I am. I should be a rich writer by now. Not a struggling writer."* Maybe he should quit for a while too. Me, when I drink, I just get mellow happy.

"We don't have to talk about it if you don't want to," I say.

"Anna still in bed?" he asks.

I'm guessing the abrupt change in conversation direction is his way of saying, *I actually don't want to talk about it.*

"She's twelve, almost thirteen," I say. "You gotta ask?"

He laughs. "Can you believe we were thirteen once? Now I'll never see fifty again."

"I'm coming up on it faster than I'd like," I say.

He turns to me. "You know what, Rose?"

"You have my attention."

"You are one hot close-to-fifty lady," he says, grinning. "A real MILF."

We both almost fall off the table laughing. And that's when he steals a long, loving kiss. Never mind the combination cigarette smoke and coffee breath, it's the sweetest kiss I can remember receiving from anyone, next to that first kiss he laid on me last night.

Speaking of last night . . .

"Tim," I say, as we come up for air and he tosses his spent cigarette to the ground, stamping it out with his boot tip. "I saw something last night, and the night before, that kind of disturbed me."

"Where?" he says. "When?"

His face is now genuinely full of concern.

"It happened after you left. After you left on both nights, actually. In the back, behind the log pile, I saw something scoot out from around the side of the house and then disappear into the Paradox Lake trailhead. It's the spookiest thing in the world."

He ponders what I'm telling him for a long beat or two.

"Are you thinking the *something* could be human?" he asks.

"That's just it," I say. "Whatever it is, it moves so fast, and on all fours, it almost seems sort of . . . and I can't believe I'm saying this . . . inhuman, you know?"

He nods some more, pulls out a second cigarette, and lights it up.

"That's because it probably is inhuman."

"Excuse me?"

Exhaling the initial drag of smoke, he says, "If you ask me, it's just a deer."

I find myself smiling. "That's what I keep telling myself." I place my hand on his hard-as-rock thigh.

"But I'll tell you what," he says. "Why don't I come by after dinner tonight? We'll make a fire and we'll see if we can spot whatever the heck it is, together. If it's a deer, chances are it will be there. They are creatures of habit."

"That would be wonderful," I say.

Of course, I'm not sure if I'm saying this because he's taking charge of the situation or because I'm going to have yet another date with him tonight. Maybe a little of both.

"One thing that worries me is that it's another kind of animal," he says, "like a black bear or a mountain lion or even a wolf."

"Jeez, a wolf, really?"

"The climate is changing, Rose. More and more wolves are coming up from the south, seeking lower temps. They're being spotted more and more while they make the trek to Canada and farther north."

"Are they really that dangerous?"

"Let's put it this way. If it's okay with you, I'll bring my pistol."

A shot of adrenaline injected into my bloodstream.

"You mean like a real gun?" I question.

"That would be the idea."

"I haven't been around guns very much, being an art professor. But I guess up here you need them. My father had a hunting rifle, but he kept it locked up."

"I'm fully licensed," he says. "If something is out there, we don't want Anna getting hurt, now do we?"

"We most definitely do not, Tim."

I drink some more coffee. When I look up, Creepy Ed is standing there. His sudden presence startles me. Has he been there the entire time? He must have come from around the back of the building. Did it silently, stealthily. Like always when I'm in his presence, he's staring at me with his blue eyes.

"What is it, Ed?" Tim poses.

"I need to go home for a minute. Is that going to be a problem, Mr. Ferguson?"

"No, Ed. The morning rush is over. Just get back as soon as you can, and start refilling the shelves."

"Yes, Mr. Ferguson."

He shifts his focus to me again.

"Hello, missus," he says. "How is your little girl?"

Just his asking for my Anna sends a cold shiver up my spine.

"She's fine, thank you," I say, my eyes now drawn to the wolf tattoo on his neck. The tattoo is pulsing with his every breath.

He nods.

"I'll be going then," he says.

Together, we watch the barrel-chested man get into his battered pickup. Starting it up, he pulls out of the lot and heads in the direction of the lake. For a time, we sit there in the quiet, until Tim finishes his cigarette and stamps it out. He slides off the table and faces me.

"You don't like Ed, do you?" he says, a sly grin painting his face.

"It's not that I don't like him," I say. "It's just that I feel like he isn't looking at me, so much as through me. Through my clothing. And that black wolf tattooed on his neck. All this talk about wolves suddenly . . . Frankly, it's unnerving."

Tim laughs a little. Not at me, but at the situation.

"Trust me, there's no need to be concerned about wolves or Ed. If there's a wolf in the area, I'll take care of it. And as for Ed, well, he's a good man. Like I said, he's a little slow. He's lived in the North Country his whole life with his family and extended family in a farmhouse in the middle of the Paradox Preserve. You should see the place. No electricity or running water. It's completely off the grid. It's like a place caught up in a time warp. You can see it from the Paradox Lake Trail if you look hard enough. The house is accessible from the Paradox Lake Road only by a narrow two-track that runs for miles in the deep forest. You wouldn't even know it was there unless you were looking for it."

"I won't be looking for it, thanks," I say, sliding off the table. "I'll be letting you get back to work, Mr. Ferguson."

He takes hold of my arm, pulls me towards him, and plants one on my mouth. It makes me want to melt on the spot.

"Oh my," I say, as I pull back. "Yes, you may make violent love to me in the parking lot."

"I'm sorry," he says. "I couldn't help myself. It's just that you're so stunning, Rose."

"You really think so? Or is that what you tell all your girlfriends?"

"You know it's true," he says. Then, kissing me more gently this time. "See you later, when we do a little hunting."

"Sounds like a plan, Stan," I say.

As he heads back to the store and I go to my car, I feel the weight of true love bearing down on my heart.

CHAPTER 20

I CAN'T HELP myself. The egg sandwich smells so good, I peel back the aluminum foil and steal a couple of bites while I'm driving back to our house on the lake—I'm breaking my own *no eating in the Mini Cooper* rule. By the time I'm pulling up in the driveway, I've finished half the sandwich. Getting out, I come around to the passenger side, grab the tray, and bring it with me into the kitchen. Then I head back into the living room, stationing myself at the bottom of the stairs.

"Anna, you up, honey?"

I wait. No answer. No surprise there.

"Anna, wake uppppp . . ." Now I'm using my singsong wakey-wakey voice.

The point to all this is that I want her to shift from her summer sleep-in schedule to her everyday school schedule since the Labor Day weekend is almost upon us. Maybe my daughter is about to be homeschooled, but we have to take it all very seriously. That means getting up on time, five days per week, minus traditional school holidays, of course.

"Anna, come on," I call out again. "I have a hot chocolate and an apple fritter for you. Your favorite."

Still no answer.

"Sure," I say, "force an old lady to make the stairs."

I trudge up the staircase and come to the second-floor landing. Hooking a right, I then make a quick left into Anna's bedroom. She's not there. My lungs go tight and I have trouble breathing.

"Relax, Rose," I whisper to myself. "I'm sure she's in the bathroom."

About-facing, I cross the hall into the upstairs bathroom. She's not there either. I open the shower curtain. The shower is empty.

"Anna!" I bark. "This isn't funny."

I speed-walk the short hallway into my bedroom. Anna is not there. Open the closet. She's not there either.

"Oh Christ," I say, the panic starting to kick in. "I never should have left her alone."

I go to the closet in her bedroom, throw the door open. Empty again.

"Oh sweet Jesus," I say aloud.

Then, coming from outside the window: "I got one!!!"

I go to the window, look out onto the dock. I'll be damned. Anna is standing out on the dock in her black one-piece bathing suit. She's got a fishing poll in her hand. A sunfish—or what I'm guessing is a sunfish—is dangling off the end of her line. The live fish is throbbing, jerking, and struggling to get free.

I can't help but smile, but that's also when I realize my eyes have filled with tears. The tears are proof that I will never get over the pain and fear of losing a child.

Take it easy, Rosie. You gotta learn to let go.

I know, I know, Allison. It's just that I still feel the pain of losing you and I can't bear to lose another.

You won't, Rosie. But the more you try to protect her, the more she won't be able to protect herself. You get what I mean? If you could have transferred my cancer to yourself, you would have. You would have gladly died in my place. But you see, it's impossible to do any of those things. Life has its own way of working things out.

So does death, I guess.

Correctamundo.

I picture my sandy-blond-haired daughter sitting on Anna's bed. She'd be dressed in her jeans and flip-flops, and maybe a Nirvana t-shirt. At least, that's the way I picture her as the teenager she never got to be. She might be gone, but she's still with me, just like all my ghosts are with me.

Allison, do me one favor.

What is it, Rosie?

Just for once, call me "Mom."

Love you, Mom.

Love you, Allison.

I quickly head back down the stairs, wiping my eyes with the backs of my hands so that Anna can't tell I've been crying. I want her to know that I trust her . . . that I trust her enough to start taking care of herself now that soon she'll be a teenager.

"What a fish, Anna," I say. "Bravo."

She's still holding the rod with both hands, the fish never still.

"So what the heck do I do with it now, Rosie?"

"Let me help," I say, jogging onto the dock.

"I don't want to touch it," Anna says.

"Then why go fishing, silly?"

Taking hold of the fish between forefinger and thumb, I then pull out the hook. Before tossing the sunfish back, I ask Anna to give me her hand.

"Really?"

"Really," I say. "Consider this our first lesson in homeschooling."

"Well, okay," she says. "So long as I get an A for participation."

"Most definitely."

Reluctantly, Anna touches the fish.

"It feels cold and scaly," she says. "But not so bad."

"See, I told you," I say. "Always remove the hook as gently as possible. If the hook is buried too far inside the fish, cut the line and throw the fish back in the water anyway. Unless, of course, you plan on having a fish fry that night."

"Toss it back with the hook still in it? Won't that hurt it even more?"

"The hook will dissolve in no time, honey."

She scrunches her forehead.

"How do you know all this stuff, Mom?"

"I grew up with your uncles and a dad who would rather fish than work. He took me out in his boat a lot on Lake George when I was your age."

"Do you think we can get a boat?"

"You never know," I say, making a mental note to ask Tim about it later.

She casts the lure into the water, slowly reels it in.

"Got you some breakfast," I say. "An apple fritter and a hot chocolate."

"Oh good," she says, setting her pole down thoughtlessly on the dock. "I'm starving."

We head back into the house where I microwave her now-cooled hot chocolate. I also microwave her apple fritter for ten seconds since Anna likes it warmed up. Together, we sit at the kitchen table and dig into our breakfasts. Since I only have half a sandwich left, I'm done in no time. I sip my coffee while Anna continues to work on hers.

"So you went to the general store this morning," she says, after a time. "Did you go just to get us some food? Or did you go because you were hoping to see someone?"

I can't help but smile.

"Snagged," I say.

"This is getting serious, Rosie," she says, while popping a piece of apple fritter in her mouth.

"We've only just met one another," I say. "It's way too early for getting serious."

"When are you going to tell Tony?" she asks. "He should probably know. What's that you're always preaching? Honesty is the bestest policy."

I nod, feeling a definite sadness in my chest. I still love Tony. I'm just not *in love* with him anymore. There's a distinct difference. I could attempt to explain this to Anna, but now that she's done with her breakfast, all I wanna do is grab a quick shower and get to work.

"All done?" I say, pushing out my chair and standing.

"Finished," she says, while getting up and tossing her empty paper cup into the garbage. "And way to change the subject, Rosie."

"Very funny," I say. "I'm going to grab a quick shower since I stink, and then get some work in. Don't forget to wash your dish."

"Aye aye, Captain."

"At ease, sailor."

"Let's get a boat," she says, as I exit the kitchen, scoot across the living room, and bound the stairs two at a time to the second floor.

*   *   *

Undressing down to my birthday suit, I go to the hall closet and search for a couple of fresh bath towels. There's a stack on the mid-level shelf. The lower shelf houses the bedsheets and blankets. The top shelf holds three or four extra pillows. It's while glancing at the pillows I can't help but notice something stuffed in the far corner. Newspapers. Maybe three or four of them. It's almost like someone shoved them there at the last minute and then hid them with the pillows.

I pull one of them out. It's so old it feels like it's about to crumble in my hands. The date is September 8, 1986. The paper is the *Glens Falls Eagle* and the headline is the same as the one I read online two nights ago about Sarah Anne Moore having gone missing. There's a beautiful black-and-white photo of her below the headline. The photo must have been snapped by a school photographer, perhaps for her yearbook. She's got long, thick, dark hair parted in the middle, and stunning dark eyes, a perfectly chiseled nose, full lips, and her expression is one of hope and youth. If I had to wager a guess, the concept of death is the furthest thing from her mind.

But here's the strange thing. Sarah looks so much like my Anna, it's scary. Maybe I'm letting my imagination get the best of me, but I swear she could be a dead ringer.

I flip through the papers. Each one carries one dreadful headline after the other. "Sarah Anne Moore Gone Missing Along the

Paradox Lake Trail." "Still no Sign of Sarah." "Sarah Anne Moore's Body Discovered on Paradox Lake Trail." "Theodore Peasley Arrested in Connection with Moore Murder." This final headline is accompanied by another black-and-white photo of a short, heavy-set man with his wrists cuffed behind his back. He's being led to what looks like a state trooper cruiser car by two gray-uniformed troopers. You can't see his face because it's hidden by long, scraggy dark hair under a hooded sweatshirt.

"Sarah Anne Moore," I whisper to myself. "You look too much like my daughter."

I go to place the newspapers back in the spot in which I found them, but something inside me tells me to hang onto them. That maybe I was meant to find them. The towels in one hand and the newspapers in the other, I go back into the bedroom, set them on the bed. Then I head back to the bathroom and quickly shower. After drying myself off, I put on a fresh pair of jeans and a plain black t-shirt. As always, I slip into my favorite pair of brown cow-boy boots. Taking hold of the newspapers, I carry them down into my studio with me. Already, I feel my creative left brain warming up.

CHAPTER 21

SEATED AT MY little round stool, sculpting knife in hand, I go to work on the face. One eye on the newspaper photo of Sarah Anne Moore, the other on the clay head, I begin to carve the eyes. I'm not in charge of my movements at this point. A higher being, like an angel or a ghost, is doing the work for me. My fingers and arm muscles are merely conduits for what the muse wishes to construct. I gaze once more at Sarah's picture and my fingers rapidly cut away at the clay, forming one eyeball and then the other, until I find myself working on the nose, and then the mouth, using my thumb pad to smooth out the thick lips.

I hardly even notice that an hour has passed since I first started working. My brow is covered in sweat and I swear there's clay in my hair—looks like another shower is in store for this afternoon or maybe a quick swim off the dock—and the back of my t-shirt is wet with sweat. My hands are covered in clay, but that goes without saying. I stand, stretch my back. When the hell did I take scissors to the newspapers and tack the pictures of Sarah Anne and Theodore to the wall? When did I cut out the headlines and tack those to the wall under the pictures? When did I tack the little piece of yellow crime scene ribbon to it?

Of course, I recall having done it sometime in between my carving the cheeks and the chin. I was so excited, so pumped with adrenaline, that I didn't think about it. I just picked the scissors up off the worktable and started cutting. Now I can't help but feel a little guilty. The newspapers weren't mine to destroy. But then, Sarah Anne's entire family is deceased now. Who would want the newspapers? Certainly not anyone who's renting this place out on Airbnb, excepting myself, of course. It almost feels like someone, somewhere, left them in the closet specifically for me to discover.

Wiping my hands off on a rag, I head into the kitchen, pour a tall glass of water. Gazing at the crucifix on the wall, I can't help but picture the Paradox Lake Trail, and the spot in which Anna and I discovered the crime scene tape. I know I should head right back into my studio for another round of sculpting. But there's a feeling growing in my gut . . . something physical that's gnawing at me to head outside, go back to the trailhead, and revisit the site of Sarah's rape. Sarah's murder. Her spirit is occupying precious space in my head now, and there's nothing that's going to get her out of there.

I go to the staircase.

"Anna, I'll be right back. Going outside for a few minutes."

"Don't get lost, Rosie," she says.

"Very funny. One hour of screen time, young lady, and then I need you to help give the place a little bit of a cleaning."

"Yeah, yeah, yeah," she says. "I'm at your service, Rosie."

"Excellent," I say. "I'll be right back."

"I repeat," she says, "don't get lost in the jungle."

Turning, I head for the back door. I also tell myself that it's too late. I might not be lost in the jungle, but I am already lost in Sarah's world.

* * *

Entering onto the trailhead, I immediately feel the cooling effect of the thick tree cover. Although some heavy clouds are moving in—heavy thunderstorms are predicted for this weekend—the sun is almost completely blocked out. Only narrow rays make their way in through the small openings in the tree canopy. I walk as fast as I can in my cowboy boots—hiking boots would be better—making my way over the occasional felled tree trunk and tree root. But this portion of the trail is clearer than it was before Anna and I cleaned it up.

I walk for twenty minutes, working up a cool sweat under my t-shirt, until I make out the lake on my right-hand side and the secluded beach that accesses it. I head for the beach via the narrow path that connects to the Paradox Lake Trail. Exiting the forest, the sun's warmth blankets me immediately. Despite the thick clouds that are moving in, the sky is still mostly sunny and the sunshine reflects off the gray-white sand.

Going with my gut, I go to the place where we uncovered the piece of crime scene ribbon, and drop to my knees. I start digging with my hands into the loose sand. It's easy at first, but soon the sand becomes more like packed gravel and dirt. I find a stick behind a felled tree and I use it like a small shovel.

I dig like a woman possessed. Mostly I just find rocks and the occasional nickel or quarter. I find a Bic lighter and an old rusted Budweiser can. But then I find something else. I find a cross-shaped pendant that's attached to a silver chain. Most of the chain is gone now, but a length about the size of my index finger remains. Shifting myself, I sit down on the tree, the sweat pouring into my eyes and down my face and onto my lips.

Could this belong to Sarah? It looks old enough to have been in the ground for more than three decades. The silver is so tarnished it's almost black. Judging from the rusty ends on the chain, the metal has disintegrated over the years. My hands are shaking. If only I'd brought along one of the newspaper photos of Sarah, I could maybe check to see if she's wearing a silver cross.

But that's when it hits me. This is the 21st century. I can access the photos with my smartphone. If Anna were with me right now, she'd probably say something like, "Duhhhh." I pull the phone out, type in "Sarah Anne Moore, Paradox Lake." I get the same results as I did with my laptop the other day. My hands now going from shaking to outright trembling, I click on the first link and once more see the first archived newspaper front page. Using my fingers, I blow up the photo of Sarah.

"Oh sweet Jesus," I whisper. "She's wearing the cross."

That's it then. The cross I'm now holding in my fingers belonged to Sarah. No question in my mind about it. What significance does this pose? What importance? It doesn't, other than the fact that I am now physically connected with the murdered girl. Physically and emotionally. I scroll once more through the newspapers. I come to the last one with Theodore Peasley being led to a state trooper cruiser by two uniformed troopers. I blow the picture up and stare at it, like it's going to reveal something to me. Some sort of clue about who he was and why he did what he did to such a sweet young girl.

He's a short, stocky man. A strong, barrel-chested man by the looks of it. A man who was far too strong for a thin, if not skinny, girl like Sarah. He's wearing a hoodie and his scraggly hair covers his face, so it's almost impossible to make out his face. He's wearing work boots and farmer's overalls over a t-shirt.

A connection flashes in my brain. The creepy worker, Ed, who works in Tim's store. He's a short, stocky man who wears farmer's overalls over a ratty t-shirt. He doesn't have long hair, or any hair at all, for that matter. Of course, the man in this photo would be thirty-three years older by now. He'd have gone from a young man to a middle-aged man.

"Jesus, could he be the same man?" I say aloud. "And if he is the same man, what the hell is he doing out of prison?"

Tim mentioned to me that Ed lives in these very woods. His house is visible along the Paradox Lake Trail. I stand and gently place the cross in my jeans pocket. Turning away from the water, I head back onto the trail. I have to get back for Anna. But something is pulling me in the opposite direction. It's the urge, or should I say need, to see Ed's house. I need to know if this man is the same man who killed Sarah all those years ago.

I glance at my watch. It's only a little after eleven in the morning. Anna will still be chatting with her friends on her phone for another half hour at least. If I explore the trail for another mile or so, I'll certainly come upon Ed's house in the woods. Like Little Red Riding Hood, I move in the opposite direction of my house and head deeper into the dark forest.

CHAPTER 22

NOW THAT THE cloud cover is blocking out the midday sun, the woods are even darker than normal. Squirrels scatter about, and birds scoot and shoot from branch to branch. I bust through one spider web after the other. The sensation of the webs against my face and exposed arms creeps me out. The deeper I go, the more intent I am on keeping an eye out for the house. I'm not sure what to expect. Does more than one house exist in these deep woods? Or just Ed's old family farmhouse?

I keep walking. But then, walking isn't the right word. More like slow jogging. I'm on a mission that has no rhyme or reason. Or does it? I'm trying to put two and two together. Trying to determine if Sarah's killer is still alive, out of prison, and living in these very woods. If he is all of these things, it bears the question, why in the world would a man like Tim Ferguson hire him? After the way he brutally murdered Sarah, covering her body in hundreds of bites, including trying to bite her face off, why would Tim be so nice to him? Is Tim's soul that forgiving, that compassionate? Maybe.

I keep moving, over tree stumps, roots, and felled branches. I feel like I've been walking for miles when, in fact, I've only covered a half mile, or a little more than that. But that's when I begin to smell something. Smoke. Definitely smoke that's coming from a fireplace or maybe a firepit. The farther I go along the trail, the stronger the smell gets. My breathing is growing shallow, my heart pumping in my throat. I'm drenched with sweat. I also need water. Still, I keep on moving towards the smell of smoke.

Then, I see it, out of the corner of my eye. It's a structure built in the middle of the thick forest. A two-story farmhouse by the looks of it. I stop and take a long beat or two to observe the place. It's tough to make out with so many trees and so much brush blocking my view. I move off trail and slowly make my way through the thick stuff until I come to a spot where I can see the entire spread.

The house is old. Very old. It's got a run-down porch in front and the wood siding is grayed with age and much of it covered in the same green mold that covers the roof. A dog—a mutt by the looks of it—is attached to a chain in the front, and there's a chicken coop set beside an old wood shed. The lawn is overgrown, and all sorts of junk and scrap are stored on the front porch. Thick smoke is coming from the chimney. It's the same smoke I've been inhaling for a while now. Parked in front of the house is the same old rusted pickup that Creepy Ed drives. It tells me that, without a doubt, this is his home. It also tells me he's still home.

Something else catches my eye. Beyond the shed is what I first thought was a clothesline. But it's not a clothesline. It's a kind of rack made from two thick poles buried in the ground. Attached to both polls is a long horizontal beam. The purpose of the setup is to dry skins. Animal skins, I can only assume. Maybe deer or bear. My throat closes in on itself. My stomach goes tight. I don't like what I'm seeing. Even if it's an entirely innocent operation, there's just something about it I don't like . . . something that doesn't sit well in my gut.

I'm about to turn tail and head back to the trail, when I see a man emerge from the front door of the house. It's Ed. He's wearing his usual overalls and work boots. He's cradling something in his arms. It's a pale skin and it appears to be somewhat heavy, judging by the way he seems to be struggling to carry it. Whatever it is, the dog is going nuts, barking and growling, thrusting itself against the chain, like the poor thing is purposely trying to choke itself. Ed kicks the dog with his right foot. The dog yelps and curls itself up in a fetal position.

"That'll teach you to shut your trap!" Ed barks.

My heart aches for the poor dog. But it doesn't ache for Ed. He carries the animal skin around to the rack where he proceeds to hang it from what I can only assume are meat hooks embedded into the crossbeam. Whatever animal the skin belongs to, it's pretty big and dark. It can only be the skin of a big deer. But then, what the hell do I know?

When he's through, I watch him come around to the front of the house again. He goes inside for a few moments, until he comes back outside, his truck keys in one hand and what looks to be a chunk of bloody raw meat in the other. When he tosses the meat to the still ailing dog, the animal seems to forget all about its pain. It bounds up and snatches the meat right out of the air and begins to ravage it, like it's his last meal.

Wiping his bloodstained hand off on his overalls, Ed heads to his truck. He gets in, starts it up, and pulls away. I don't move a muscle until all signs of him disappear.

Choices. I can play amateur detective and examine Ed's house. Or, I can head back to my house since Anna will be worrying about me by now. I check my cell phone. No texts. In fact, there's no service this deep in the thick woods. Go figure. Okay, it's settled then—I'll head back to my house. Turning, I head for the Paradox Lake Trail, happy to be putting some distance between me and what appears to be a very unhealthy place.

*   *   *

It seems to take me forever to get back to the house. But when I do, the first thing I see is Anna laid out on the dock on her tummy on a beach towel. She's wearing sunglasses and she has what appears to be a tall glass of lemonade by her side. Naturally, she's staring into her iPhone.

"Anna," I say, truly happy to see her, "glad to see you getting some air."

She turns to me. "'Bout time, Rosie. I was beginning to think a wolf ate you up."

More wolves . . .

I wipe the sweat from my brow.

"Decided to go for a longer hike than I thought," I say. "You getting hungry?"

"Starving," she says.

"I'll whip us up some lunch and we can eat outside." Gazing up at the sky, I see that the sun is still shining in between the heavy clouds. "Doesn't look like it's gonna start raining till later tonight."

"Sounds good, Mom," she says.

"I like it when you call me 'mom'," I say, recalling my earlier conversation with Allison. "I know you like to call me Rosie, too. But mom is nicer. So is mama."

"Whatever, Rosie mama," she says.

Anna . . . she's always got to have the last word, just like Charlie and Tony.

Heading into the house, I immediately go to my studio. I dig into my pocket for the silver cross, pull it out, and feel its light weight in the palm of my hand. I gaze at the photo of Sarah hanging by a thumbtack on the wall over the work desk. I focus in on the cross.

"I've found your cross, Sarah," I say, my eyes veering from her to the cross and back again.

My eyes fill. I'm crying for a girl who died when I was sixteen years old. But now I'm nearly fifty, and she is still twelve. She will always be twelve. I head back into the kitchen, run the cross and what's left of the chain under warm water. I use my thumbnail to scrape off any dirt that's still attached to it. I look under the sink for something that might clean the cross and return its original silver sheen.

I don't find much of anything. But I do recall a box of baking soda stored in the fridge. I remember my mom cleaning the family silverware with baking soda and boiling water. Retrieving the baking soda from the refrigerator, I fill a small pan with water and a couple tablespoons of the white powder. I then set it on the stove to boil. In the meantime, I set the cross on a dry paper towel on the counter. I go about making some ham and cheese sandwiches which I set on a dinner plate. Pulling out a bag of potato chips, I place a generous handful in the center of the sandwiches. Lastly, I grab two bottles of spring water from the case set on the floor near the back door.

Before heading outside with our lunch, I take hold of the cross and place it in the now boiling water. Closing the gas burner, I allow the cross to just sit. If my experience serves me right, the cross will be entirely cleaned up by the time we finish our lunch.

*   *   *

"So what did you discover in the woods, Rosie?" Anna says, after a time.

She's already scarfed half a sandwich and now she's starting on another half. Instead of eating her potato chips one by one like normal people, she opens the sandwich up and adds a layer of chips on top of the ham and cheese. It's such a great idea I find myself doing the same. After all, the chips add some crackly texture to the otherwise soft sandwich, aside from the extra salty flavor. If I'm addicted to anything besides my art and parenting, it's potato chips and homemade chocolate chip cookies.

But I digress.

I could tell Anna the truth here . . . that I not only found Sarah's cross but that I also discovered the house where Creepy Ed lives and the many animal hides he's drying on an outdoor rack. But I think every bit of this information would only scare the daylights out of her. As it is, I'm tempted to tell her to pack her things, we're leaving Paradox for a safer Adirondack lake. A lake and a house with no history of rape and murder. No history of violence. But before I make that kind of rash judgement, I'll talk with Tim about it. If anyone knows Creepy Ed, it's got to be Tim. He alone can tell me if the general store worker poses a threat or not. He's already referred to Ed as harmless, and I have no reason thus far not to trust Tim.

"I was just doing more work on the trail," I fib.

"You like that trail a lot, Rosie," she says, taking another bite of her sandwich. "You sure you weren't looking for something else?"

"Like what, honey?"

"I saw your studio," she says. "It looks like a memorial to Sarah Anne Moore, the little girl who was murdered a hundred years ago."

There, she said it. And it's not her fault that she knows about the murder. I tacked the newspaper accounts of it to my studio wall for God's sake. What the hell was I thinking?

"My bad," I say. "You weren't supposed to see that stuff. It's for my new project."

"Good job at hiding it," she says.

I eat some sandwich, but my appetite has suddenly vanished.

"Then you know who lived in this house and what happened to her back in 1986," I say. It's a question for which I know the answer.

"Let me guess," she says, finishing off the last bite of her food. "You think I'm scared now."

"It crossed my mind that news of the event might frighten you."

"Maybe if I were a little girl, Rosie," she says. "But I'm gonna be thirteen in a few months. I think I can take it."

"You sure?" I say. "You telling me the truth?"

"Here's the way I see it," she says. "If there was anything to worry about, I believe Tim would have said so, don't you?"

I find myself smiling. My daughter is maturing right before my eyes. Maybe I am doing a decent job at parenting after all.

"I couldn't agree more, honey," I say.

While we're on the subject, I come clean about the shadows I've been seeing coming from the Paradox Lake trailhead. Might as well be honest about everything.

"Shadows?" she asks, taking hold of the half sandwich she knows I'm not going to eat.

"Tim thinks it's nothing more than the deer who move around at night."

"He's probably right. You were wrong about the loon."

She makes a good point.

"He's coming over later to check on the shadows anyway," I say. "I hope you don't mind, Anna. I know it seems like we can't spend a night without Tim."

"It's okay, Mom," she says. "Like I said, Tim is cool."

I know what's coming next.

"You, umm, spoken with Tony yet?" she adds.

I feel my cell phone pressed against my ever-expanding butt. I also feel an annoying pit in my stomach every time my daughter mentions my boyfriend.

"No, I haven't, thank you very much," I say.

"Don't bite my head off, Rosie," she says. "Just asking."

She eats the rest of my sandwich, and scarfs the last potato chip.

"You're absolutely right though," I say, standing up from the picnic table. "I've got to be honest with him sooner rather than later."

"Is love always this hard, Mom?" Anna asks as she gets up, taking hold of the now empty plate.

"Let me tell you the absolute truth," I say. "It never gets any easier."

"Oh," she says, "now that's the kind of encouraging wisdom every preteen girl wants to hear."

*   *   *

We head back inside the house. I immediately go to the stove and what I see takes my breath away. The silver is so clean it's practically shining inside the small pot of water. Wrapping a dish towel around my hand, I grab hold of the pot by its handle, bring it to the sink, pour some cold tap water into it to cool it down. Then, I reach in for the cross and pull it out. It feels solid between my fingers. It's like new again.

"Where'd you get that?" Anna says.

"I found it on that secluded beach off the trail," I say.

She looks into my eyes. "You don't think it belonged to Sarah Anne, do you, Mom?"

It's the obvious question. The million-dollar question.

I inhale, exhale. "It's exactly what I've been thinking, honey."

She holds out her hand.

"Can I see it?" she asks.

"Sure," I say, handing it to her.

She stares not at it, but into it, as if she's imagining the things, both good and bad, this cross witnessed when it was being worn by the girl who used to live in this very house. She looks into my eyes.

"What were you going to do with it?" she asks.

I draw a blank, because I hadn't really thought about that. It's exactly how I put it to her.

"Do you think I can have it?" she asks. "I can bet Sarah would want it that way. You said yourself that we sort of look alike. Maybe you were somehow meant to find it for me. You know, like you were somehow destined to find it."

Her words hit me like a ton of bricks and rocks. Was I destined to dig up this cross? If that's the case, were we drawn to this house in the woods not by chance but by some kind of divine intervention? Jesus, will you just listen to what I'm saying? It sounds like something you might hear on the Hallmark Channel or a romance novel by Nicholas Sparks.

Still, my very perceptive, very sharp young daughter has made herself a very important point. It's almost like I was meant to find this cross and to hand it over to her so that perhaps, just perhaps, Sarah Anne's spirit can live once more. There, I said it. I know it sounds corny, if not downright weird, but there you have it.

"Come with me," I say, heading into my studio.

Opening the drawer on what I've designated as my worktable— I have to wonder if Sarah Anne used this very same table to do her homework on—I pull out a clear plastic box that's filled with all sorts of jewelry making junk, including some thin chains, leather laces, assorted beads, fishing line, and other useless stuff. Since there's not enough chain to make a necklace, I pull out one of the spaghetti-thin black leather laces. Attaching a new ringlet to the top of the cross with my pliers, I then run the lace through it and tie the ends together in a fisherman's slip knot. Solemnly, I place it over my daughter's head and allow it to rest on her chest.

Anna uses both her hands to draw her long hair over the leather necklace. She then touches the cross gently with the tips of her fingers. It's almost like she can feel it working some sort of magic, if that's at all possible. She smiles and I swear I see her eyes tear up. She takes a step forward and gazes at the junior high yearbook picture of Sarah, and again places her finger on the cross that is now hanging from her neck.

"Thank you, Sarah," she says. "I'll make sure to take good care of it."

My daughter then does something extraordinary. She wraps her arms around me and hugs me tightly. Now I'm the one with tears in her eyes. I kiss her cheek.

"You're a sweet girl," I say. "The sweetest in the world."

"And you're the bestest Rosie mama ever," she says.

We might release one another and go about our day then, but instead, we hold onto one another like our lives depend upon it.

CHAPTER 23

THE BIG BAD WOLF sits behind the wheel of his pickup outside the general store. He should be heading back inside to stock the shelves, but in his head, he's reliving the events from the morning. His hiding in the bush, watching Anna's mother down on her knees on the beach, digging in the sand with her fingers, then using a stick to get down deep.

He watched her intently, without breathing, without blinking, and he felt himself getting aroused.

What big eyes you have.

The better to watch you through the trees.

But when she pulled out the cross . . . Sarah's cross . . . he thought he might faint from the excitement that filled his veins. He recalled how she was wearing it on the morning he followed her to this very spot thirty-three years ago almost to the day. The moment he sprung himself on her with all the speed and agility of a wild beast.

What big legs and arms you have.

The better to pounce on you.

He recalls tearing her blue, one-piece bathing suit off in one swift swipe of his claw-like hand. How she tried to scream, but was too afraid to scream. How her voice just would not come. How she hyperventilated when he grabbed a fistful of her hair and threw her down on her back. How her eyes went wide at the sight of him straddling her, pulling himself out.

What big sex you have.

The better to ravage you.

He was just getting to the best part of his remembrance when Anna's mother got up from the log and stuffed the cross in her jeans pocket. He backed off and hid in the woods beside the lake trail. He saw how she hesitated, how she weighed going back home with exploring the deep woods. In the end she decided to explore. That was his cue to head back home by bushwhacking through the same thick woods he's known for his entire six decades on earth. Doesn't matter that he spent half those years locked up inside a maximum-security psychiatric prison, he can find his way through the forest even on the darkest night. Not only does he know every tree, and every branch on every tree, he knows the terrain. The inclines and the declines. Most of all, he knows the lake.

He didn't need to see Anna's mother hiding in the trees to know she was spying on him. He could smell her presence, the same way a wolf sniffs out its prey.

What a big snout you have.

The better to smell your scent all the way out here in the woods.

He knew he was being watched while he hung his skins, while he fed his hungry dog some fresh meat from a fresh kill—the kind of meat the dog lives for. He was aware of being watched all the way up until the time he got back in his truck and drove away from the old family farmhouse in the woods. He wondered if she would have the guts to approach the house and have a look inside. He wondered if she would be horrified at what she saw inside his kitchen.

But in the end, he knew she wouldn't have the guts to trespass on his property any more than she would want to leave her precious Anna alone for too long. And by then, it had become far too long.

Now, as he opens the door to his pickup and begins making his way around the back of the general store to the employee's entrance, the excitement is not leaving his veins. It is only building, like a big winter wind that blows off the lake. The time for the Big Bad Wolf to feed is rapidly approaching.

CHAPTER 24

THE SUN IS beginning to set as we finish a dinner of fresh trout cooked over burning charcoals. Anna used to hate fish, but now that's she's growing up, it's become one of her favorite foods. As I've told her a half dozen times since we arrived, you can't find a better place for fresh fish than Paradox Lake.

"Then how come you bought our fish at the Price Chopper in Schroon?" she says.

"Okay, but I can bet the trout was still pulled out of the lake," I reply. "Next time, we'll catch our own. How does that sound?"

"We need a boat, Rosie," she says as we both chip in at clearing the dinner dishes.

As if on cue, a horn blows from out on the lake. A small boat is approaching our dock. Standing in the boat's open cockpit is a tall, bearded man. He's waving at us.

"It's Tim," Anna says.

She raises her free hand, waves back at him. I wave too. The closer he comes, the more I can make out his sweet smile.

"Give me a hand," he shouts.

Without hesitation, Anna sets the plates back onto the picnic table and heads down to the dock. I don't hesitate to follow either. Tim slows the boat to a crawl, and while the outboard engine idles, he drifts up against the dock. He tosses Anna the bow rope while I reach for the stern rope. I tie my end to the metal cleat that's embedded in the wood dock. Anna isn't at all sure how to use the rope, so she just holds it. As I said, my dad had a boat so I know how to tie it down.

I start making my way to her, but Tim beats me to the punch when he hops off the boat onto the dock and says, "Let me show you how it's done, Anna."

As usual, he's wearing Levi's jeans and his feet are bare. He's also wearing a Levi's jean jacket over a blue work shirt and a baseball cap that has the words "Ferguson General Store" printed on it in green lettering. He kneels and, in turn, Anna kneels beside him.

"You twist the rope around each end of the cleat, just like this," he says. Then, untying it, he adds, "Now you try it."

Anna takes the rope into both hands and starts on slowly tying the rope around the cleat. That's when Tim places his hand on her back, moving it gently in an up and down manner. The gesture is sweet, but it also sort of catches me by surprise. Don't get me wrong, he's not being weird with her. He's being kind and gentle. Or so I can only assume. Of course, we've only known Tim for a few days, but he doesn't seem like the predatory type. Okay, now my imagination and overprotective nature are really coming out.

When she's done making the knot, Anna peers up at Tim's smiling face.

"How's that?" she says.

They both stand. He presents her with his fisted right hand. She happily fists bumps him. He shoots me a glance along with a wink of his eye, like, *How'm I doing?*

I'd say you're doing pretty darn well . . .

"You see, Anna," he says, "if you're going to be piloting a boat, you have to learn a thing or two."

She looks at me.

"Well, we don't have a boat, Tim," she says.

"You do now," he says.

Anna's eyes light up.

"You mean . . ."

"Yes, I *mean* this is your boat," Tim says. "On loan, of course. But you have full use for the duration of your stay."

My spirit lifts and my heart is beating happily. Where did this sweet man come from?

"Are you sure, Tim?" I say. "I mean, what if we . . . I don't know . . . break it."

He laughs. "No worries. It's an old boat I've had around since I was a teenager. Plus, it's fully insured. It's not very fast, but it's a Boston Whaler. That means it's rugged as heck. You can't destroy it no matter how much you try. Come on, Anna, I'll take you for your first lesson. If it's okay with your mom, of course."

I gaze up at the sky. The thick, gray/black storm clouds are still gathering. No rain or thunder yet, but it's coming for sure.

"You think the weather's okay, Tim?" I ask.

"Don't be a worrywart, Mom," he says. "The storms aren't projected to hit until later tonight and tomorrow. We'll be fine."

"Oh please, Mom," Anna begs.

They're both looking at me like the fate of both their worlds rests with me. Who am I to play spoiler, especially when I'm always looking for ways to keep Anna entertained and happy?

"Sure, guys," I say. "I'll clean up the dishes. Tim, you in for some desert when you get back?"

"Haven't had dinner yet," he says, "but one of my favorite things in the world is desert first."

"Great!" Anna says.

"Okay, mate," Tim says, "you get the bow rope, and I'll get the stern."

Together they begin to untie the ropes. They then climb aboard the small white Whaler. Anna is a little unsure of her balance so she quickly takes a seat on the cockpit bench.

"Oh no you don't," Tim says. "You're taking the wheel."

"You mean like now?"

"No better time than the present."

He fires the engine up, and with his guidance, Anna backs the boat out and away from the dock. She then slowly pulls forward and out towards the lake's center. If only you could see the smile on her face, you'd feel it in your heart, just like I do. I watch them head off into the sunset until they are out of sight entirely. I then go to the picnic table, collect all the dishes, bring them into the kitchen with me, and set them down in the sink. It takes me a few minutes to wash and dry them, then put them away. But during the process I find myself whistling and humming a happy tune.

As I'm drying my hands, my eyes gravitate to the crucifix. Maybe Anna and I have once more brought some happiness to this house. I surely hope so. I get the craziest sensation of deja vu then. Like I've been here before, washing these very dishes at this very sink. It gives me goose bumps, like a ghost has just passed through my body.

My vibrating mobile phone breaks me out of my spell.

It's set on the kitchen table. Instead of grabbing it right away, I just sort of stare at it. My first thought is that somehow the boat engine malfunctioned and now my daughter is stranded out in the middle of the lake with a strange man and an electrical storm brewing. Why did God feel it necessary to gift me with such an overactive imagination?

But my other thought is that it can only be Tony. Let's face it, I've been pretty much ignoring him, and if there's one thing on earth he can't stand, it's being ignored. Finally, I pick up the phone. While I'm relieved to see that it's not my daughter calling, I am not relieved to see that my gut was spot on. Tony. I guess I have to speak with him sooner than later.

I press the *answer* icon.

"Hi, Tony."

"Are you really having that good a time you can't check in with me once in a while, Rose?"

He's right, of course.

"I'm sorry," I say. "It's just been very, very busy."

In the background, I hear bar patrons talking and laughing. I hear beer bottles and wineglasses clinking. It's no surprise to me that Tony is holding court at the bar.

"Tell me the truth, Rose," he says, after a time. "You didn't happen to meet someone up there, did you?"

A chill shoots up my spine.

"We've only been here a few days, Tone," I say. "There hasn't been a whole lot of time for socializing."

"Paradox is a small town. I Googled it. Word of a beautiful woman and her cute daughter arriving for the fall will spread like wildfire. All the local single sharks will come hunting, believe me."

In my head, a little voice says, *Tell him the truth. You'll feel better and at least he'll know you're being honest.*

Inhaling and exhaling a deep breath.

"Okay," I say, "if you must know, I have made a friend."

He exhales. "A male friend."

"Yes, a friend who happens to be male. He's been helping us out."

"Oh God," he says, "I knew this kind of thing was going to happen."

In my head I see him seated at the bar, dressed in his boots, jeans, and bush jacket, maybe his Ray Ban Aviators set on his receding hairline, his round face scruffy and tired.

"We're just friends, Tone," I say. "He owns the general store and he's letting us borrow a boat for the duration of our stay. In fact, Anna is out on the water with him right now. He's the man who helped us move in. Tim."

"She likes him better than me?"

Oh my God . . .

"It's not like that at all," I say. "He's a nice man and I'm already finding it hard to keep her occupied and happy. So if a nice man is willing to show her how to use his boat, I'm all in."

"You sure you know this guy well enough for Anna to be spending alone time with him?"

His question makes a lot of sense. It also makes my stomach tight and my pulse pick up speed.

"He can be trusted," I say, although I'm not entirely sure I believe myself. "He's been very nice, Tony."

He pauses for a second or two. It tells me he's stealing a drink of his beer or maybe a Jameson chaser, or both. Something he needs to curb now that his doctor has put him on high blood pressure medication.

"Whatever you say, Rose," he says. "So then, when do I get to pay a visit to my girls? How about tomorrow since it's Saturday?"

I'm reminded of my dinner date with Tim in Schroon. We'll be gone from late afternoon into the evening. Tony's sudden presence would surely put a damper on things.

"Listen, Tone," I say. "I really, really want you to come out. But like I've already said, give Anna and me a chance to adjust to the place first. I really want to use this time to get closer to her. Before we know it, she'll be in high school, and we'll never see her other than when she makes the occasional pit stop for food, clothing, cash, and sleep."

He hesitates for a long beat, like he's debating in his head whether he should press the issue. My eyes are focused out the big picture window that overlooks the lake. The sky is getting very dark now along with the cloud cover. I'm starting to feel slight pangs of worry. Will Anna and Tim be coming in soon? Or has tragedy struck and the boat sunk?

Don't overthink it, Rosie.

I'll try not to, Allison. But you know me by now.

"Rose, you there?" Tony begs. "Rose?"

"Yes," I say. "I'm here."

"Okay, 'cause you went AWOL for a second or two."

"Sorry, Tony, just keeping an eye out for Anna." Then, I see the green and red running board lights on the Whaler slowly approaching the dock. My heart feels one hundred times lighter. "Look, I've got to go. Anna is coming back in."

"Anna and Tim, you mean," he says.

"Tone," I say, "stop worrying."

"Whatever you say," he says. "But I'm coming next weekend even if it's only for an afternoon. I miss my girls."

"Okay," I say, "we'll talk about it this week. I've got to go. Oh, and don't forget to take your medication before bed."

"Love you, Rose," he says.

"Love you, Tone," I say.

"I hope so," he says, hanging up.

"I hope so too," I say to myself while setting the phone back down on the kitchen table.

* * *

Heading back outside, I greet Anna and Tim at the dock. I grab the bow rope and tie that off, while Anna enthusiastically jumps out of the Whaler and ties off the stern line.

"So how did the first lesson go?" I ask.

"She's already a seasoned captain," Tim volunteers as he hops onto the dock with his cowboy boots in hand. "She's a natural."

"It was a blast," Anna says. "We can go fishing tomorrow morning, Mom. I'll be your captain."

"If it doesn't rain," I say. "Sounds like a plan."

"It's getting dark," Tim says, coming off the dock. He sets himself on the picnic table and slips into his socks and boots. "How about I build you guys a fire in the firepit?"

"How about some dessert?" I say. "Or how about some dinner leftovers first?"

"I'm all in for dessert," Tim says, making his way to the woodpile where he starts gathering fresh logs.

That's when Anna gives me a wink and a sly grin.

"How's about I give you two a little private time?" she says, slyly.

I can't help but smile.

"Listen, honey," I say with my back to Tim so he can't hear me, "Tony called and he was asking for you."

"I should really call or at least text him," she says. "You should talk to him, too, Mom. Tell him the truth."

There's that pang in my stomach again.

"Yes," I say, "you should at least text him and I should have a talk with him. A real talk, I mean. He misses us. He might come out next weekend for the day."

"That's good," she says. "Right." The "right" comes out sounding like a loaded question.

"Yes, honey," I say, "of course it's good. I miss Tony."

"I'm sensing a *but* coming, Rosie."

I nod.

"But him," I say, gesturing towards Tim as he gathers wood to make the fire.

"But him," she says. Then, "I'm gonna go see what that little scoundrel Jake Walls is up to."

"About five foot three," I say.

Anna laughs aloud because she towers over him when they're together. But, still, they like one another.

"One day he'll go through a growth spurt," I add, "and shock us all."

"That's what I'm betting on, Rosie." Then, turning to Tim. "Later, Tim. Thanks for the boating lesson and thanks for letting us use it."

"My pleasure, Anna," he says, his blue eyes reflected in the small flames now shooting up from the firepit. "She's all gassed up for you too. You've got a twelve-gallon tank there."

Anna scoots back into the house where she'll take the stairs two at a time to her bedroom.

"How about some leftover apple pie, Tim?" I ask.

"I'd love some," he says.

I head inside, retrieve the pie and a couple of coffees, which I take back outside on a tray. As I'm setting the tray down on the picnic table, he comes to me and kisses me tenderly on the lips.

"Couldn't wait to do that," he says.

"Neither could I," I say, feeling a hard lump on his left hip.

"What's that?" I say, patting the lump.

He opens his jean jacket.

"Told you I'd come packing," he says, revealing a pistol.

I'm not sure why, but it more than takes me by surprise.

"The shadow," I say, recalling our conversation of this morning.

"Hopefully that's all it is," he says. "A shadow."

I feel a wave of warmth wash over me. I am most definitely falling hard for this man.

"Tim," I say, "can you do me a favor?"

"Name it," he says, taking hold of both my hands.

"Kiss me again," I say.

We make out to the sound and the heat of the roaring fire.

CHAPTER 25

By the time our desert is finished, complete darkness has enveloped Paradox. Some lightning can be seen flashing off the opposite west side of the lake. The thunder rumbles moments later. We both occupy our respective Adirondack chairs, our hands wrapped around our coffee mugs, which are set in our laps, our eyes staring not at the fire but into it.

Shifting my eyes to the Paradox trailhead, I somewhat nervously await the nightly dark figure that always seems to emerge from the woods not long after full dark. This time, I'll have Tim here to tell me precisely who or what the dark shadow belongs to. If it's something dangerous or threatening, I guess Tim will have no choice but to shoot it. I'm praying something like that doesn't happen. How would I explain it to Anna?

"See anything yet, Tim?" I ask.

His eyes are focused on the trailhead.

"Not yet," he says, his voice lowered to little more than a whisper. "But don't worry. If it's out there, I'll see it."

"Probably just a deer, right?"

He turns to me, smiles devilishly.

"Or a monster," he says. "Like a big bad wolf, only worse."

"Thanks," I say, reaching out for his hand. "Way to scare me."

He takes my hand, squeezes it.

"Just having a little fun with you, Rose."

I'm just about to tell him about the cross I found this morning, when my eyes catch the shadow coming from the trailhead, quickly scooting past the woodpile and disappearing around the side of the house.

"There," I say, jumping up. "Did you see it?"

Like always, it appears to be an animal on all fours.

He stands. Dumping what's left of his coffee, he sets the mug onto the picnic table.

"Stay here," he says, pulling out his gun.

"If you insist," I say.

He disappears around the side of the house. My heart is pulsing in my neck, precisely because I'm not sure what to expect right now. Is there going to be a scuffle? Man versus animal? Maybe I'll hear a shot and see a bright muzzle flash. Anna will be scared out of her wits. But that never happens. Instead, Tim returns, walking nonchalantly around the woodpile. His pistol is no longer gripped in his hand, but returned safely to its holster.

Placing both his hands on my shoulders, he purses his lips.

"Just like I expected," he says. "It's a deer. Good-sized buck, too. Something to keep in mind come November because me and my thirty-thirty have definitely got our names on it."

"Deer hunting season?" I ask.

"Do you hunt, Rose?"

I laugh.

"I'm an art professor from Albany," I say. "I'm supposed to hate guns. But my father and brothers used to hunt."

"Well, if you'd like to learn," he says, "I'd be happy to teach you. One buck can provide you with enough venison for a whole year. And it's delicious."

"I'll think about it, Daniel Boone," I say.

He looks at his watch.

"I really should be getting back," he says. "Long day tomorrow. But I hope I've put your mind at ease."

"You have, Tim," I say. "Whatever would Anna and I do without you?"

"Ha-ha," he says with a grin, "you'd get along fine."

Then, something dawning on me.

"Hey, you came by boat," I say. "How are you getting home?"

"I can call a friend to pick me up."

"Nonsense. I can give you a ride back into town. Anna will be fine for a few minutes."

"You sure, Rose? I hate to be a bother."

"After everything you've done for us," I say, "it will be my pleasure. Besides, now that I know the shadow monster is only Bambi, we have nothing to fear."

"Okay," he says with a happy face. "If you insist, Rose."

Back inside, I lock the kitchen door behind me, and then head up to Anna's room. I tell her I'm dropping Tim back off at his house in town and that I'll be back in a few minutes. Everything is locked up, I assure her.

"Have fun, Rosie," she says, with yet another one of her winks.

"And what's that supposed to mean, young lady?" I beg. "Excuse me . . . young, inexperienced-to-the-ways-of-the-world lady."

"Don't do anything I wouldn't do," she says.

"Let's hope you don't do anything."

I head back downstairs to my daughter's laughter.

"All set?" Tim says.

I grab my car keys off the small table that's set between the front door and the old leather couch. That's when I notice he's placed the keys to the boat there as well.

"Let's rock n' roll," I say.

I remember to grab my phone and lock the front door on the way out.

*   *   *

Tim slips in the passenger seat and I get behind the wheel.

"Mind if I adjust the seat?" he asks. "Damn my long legs."

I can't help but be reminded of Tony's short legs.

"Knock yourself out, Tim."

I start the car, throw it in drive, and pull out of the driveway, hooking a left onto the country road that will take me to the two-track that leads to the Paradox Lake Road. We're not driving for more than a minute, when I feel his hand on my thigh.

"Is this okay?" he asks.

I could tell him to remove it, but it feels so damn good, I don't dare. I squeeze his hand with my free hand.

"It's more than okay," I say.

"Question," he says. "I overheard Anna speaking about a man named Tony. She referred to him as 'Mom's boyfriend.' Am I intruding on something I shouldn't be, Rose? Because I don't want to cause you any trouble."

It's time to fess up with the truth. Maybe Tim doesn't want to cause me any trouble, but I don't want him to think of me as a liar and a cheat either.

"Tony and I have been together since my husband, Charlie, died," I say. Then, realizing what I just said, "Correction. Tony came into my life not long after Charlie died. He was a friend of Charlie's going back to their college days together at Providence College in the mid-'80s. When Charlie passed, Tony just sort of started hanging around, making sure Anna and me were okay, and just being our helpful friend."

"Like he would fix things around the house, mow the lawn, stuff like that?"

I can't help but laugh. "Tony fix something or mow the lawn? I took care of all of that. He's a writer, and trust me when I say his writing comes first. But then at the end of the day, he'd show up and drink some beers at the kitchen table while we went about our evening. He would just sort of be there, and eventually I . . ."

My thoughts trail off because I'm genuinely not sure how to explain how Tony and I first became lovers.

"And eventually you, ummm, what?" Tim presses.

"Well, you know," I say, slowly removing my hand from his. "One thing led to another and we got intimate."

"Oh," he says. "Intimate."

He gives my thigh a pinch.

"Okay, now you're making fun of me."

We both have a laugh.

"I'm sorry," he says. "Couldn't resist. So where do things stand now? Do you love Tony? Should I back off, Rose?"

I inhale and exhale.

"The truth?" I say. "I'm not sure if I ever actually fell in love with Tony. Like I said, he was just there. But I do have love for him. So does Anna. He's been very good to us over some pretty hard years. I lost my first daughter and then Charlie, and Tony came into our lives when we needed him the most."

"You lost your daughter? I'm awfully sorry to hear that. What was her name?"

"Allison," I say. "She would be eighteen now. Leukemia took her. Charlie couldn't take the grief and he took his own life while I was still pregnant with Anna."

"My God, Rose, I'm so sorry. You've been through hell and back."

"We got through it, Anna and me, and Tony was there for us. That's why I love him."

"But you're not *in love* with him."

"There's a difference," I say. Then, pausing for a few long beats, "Which is why if you and I . . . if we do something more than just kiss . . . I don't want you to get the wrong idea, Tim. I'm not the kind of girl who sleeps around or cheats on her husband or anything like that. I truly consider myself loyal to the core."

He squeezes my thigh again like he gets it. Or what the hell. Maybe I'm just naïve and he's super horny. The town lights are visible just up ahead.

"I understand completely," he says. "My guess is you haven't married Tony after all this time for a reason."

"Exactly," I say. "We don't even live together. And to be even more truthful, if we have, well, you know what, three times a year, that's a lot. Tony is more interested in his writing, his drinking, his working out, and his traveling."

"He sounds like the boy who never grew up."

"Well, the boy who never grew up is now pushing sixty," I say. "He's got high blood pressure, or so he just found out."

"Poor guy."

"Well, he should be okay if he takes his meds and keeps up the exercising."

"I wish him the best," Tim says. "You should know that. And thanks for sharing your story, Rose. It means a lot that you can trust me."

Once more I wrap my fingers around his and squeeze. The more I reveal to him, I swear, the more I'm falling in love with him.

"Okay, Mr. Ferguson, we've arrived in Paradox. Where to?"

The general store is coming up on our right-hand side.

"Right here," he says. "Just pull into the store."

"Here?"

"Yup," he says. "I live in the apartment upstairs. It's actually quite nice. Why don't you come up for a quick drink and I can show you the place. That is, if you don't have to get back to Anna right away."

Heart beats a mile a minute. Mouth goes dry. Stomach cramps. I also feel a little something happening in what my mother used to refer to as my private area. A certain tingling sensation.

Go for it Rosie. You only live once. Trust me on that.

You really think I should, Allison?

I know so. Pops, what's your opinion on this matter?

You have my blessing, Rose darling. Just spare me the details later on.

Thanks, Charlie. I still love you the most.

So that's it then. I'm going up to Tim's apartment. I park the Mini Cooper along the side of the building. Together we get out. Tim leads me around back to a wood staircase that accesses the second floor. We climb the stairs like we're ascending the stairway to heaven.

CHAPTER 26

PULLING OPEN THE old rusted Bilco doors that access the Moore house basement, the Big Bad Wolf stares down into the cobweb-covered black hole. The metal doors aren't locked. It's Rose's bad luck that she never bothered to inspect this side of the house. But then, a whole bunch of overgrown brush covers almost the entirety of that side of the house, and you'd only make out the Bilco doors if you were looking for them. He descends the old wood steps to the cold, damp, dark basement.

He has better than 20/20 vision. The basement is pitch dark, but somehow, he can see his way along the packed dirt floor.

What big eyes you have.

The better to see you when I spy on you in your bed, Little Red Riding Hood.

Spider webs cling to his face and arms. He feels a spider scuttling across his forehead. He slaps it off before it bites him and lays its eggs under his skin. He recalls waking up one morning in his bedroom inside the house in the woods. He'd been bitten on the arm by a big brown wolf spider during the night. That afternoon, when he was cleaning out the chicken coop, he noticed a big purple lump growing on his forearm. The lump was tender, and it itched liked nobody's business. By the end of the day, the lump

was as big as a golf ball. The itch was so bad, so unrelenting, he had
no choice but to pull out his pocketknife and poke a hole into the
tip of the lump.

Blood and yellow puss not only oozed from the lump, but so
did something else. Thousands of baby spiders came crawling out
of his arm. So many, they covered his arm and hand entirely. He
was so horrified he screamed bloody murder. For a second or two,
he considered cutting his arm off entirely just to rid himself of the
spiders. Instead, he ran into the house, went to the kitchen sink,
and poured hot tap water over them until every one of them cir-
cled the drain along with his blood.

Was that the day he became the Big Bad Wolf?

Maybe.

Or maybe he was always a wolf.

But that was then and this is now. The Wolf makes his way
across the basement floor until he finds the single bare light bulb
that hangs from a wood ceiling beam. He pulls on the string and
the stonewalled basement lights up in an eerie yellow glow. To his
right, a bunch of old furniture is stacked up against the wall. The
furniture used to belong to the Moores. Now it's all covered in
green mold and spider webs. To his left is the breaker box. For a
brief moment, the Wolf considers killing the power in the house.
He's not ready for that, however. A time will come very soon when
the darkness will work well for him. But not now.

He faces the old wood staircase. Acting on instinct, he drops to
all fours, and begins taking the stairs like a hungry wolf. It's the
same way he traverses the woods and the opening between the
Paradox Lake trailhead and the Moore house. It's something he
has not lost during his many years in prison. He hasn't lost his
speed, nor his hunger, nor his desire to feed.

What great speed you have.

The faster to catch you and tear you to pieces, my dear.

He enters into the kitchen, quickly trots his way into the living room, and then up the stairs where he pauses right outside the open door to Anna's room. Or should he say, Sarah Anne's room. He hears her talking to someone on her phone. She's telling whoever is on the other end that she loves him. He breathes in deep, smells her fragrance. It's the smell of a budding young woman. A fresh young woman, just waiting to be ravaged.

What a big nose you have.

The better to sniff you up and down.

He knows that, at any moment, she can get up off the bed and discover him in the hallway. But he won't allow that to happen. He's too fast for her. Too swift. Too stealthy. His wolf-like powers make him superhuman. He only grew stronger in prison. Smarter. Hungrier.

For now, he is satisfied with listening to his prey and inhaling her scent. Because, in a matter of hours, he will be devouring her.

What big teeth you have.

The better to eat you all up.

CHAPTER 27

THE RAIN IS finally beginning to fall as Tim gives me a quick tour of his apartment over the general store. It's nothing too big. Just a living room, a small galley kitchen, a vestibule, and a bathroom. Beyond that is the bedroom. Tim lives simply, with not a lot of furniture or amenities. I mention this to him.

"I like to live an uncomplicated life," he says, while removing his jean jacket and setting his pistol on the small table in the vestibule. "Or, as uncomplicated as I can possibly make it."

Hanging on the wall in the living room are pictures of his two sons during their teenage years. They are handsome kids like their dad. I can't help but wonder what their mother looks like, but I can bet she's very attractive.

"How about a drink?" Tim says.

I look at my watch.

"It's after eight," I say. "I really should be getting back."

"Just a half glass of wine?"

His question surprises me.

"Thought you didn't drink?" I ask.

"Well, truth be told, I still enjoy a glass or two, now and again. Right now, I have a nice red going."

His words come as a bit of a shock. I wonder why he felt the need to lie about his drinking before. He said he becomes a different person when he drinks, so he had to stop. Or, maybe he wasn't lying at all. Maybe he was simply not telling me the whole truth. We are just getting to know one another after all. Even people who appear to live simply can have complicated personalities.

"Okay," I say, "I guess a small glass can't hurt. But let me text Anna, let her know I'll be a few minutes more."

"Good idea," he says, heading into the kitchen to grab the wine.

I pull out my phone. Thumbing the text icon, I write: *Having a quick drink with Tim. All okay? I'll be back very soon unless you want me to come right now.*

Not bothering to put my phone away, I continue to hold it in my hand since I expect her to answer me right away. Knowing she's talking to Nicole or Jake, I can almost count the seconds until she responds.

Then: *All good Rosie Take your time.*

Smart ass that my precious daughter is, she adds one of those winking smiley-faced emojis at the end of the sentence. Does she think I'm about to get laid? Do *I* think I'm about to get laid?

It's entirely possible . . .

Tim comes back in. He hands me a long-stemmed glass of red. He's holding an identical glass. He stands before me, looking into my eyes.

"So what shall we drink to, Rose?" he asks.

"To Paradox Lake?" I suggest.

"How about to us," he says.

I feel my face fill with warm blood. My stomach goes even tighter than before, and whatever is happening in my most sensitive of areas is not entirely unpleasant, I must say. I steal a nervous sip of wine. In fact, I drink almost half the glass. He, too, takes a sip, but it's a careful sip. That's when something happens. Something magical. Almost on cue, we both set our glasses onto the coffee table. We don't proceed to take one another in our arms. We freaking lunge at one another.

Next thing I know we're on the couch, kissing passionately, our tongues and lips playing, our teeth nibbling. Tim places his hands on my breasts, and I feel electric shocks swim up and down my body. He skillfully uses both hands to pull my t-shirt up and over my head, exposing my black bra and the breasts that fill it. Almost unconsciously, I've got my hand on his midsection and I'm rubbing his considerable erection through his jeans. He's responding by gyrating his hips.

He reaches around my back, unclasps my bra. It falls off of me, and he immediately begins to suckle on my hard-as-a-rock nipples. The way he sucks and nibbles on them with his lips, tongue, and teeth drives me insane. I feel his hand unbuckling my belt, and then unbuttoning my jeans. I feel his hand slip inside and his fingers on my wetness. He knows precisely where to touch me. That's when I return the favor by unbuckling his belt buckle and unbuttoning his jeans. I pull his pants and boxers all the way down to his boots and he does the same for me.

Rolling onto my back, I open my legs for him, and he enters me. He takes it slow, and gentle, and sweet. I'm so ready for him, it's like I've been waiting for this very moment in time for all my life. I want all of him in me, and I want him to be me and I want to be him, and I never want us to separate. He places his hand on my face and runs his fingers through my hair and never once does he stop looking into my eyes with his deep blue eyes. His motions are slow at first, and I try to move with him, in synch with him, until he begins to go faster and faster.

I can hear myself moaning now, and I listen to his breaths while our thighs thrust against one another's. He dives into me and bites my neck, and it makes me crazy with pleasure. I can tell then that we're coming to that wonderful place together . . . that place that I never want to end, but to go on and on forever. When his lips connect with mine, he releases and I release and it's like we're never, ever going to be separated from one another.

When the time is passed, he doesn't just back off and get dressed as so many men will. Instead, he continues to hold me, continues to run his hands through my hair, continues to kiss my neck, continues to stay inside me, his hardness not abating in the least. When he begins his motions again, I can hardly believe it. Is Tim really a middle-aged man? Or is he a seventeen-year-old in disguise? The thought almost makes me laugh while he picks up speed and I pick up speed along with him, and before we know it, we are both revisiting that special place for a second time. It's pure magic. It's also sweet love. Love like I've never before experienced. Not even with Charlie, God rest his soul.

Minutes later, we're both sitting on the couch, still undressed, but not shy about our nakedness. We're drinking another glass of wine and laughing like we're not two acquaintances who only met a few days ago, but instead, two old lovers who've known one another forever and ever. It is, quite possibly, the most precious time I have ever spent with a man. And I am most definitely falling in love, although this is nothing I would ever tell Tim. Not yet anyway.

I finish my wine and feel a start in my heart.

"Oh dear Lord," I say, setting my glass down on the coffee table and standing. "I've really got to go. Anna will be worried sick."

Pulling up my underwear and jeans, I finish getting dressed. Tim gets up and gets dressed too.

"My apologies," he says. "I've kept you too late."

I check my phone. Nothing from Anna. No texts, no calls. I'm sure that's a good thing. It means she's distracted with her friends. Turning to Tim.

"That was one of the shortest, but sweetest, dare I say it, loveliest dates I've ever had," I say. "I love the spontaneity of it all."

I wrap my arms around his neck and plant a kiss on him. He kisses me back and holds me tightly.

"You ain't seen nothing yet," he says. "Just wait till tomorrow and our dinner date. It's going to be quite the night."

Heading around the couch, I grab my keys.

"What time, Tim?" I ask, wishing it were already tomorrow.

Coming around the couch, he meets me at the vestibule.

"Not sure how much you'll be into this or if you're even a Catholic, but I generally make the four-thirty Mass in town on Saturday. I'll understand if church is not your thing. But if you're into it, we can go together and then head over to Schroon right after. It's always a short Mass since the priest likes to belly up to Bunny's Bar as fast as possible on a Saturday to start working on his Sunday hangover."

I can't help but laugh at this. Welcome to small-town life . . .

"Well," I say, "in truth, I haven't been to church since . . . well, I don't know the last time I was in church. But sure, I'd be happy to attend Mass with you."

"Great," he says. "I'll pick you up at the house at four fifteen. And, as an added bonus, I know you'll need to think about dinner for Anna. We have delicious homemade premade meals in the general store. What does she like? We have just about anything you can imagine."

Where on God's earth did this man come from? He makes love like he invented it. He owns his own business. He's brave enough to chase after a wild animal—or a potential wild animal, anyway. He believes in God and he practices his faith, and he is perhaps the most thoughtful man I have ever met in my life. Perhaps even more thoughtful than Charlie, and that's truly saying something. And, yes, even more considerate than Tony.

"Do you have cheese and macaroni?"

"Do we have cheese and macaroni?" he says, wide-eyed. "We have the best cheese and macaroni this side of Lake Champlain. My sister, Kathy, makes it herself inside her kitchen at home. I'll bring two. One for Anna and another for you the next day."

"You are a very generous man," I say.

He wraps his arms around me once more, kisses me.

"I'm not too bad in the hay either," he says.

"I can second that," I say. "I hope I'm no slouch."

"You rock my world, Rose."

With that, I squeeze him and kiss him one last time. Then, opening the door, I blow him a kiss and head back down the steps to my Mini Cooper. Before I get to the final step, it dawns on me that the last time I was in church was for Charlie's funeral.

CHAPTER 28

HIS BIG EARS make out a car pulling up in the driveway. How the Wolf hates to leave Anna all alone in her bedroom. He's had the most wonderful time listening to her, smelling her scent, fantasizing about all the things they will soon do together. Turning away from the bedroom, he silently heads back down the stairs on all fours, gallops across the living room floor into the kitchen and down the basement stairs.

Raising himself up on his hind legs, he pulls the string on the overhead light and returns the basement to blackness. He makes his way on two feet back through the fresh spider webs to the Bilco door. He exits the Moore house and, once again dropping to all fours, scoots his way back into the forest through the Paradox Lake trailhead.

What incredible speed and power you have.

The better to chase you down and rip you to shreds, my Little Red Riding Hood.

CHAPTER 29

COMING THROUGH THE front door, I immediately call out for Anna.

"Hi, Mom," she says, much to my relief. "That took a while. Wonder what you were doing all that time? Oh wait, you don't have to tell me."

Oh good, she's still being a wise ass. That's a good sign. A very good sign. But that still doesn't take away from the guilt I'm feeling, first, for leaving Anna alone for so long, and second, for drifting from Tony.

"I'll be right up, honey," I say. "Are you hungry? Do you want me to bring you a snack?"

"How about some popcorn and some Netflix before bed?"

"Sounds like a plan," I say, even if it is getting a little late.

But truth is, I need something to take my mind off of Tim and Tony, and maybe a little quality time with my girl will do the trick.

Setting my keys onto the end table beside the boat keys, I head into the kitchen, grab a clean dish towel under the sink, and dry my hair with it. That's when I notice the door to the basement is open. Not all the way, but it's definitely been opened. For a split second, I think about calling back up to Anna to see if she went downstairs. But then, why the heck would she want to go down there into that spider-infested cave? The wind is picking up outside and the rain is falling harder and harder. Jagged streaks of lightning are flashing over the lake, rumbles of thunder reverberating against the many mountains that surround the big body of water.

Maybe the wind somehow affected the door and caused it to open. Or maybe the ghost of Sarah Anne opened it—ha-ha. But this stuff is no laughing matter. Ghosts of loved ones have surrounded me most of my adult life. I am never far from their memory, never far from hearing their voices or feeling their presence, even if they no longer exist on this good earth.

I close the door. If it had a lock, I'd engage it, but it doesn't.

I go to the cabinet above the stove, find a bag of microwave popcorn, place it in the microwave, and press the popcorn icon on the machine. While the bag spins and inflates and the kernels begin to pop, I open a beer and take a long drink. After what I experienced tonight with Tim, it is positively the best beer I have ever tasted. My heart is pounding for him right now, and I feel as if my entire body is falling into a bottomless pit of ecstasy and pure love. But damn, if I don't feel guilty about Tony.

Drinking some more beer, I pull my cell phone from my pocket, check to see if he has called or texted. I'm a little surprised to see that he hasn't. It's going on nine and he's quiet. But then it dawns on me that it's Friday, which means he'll have been at Lanies Bar since maybe three that afternoon. If he isn't already two sheets to the wind whooping it up with both his guy- and girlfriends, he's quickly on his way to getting there. My gut speaks to me, however. It tells me to get ahead of the situation before he decides to call at midnight, drunk as a rabid skunk, feeling sorry for himself and calling me a selfish jerk for leaving him all alone—Tony would never, ever call me a bitch even under the worst circumstances.

While the popcorn pops machine-gun style inside the machine, I text, *Heading to bed Tone. Goodnight XO.*

Again, the XO is not me being hypocritical. It is me averting what would surely be a panicked phone call from him. I lower the ringer volume then to emergency calls only. It's only a matter of time until he texts back and there's no telling how upset he might be with me. Or perhaps I'm blowing this entirely out of proportion. One thing is for sure, when he arrives next Saturday, I am going to tell him the truth about Tim and me. It's the least I can do for a man who has been so good to me and my daughter over the years. Naturally, he's going to be mad and upset with me—okay, that's when he might finally use the B word—but I truly hope we can one day be friends again and that he wants to remain in Anna's life.

Shoving the phone back into my pocket, I open the microwave and pull out the bag of popcorn. Opening it in a way that the hot air doesn't scald my face, I carry it and my beer to the back door. I make sure it's locked. Then, I head into the living room, make sure the front door is locked. Satisfied that all the hatches have been battened down, I once more leave the light on in the kitchen.

It's the little things that put me at ease in the old house on Paradox Lake.

*   *   *

I fall for it again. I fall asleep with Anna in her bed after three back-to-back episodes of *Grey's Anatomy*. Sleep comes easy with the cool breeze coming off the lake and the lonely loon crying, *Saaaarrrrr . . . Saaaarrrrr . . . Saaaaaarrrrrrrrrrr . . .*

*   *   *

I'm walking the Paradox Lake Trail. It's not dark under the canopy of trees, but instead an almost heavenly light washes over it. Every leaf on every tree sparkles and radiates in the sun's brilliance. It warms me from the inside out, like a heated blanket. I have no fear. I only feel the need to keep moving, deeper and deeper into the thick forest.

Then, up ahead, I see a person. It's a girl. I only see her back so it's impossible to make out who exactly she is. She's tall. Her hair is long and dark. She's wearing white Keds sneakers, cut-off jean shorts, and a red t-shirt with the four faces of the Beatles printed on the back.

"Anna," I call out. "Wait up. Anna, wait up."

The girl stops, turns.

"Anna isn't with us any longer," says Sarah Anne Moore.

*   *   *

I wake up with a start, heart pounding in my chest, sweat covering my brow, my t-shirt nearly soaked through. The sun is up, but it's raining hard outside. A flash of lightning strikes close by. It's followed by a huge crash of thunder that seems to rock the house. I glance at Anna. Her eyes are open and she raises her head up off the pillow.

"What the heck was that?" she says, groggily.

"Just a storm, honey," I say. "Go back to sleep. It's early."

Slipping out of bed, I go to the window and close it. I glance at my watch. Five fifty in the a.m. Do I head to my bedroom and sleep for another hour? Once I'm up, I'm up. Heading into the bathroom, I flick on the overhead light, but it doesn't work. Must be the bulb is out. I make a mental note to change the light bulb. Washing my face and brushing my teeth, I then head into my bedroom and slip my feet into a pair of new flip-flops I picked up at the Target along with a new bathing suit and some underwear. Making my way downstairs to make the coffee, I feel a chill run up my spine. It's downright cold in the house, so I decide then and there to start the fire Tim prepared for us in the living room fireplace the day we arrived.

"Good old Tim," I say, now recalling our lovemaking from the night before.

I also recall my dream about seeing Sarah Anne in the woods, and I try and shake it out of my head. My subconscious loves to play dirty tricks on me sometimes. Nightmares. I guess it's how we all deal with our deepest fears. I make my way into the kitchen and turn on the light. It, too, doesn't go on. I flick the switch a couple of times but no luck. Another lightning bolt flashes and yet another thunderous explosion takes my breath away. Apparently, thunderstorms on the lake are almost Biblical events.

I glance at the clock on the microwave. It's not working.

"Damn," I whisper to myself. "Power's out."

I recall Tim telling me the breaker board is down in the basement. Why does it have to be in the basement, for God's sake? First things first. Since I know the gas stove will work if I ignite the burner with a lit match, I decide to make some tea. Pouring some tap water into a pan, I put it on the stove, then open the gas valve. A pack of matches is stored over the sink in a shot glass. I grab the pack, strike a match, open the gas on the burner, and fire it up. With that done, I head into the living room and strike another match. Taking a knee, I bring the lit match to the newspaper stuffed under the dry logs in the fireplace, and pray that it takes.

Turns out Tim's fire-building skills are top notch, because it takes right away. Or perhaps the draft on the chimney is that good. Probably a little of both. By the time the fire is going strong and warming the house, my water is boiling. I pour it into a mug that's loaded with a fresh tea bag. Now that I have no choice but to attack the electrical problem, I go to the counter and grab the flashlight. I test it to see if the batteries are still working. The light is bright and strong. I really have no excuse not to head down into what is surely a creepy dungeon.

Opening the door, I shine the light on the old wood stairs. The rough wood beam ceiling is covered in spider webs. A big black spider crawls along one of the beams, trying to escape the light. It makes my skin crawl. Still, I take my first step and a second, and so on until I come to the packed dirt floor. I scan the flashlight on the wide-open room. There's not much to see but more spider webs. The smell is mold and mildew. A pile of old, green-mold-covered furniture is stacked up against the stone wall foundation to my left, while to my right, mounted to the center of the wall, is a 4x4 piece of plywood. Attached to its center is the metal breaker box.

I go to the breaker box, open it. Shining the flashlight on it, I find the tripped breakers, and pull them back into position. You can almost feel the electricity powering up the house. It's like blood being fed to the veins. The light from the kitchen overhead bleeds down the old stairs. I feel a cool breeze coming from over my left shoulder. It chills me to the bone. I can't help but shake the feeling that someone or something is standing in the pitch darkness on the opposite side of the room. I feel like it's watching me.

I feel something crawl over my foot. It's a long centipede.

"Oh Jesus," I spit, shaking the insect off.

Heart suddenly stuffed in my throat, it's all I can do to bound back up the stairs to the safety of the kitchen. I close the door and remind myself to speak with Tim about installing a dead bolt.

*   *   *

The storms come and go for most of the early morning. Now that I have power, I switch from tea to coffee and work fiendishly on my new project. I've begun to shape the neck and some of the upper chest. I've given her a small silver cross attached to a delicate chain that hangs from her neck. Creating the chain alone cost me over an hour of my time. It's precision work, but it's also something I need to get right if I'm going to pull this bust off.

Using the sculpting knife, I carve the lips into a precise kind of half smile, half pout. It's a matter of keeping one eye on the newspaper photo of Sarah and the other on the bust. As I've said before, it's not really me who's creating something here. It's a force I can't begin to explain. Only that it controls me and not the other way around. I don't consciously move my fingers. They just move. It's as though I am a conduit for some higher power or spirit. Can art be taught? To an extent, yes. But having taught hundreds of students for more than twenty years now, I'm a firm believer that true artistic talent is something you're born with, like the color of your hair, or your height, or your ability to run a mile in less than seven minutes.

Anna's sudden presence in the dining room nearly scares the skin off my bones.

"Anna," I say, "how long have you been standing there?"

"I'm sorry," she says. "You were concentrating so hard, I didn't want to disturb you."

She's wearing her long, red Lady Gaga t-shirt and her feet are bear. Her dark hair is long, and parted in the middle. Her face is smooth, her lips full, her eyes big, brown, and wet. She's glowing in the firelight. My eyes shift from the bust of Sarah to my daughter and then to the newspaper photo tacked to the wall. Maybe my imagination is running away with itself again, but I swear I'm seeing the same little girl. Only she's not so little anymore. Like Sarah was when she was abducted so many years ago, Anna is blossoming into a beautiful young woman, and doing so right before my very eyes.

Standing, I say, "I was gonna grab another coffee, honey. Do you want me to fix you something to eat?"

"I don't want to bother you," she says.

I'm sensing a sadness in her this morning. Maybe it has something to do with the weather. More than likely, it's the hormones raging through her pubescent body.

"I've been up and at 'em since before the dawn," I say. "I could use a break by now."

"That was a bad storm," she says. "Are we gonna get more of them?"

"It knocked out the power."

"How did you fix it?" she asks.

"I had to turn the breakers back on. The box is in the basement."

She crosses her arms over her chest, like the mere mention of the word *basement* gives her a case of the chills. Like mother like daughter.

"You actually went down there, Mom?"

"No choice, hon," I say, stepping out of the room. "You gotta do what you gotta do if you want power."

"I guess so," she says.

We both head into the kitchen. She takes a seat at the kitchen table and peers out the big picture window.

"Drats," she says a little under her breath. "The weather continues to suck."

I gaze out the big picture window. The lightning has abated for now, but the rain is steady.

"I have a feeling we're gonna be bailing out the boat," I say.

"If it hasn't sunk already," she says. Then, refocusing on me. "Hey, if the rain stops for a while, maybe we can go fishing."

I place my hand on her shoulder.

"Absolutely," I say. "For now, what would you like for breakfast? I'll make you anything you want."

"Even pancakes?" she says.

"It's the weekend," I say. "Even pancakes."

Her mood is suddenly elevated.

"I must have died and gone to heaven," she says, as if to prove my point.

"Bite you tongue," I say.

She bites her tongue, like the simple gesture will prevent her from dying. Ever. I go to the cabinet over the stove, pull down the box of pancake mix. My eyes fill, because I realize, suddenly, that Anna is all I have left in the world besides ghosts.

CHAPTER 30

As if the God of good weather has been listening to our prayers, the sun is managing to poke its way out of the clouds by the time we've finished a big grand slam breakfast of pancakes, sausage links, and over-easy eggs.

Carrying my plate to the sink, I say, "I'm not eating another thing until dinner tonight."

"That's right," Anna says, "I almost forgot. You have a hot and heavy date tonight with Tim."

My cell phone vibrates on the counter.

"Speak of the devil," I say. "It's a text from Tim."

Placing the plate in the sink along with the other dirty pans, I open the text.

That was wonderful last night . . . Can't wait to see you later for church . . . We can confess our sins LOL

I can't help but laugh aloud.

"What is it?" Anna says, standing up from the table and carrying her plate to the sink.

"Tim's so funny," I say.

She attempts to snatch the phone from my hand, but I'm too fast for her.

"Don't even think about it, woman," I say.

"You guys are getting hot and heavy," she says. "Better tell the big Tony."

Her words hit me the wrong way, and a sudden jolt of anger fills my veins.

"Damnit, Anna, if you say that one more time, I swear I'm taking your phone away."

Her eyes grow wide and tears fill them.

"Oh my God," she says, "I was only like joking, Mom. You don't have to freaking scream at me."

She storms off in a huff, pounding each tread as she ascends the stairs. I wait for the inevitable door slam. When it comes, my body shudders. I place both hands on the countertop, as if to hold up my heavy, dead weight. She's right, of course. She was only joking and I snapped. Maybe I'm overtired. Maybe I slept like crap last night. Maybe I'm suffering from a case of the guilts over Tony. Maybe I'm still upset over the nightmare. Maybe I'm spooked by Sarah Anne's memory and the fact that she looks so much like my daughter. Maybe I'm spooked by this house and the ghosts of the people who lived here. Maybe I'm spooked by the ghosts of Allison and Charlie. Maybe it's all of the above.

"God forgive me," I say.

Don't be so tough on yourself, Rosie. My little sis is twelve now, and her emotions are running wild.

She's right, Rose. This is all a part of growing up.

Thanks, guys, but I snapped at her and I shouldn't have.

Agreed, Rosie, you did fly off the handle a little.
But it happens.

I'll head up and apologize, Allison. Then we'll go out in the boat and hopefully forget the whole thing.

Good idea, Rose. I sure wish I could have had the chance to take my second daughter fishing, but . . .

"But you had to go and put the business end of a pistol barrel in your mouth, Charlie," I say aloud. Yeah, I guess you could say I'm still a little bitter about how my husband checked out, even after all these years.

Inhaling and exhaling a deep breath, I cross over the living room. My eyes catch sight of the now dying fire. Slowly, I take the stairs and then go to Anna's room. I knock gently.

"Anna," I say, in a singsong voice. "Can I come in?"

"Go away. I hate you."

"No, you don't," I say. "You're just mad. And you know what? I don't blame you. I did jump down your throat. And that's something I almost never do, and I promise you it won't happen again. At least, I'll try for it to never happen again."

Silence. A heavy dreadful silence.

"Anna," I say like a question. "Come on, give me a second chance."

More silence, until I hear the sounds of footsteps. Then the door opening slowly, and a beautiful, teary-eyed face peering out.

"Okay," she says, opening the door wider.

She goes to her bed and sits down on the end of it. I can't help but wonder if Sarah Anne had done this very thing with her own mother way back when. Almost surely, she did. I sit down beside her and take her in my arms, hug her tightly. Then, gazing into her eyes, I wipe her tears. She sniffles.

"Sorry I shouted at you," she says.

"Me too," I say. Then, "You know what this is all about, don't you, Anna?"

"Tony," Anna says without hesitation.

It's precisely what's on my mind. Precisely what's bothering me more than anything else.

"You feel like you're cheating on him with Tim," my daughter goes on.

"Yup," I say. "That's it exactly."

"But you already told me you plan on talking with him about it, Mom. It means you're already doing the right thing. So don't get so touchy about it. Just follow through."

I set my hand on her thigh.

"Shouldn't it be me giving you life advice, kiddo?"

"You do," she says. "I mean, you're always telling me what to do and what not to do."

"Fair enough," I say. "Here's another bit of advice for when you have kids of your own. Don't fly off the handle at them unnecessarily."

She giggles. It's a priceless giggle.

"I'm sure I'll have my moments," she says. "Especially if Jake Walls pisses me off."

We both burst out laughing at that one.

"Can you imagine your wedding day with Jake?" I say. "They'd have to make him stand on a soapbox so he can kiss the bride."

We laugh some more until I get up and point at the window.

"Look, the sun is out, sweetheart. Who knows for how long? What say you put on your bathing suit and some shorts and go bail out the Whaler. Meantime, I'll clean the kitchen and then we'll take a ride out on the lake."

She springs up, like she's been injected with a dose of optimism.

"Awesome," she says. "I'll grab a couple of fishing poles and the tackle box."

"Tackle box?" I ask.

"Yeah, it came with the place. I found it in the garage along with the poles when I was snooping around after we first got here."

I can't help but wonder if the stuff belonged to the Moores.

"We have a plan, Houston," I say, exiting the bedroom.

I enter my own bedroom and dress into my new, black, one-piece suit. Then, I grab a pair of tan shorts and slip into those too. I put my flip-flops back on while grabbing a baseball hat and a pair of Aviator sunglasses. I also grab some sun screen for the both of us.

"See you downstairs, Anna," I say.

"Be right there, Rosie."

Rosie . . .

The ship that is my fragile family has once again been righted. For now.

*   *   *

By the time I'm done with the dishes, Anna has bailed out the Whaler. I remind myself to ask Tim if he has a cover for the boat. Or perhaps there's a cover in the garage. That is, if the Moores had a boat, which I can only assume they did. I spot the two fishing poles, which have been placed inside the stern-mounted plastic pole holders—Dad had similar ones mounted on his boat—while a big, plastic tackle box is set on the bench at the front of the center console.

"I almost forgot some snacks and some drinks," I say. "I'll be right back."

"Thought you weren't eating anymore 'till your date with Tim tonight?" Anna asks.

"Something about the fresh air," I say. "It makes me hungry."

"And horny," Anna says under her breath as I head back up to the house.

"I heard that," I say.

"Ooopsies," she says.

Grabbing a box of Ritz crackers, and two bottles of spring water, I head back outside and hop into the boat.

"That's your idea of snacks?" Anna says.

"Who doesn't love Ritz?" I say.

She starts the outboard. It sputters to life and idles pleasantly.

"You mind getting the lines, Rosie?"

"Aye, aye, Captain," I say, jumping out of the boat.

I undo the bow line, toss it into the boat. I repeat the process with the stern. Then, as the boat is slowly drifting away from the dock, I jump back in.

"Sure you got this, Anna?"

"Sure as you know what, Rosie."

You should see the expression on her face. The only way to describe it is she's glowing. She grips the chrome-plated throttle and gives the boat a little gas. The outboard engine revs, and soon the boat is pulling out and away from the dock. She maintains a slow speed until we're past a red buoy. She then really gives it the gas, and we take off like a rocket for the middle of the lake.

Our hair is blowing and the cool wind that whips our faces is like heaven on earth. Boating is like flying. The motion is fast and furious, the craft never stable. But at the same time, the feeling is pure power and freedom. I just sit back and allow Anna to do the driving while she stands at the helm, her eyes poised out ahead, searching for the perfect place to slow down and perhaps drop a line. A place that Tim revealed to her. Or so I can only assume.

When we come to that place, not far from one of the lake's many small islands, she slows the boat to a crawl and allows it to drift towards the shallower water. When we've gone far enough, she kills the engine and tosses out the anchor.

"Let's try our luck, Rosie," she says.

"You fish, honey," I say. "I'm gonna work on catching some rays while we have a little sun for a change."

"Suit yourself," she says, taking hold of one of the rods.

She casts out towards the shoreline and slowly reels in. I'll be darned if she isn't a natural.

"Maybe tomorrow we can get some worms from the general store," she says. "Tim says live bait always works better than these spinners we're using."

"Your grandfather and uncles always swore by worms when they fished."

"Did you use worms, too, Mom?"

"Me, touch a worm?" I say. "Are you kidding?"

"You didn't mind touching the fish," she says, reeling in her line and quickly casting it out again.

"Worms are different," I say.

I steal a Ritz cracker and take a drink of water, then sit back in the padded seat. It's such a pleasure watching my daughter, I can't even find the words to express it. But then I hear something ominous coming from out of the distance. A low rumble of thunder. Turning, I see something that's best described as horrifying. The clouds are low lying, but they also take up the entire sky. These are not your everyday overcast gray clouds. These clouds are black and tinged with purple. Lightning is flashing from them, striking the lake. A wall of rain curtains the horizon. The cold wind that's accompanying it is already beginning to blow. Blow hard. What I'm witnessing here is not just a storm, but a major weather event.

My pulse suddenly races.

"Anna," I say, standing. "We've got to get the hell out of here."

Gazing over her shoulder, her eyes go wide and her face a distinct shade of pale. She reels in, sets her pole in the pole holder.

"Oh my God, Mom," she says.

"Should we head for the island?" I ask.

"There's nowhere to dock," she correctly points out. "We'll lose the boat and be stranded."

"Let's just go now," I say. "Head back in the opposite direction for home. Maybe we can outrun it."

Anna immediately begins pulling up the anchor. When she's done, she goes to the cockpit, fires up the engine, and pushes the stick. The Whaler engine revs and the boat lurches forward. She immediately turns the bow in the direction of the house while, behind us, the massive storm is picking up speed.

"Hurry," I shout, over the noise.

"It's going as fast as it can!" she barks.

The wind is whipping our faces. Even when we shout, it's almost impossible to hear one another. The bottom of the boat is slapping against the lake. The strange thing is, I can feel the wind from the storm against my back. It's an almost icy, harsh wind. Turning again, I can see that the black and purple clouds have overtaken us. We're about to be drenched in the pouring rain. We're in the middle of the lake, and we can't even see our home yet, much less the land it sits on.

A jagged lightning bolt strikes the lake maybe ten feet in front of us. The thunder concussion that immediately follows sounds like a bomb has exploded inside the boat. Anna screams and let's go of the wheel. The boat lurches to the side so forcefully, I'm convinced we're about to capsize. We both fall onto our sides, while the engine stalls, and the boat rights itself. Anna is crying now.

"I'm sorry!" she screams. "I'm sorry, Mama!"

I manage to get myself back up while the rain pounds us along with the wind gusts. If I didn't know any better, this storm is about to produce a tornado. If that happens, they will never find my or my daughter's body. Shifting myself to the wheel, I turn the key to restart the engine. It sputters and sputters, but won't start.

"Shit!" I bark.

Another lightning strike. This one even closer. The electricity in it causes the fine hairs on my body to stand at attention. The crack of thunder steals my breath away. Anna is screaming like she's convinced we're about to die. I try the starter again. The engine sputters once more. It just won't turn over.

"What's wrong?" Anna desperately shouts. "Why won't it start, Mom?"

"It's got to be flooded," I say, my face and eyes drowning in rainwater.

Turning, I glance at the red, twelve-gallon plastic gas tank that's attached to the outboard motor by a black rubber hose.

"Try again," she insists.

I turn the key. Again, nothing but a sputter. But there is a very loud, if not thunderous, noise coming from behind me. Spinning around on the balls of my feet, I spot something that makes my heart sink. It's a tunnel of water. A tornado, only not made of wind. It is, instead, made of water. A water spout.

"God help us," I whisper.

Turning back to the starter, I gaze up at the black-purple sky.

Please, dear God, help us. Just this once and I will do anything for you . . .

"Mom, please, we've got to get out of here!"

I turn the starter. The outboard engine sputters and sputters.

"Come on, come on," I repeat, while grinding my teeth.

Then something miraculous happens. The motor roars to life. I gaze over my shoulder and see that the water spout can't be more than fifty feet behind us. I give the throttle everything it's got. The Whaler lunges forward, and we zoom across the rough water, smashing into what has to be four- or five-foot swells. It's a hell of a rough ride with the rain pouring down on us and the severe winds whipping our faces. But at least we've got a chance of getting the hell home. At least we have a chance of surviving the severe storm.

Turning to Anna, I can see that what was just seconds ago a face filled with terror is now a happy face. She's crying tears of joy. She raises up her left hand and makes a fist. I've got both hands on the wheel, but I manage to release my right hand long enough to fist pump her. Then I make sure to place the hand back on the wheel.

It takes maybe a couple long minutes, but soon the shore is in sight, along with the Moore house. We're putting some distance between us and the storm now as it moves off in a southerly direction towards Schroon Lake. The lake calms down and even the rain stops. The lightning is still striking, but it's now far enough off in the distance that we hardly even notice it, nor can we make out the thunder over the noise of the outboard motor.

After a time, Anna pokes me on the shoulder.

"Slow her up," she says. "I'll take it from here, Rosie."

She places her hand on the wheel, and I release it entirely. We exchange places, and I breathe a long sigh of relief. Anna shoots me a big sweet smile.

"You did good, Rosie," she says. "You did real good."

"Been a while since I piloted a boat," I say. "For a while there, I thought we were in real trouble."

"Me, too, Mom," she says. "But somehow I knew Allison and Dad would protect us."

She hardly ever refers to her deceased family like that. It takes me more than a little by surprise. But it also feels good to know she's aware of their heavenly presence. She slows the boat to a crawl as we pass the red buoy. I make sure to keep quiet while she concentrates on parking the boat without slamming into the dock. Steering with her right hand, she uses her left to shift from forward to reverse and back again. For a girl who's only had one lesson on docking a boat, she does perfectly.

She kills the engine and then hits the control that raises the screw up.

The bow line already in hand, I jump out and tie it off on the cleat. Anna hands me the stern line, and I tie that one off too. Gathering the bottles of spring water and the now soaked box of Ritz crackers, she hops up onto the dock.

"That was something, wasn't it, Rosie?" she asks.

"I was never worried," I say. "Not for an instant."

"Ha," she says. "I seem to recall you screaming for your life."

I laugh.

"Okay, okay," I say, "I'll admit it was a bit hairy there for a few minutes, especially when that water spout formed. I don't think I've ever seen one of those before. Not in real life anyway."

Together we gaze out onto the lake, at the thick black and purple clouds that still persist and that are forecast to persist most of the weekend. Which reminds me of something.

"Anna, why don't you check the garage to see if there's some kind of tarp we can put over the boat. Otherwise we're gonna be bailing all weekend."

"Roger that, Rosie," she says. "What are you gonna do?"

"Do you want me to make you a sandwich?"

"I'm a big girl now," she says. "I can make my own."

"Well, if you're sure," I say, "then I'm gonna maybe steal myself a little nap. I got up way too early, and it's gonna be a bit of a long night."

Anna shoots me a wink and one of her sly smiles.

"This might come as a surprise to you, young lady," I say. "But, believe it or not, I'm not that easy."

"Sure you're not," she says, heading across the back lawn past the woodpile towards the garage.

I head into the house, knowing that it's getting harder and harder to feed my only surviving daughter little white lies.

CHAPTER 31

I MAKE MY way upstairs and head immediately into the bathroom, not only to pee, but to towel dry my face and hair. I then head into my bedroom and collapse face-first on the bed. Before I know it, I'm in never-never land.

Entering onto the Paradox Lake Trail, I feel the rainwater soaking my face. The forest is very dark due to the thick, black cloud cover. But it lights up when the lightning flashes. I'm running, but it feels like my feet are stuck in hardening concrete. I'm not sure if I'm trying to save someone or I'm running away from someone. Maybe both.

My oxygen comes and goes in shallow breaths. I feel like I'm drowning in my own air. Rainwater seeps into my eyes, burns them, makes it almost impossible to see. When the animal lunges out from the dark forest and tackles me to the ground, I feel my heart jump into my mouth. My pulse skyrockets. I try to scream but I can't. It's a wolf. A big black wolf, its furry hide is matted with fresh blood, its blood-covered claws pressing me down on the trail floor. It opens its big long jaws, exposes razor-sharp fangs covered in clear drool and red blood. I stare into its black eyes. I know that in just a matter of seconds, it's going to bury its fangs into my neck. But I manage to kick it in the groin. It shrieks and jumps off of me, yelping as it disappears back inside the woods.

Picking myself up, I about-face and make for the trailhead and my home. I can't run fast enough; it still feels like my legs are trapped in thick, heavy mud. As I reach the trailhead, I come around the wood-pile, and see that the back door has been left wide open. I also see that the ground beneath me is covered in blood. So are the steps leading up into the kitchen.

I head into the kitchen, call out for Anna.

No answer.

I call out again.

Nothing.

That's when I see a girl who looks a lot like Anna standing outside my studio. She has a silver cross hanging from her neck. It's Sarah Anne Moore. Silently she raises her left hand, points with extended index finger towards my studio. Tears fill my eyes. My throat closes in on itself. Heart is pounding against my ribs.

I can't talk, but in my head, I'm whispering, "Oh no, oh no, oh God no . . ."

Slowly, I make my way to my studio. When I look inside, the sculpted bust looks nothing like the tan/brown block of clay I've been working with. Instead, it looks like the head of a real human being. There's blood everywhere. Blood on the floor, blood on the walls and windows, blood dripping off the sculpting platform. My head is buzzing with adrenaline and panic. When I come around the head to view the face, my worst fears are confirmed.

"Anna," I say.

Her open eyes stare up at me.

"Beware the Big Bad Wolf," she whispers.

I wake up with an electric jolt. I'm so sick to my stomach I run to the bathroom, drop to my knees before the toilet, and toss my cookies. What on God's earth was that all about? Talk about the king of all nightmares. Am I that paranoid? Am I that afraid of losing Anna that my subconscious can't help but toy with me? Correction—torture me?

Standing, I flush the toilet, then come around to the sink and brush my teeth. I breathe in deeply and exhale slowly. Starting the shower, I take a look at Anna's bedroom. It's empty. Pulse lifts. I go to her bedroom window, look out onto the backyard. I feel a thousand times better when I see her placing a large tan tarp over the Whaler.

"Everything is as it should be," I whisper, as if this helps me believe myself.

Should I go on my date and leave Anna alone for a few hours? As a mother, am I doing the right thing? Or am I overanalyzing things just because of a couple of bad nightmares? A couple of very vivid nightmares. As I undress and step into the shower, I recall the horrible nightmares I had after Allison died. Also, the ones I had after Charlie killed himself. In the case of the former, I'd see her standing in the kitchen of our Albany home. She'd be the gaunt, long-haired, white-faced comatose little girl she was just moments before she died. She'd be wearing her red nightgown. It was the last nightgown I bought for her before she passed.

"Don't let me go, Mommy," she'd say, before holding out her thin, bird-like hand. "I'm afraid."

In the case of the latter, I'd see Charlie coming through the front door, like he always did upon his arrival home from work at his architecture office. He'd be wearing a blue blazer over one of his button-down shirts with the top button undone, the ball knot on his tie hanging low. He'd set his briefcase onto the floor by the door and smile for me.

"Charlie," I'd say. "You're not supposed to be here."

"What are you talking about?" he'd say. "I live here. Where's Allison?"

"Allison died, too."

"Nonsense. I'm going upstairs to see what she's doing."

That's when he'd start up the stairs and I'd see how much of his cranial cap had been blown off when he stuck the barrel of a .45 caliber semiautomatic pistol in his mouth, and pulled the trigger.

I wash my hair, then soap my body and shave my legs. I nick my calf with the razor. Blood drips down my leg and combines with the soapy water that circles the drain. I guess my hands are still trembling from my nightmare about Anna. This is not the frame of mind I wanted to be in when preparing for my date with Tim. Maybe the nightmares and the bad, ugly memories are an extension of my feeling bad about Tony. Or maybe I'm just overthinking this whole thing.

Slipping out of the shower, I dry myself, and blow-dry my hair. I then straighten my hair with the curling iron. My hair is naturally straight, but the humidity from these storms is wreaking havoc on it. Soon as that's done, I gaze into my face. A few new wrinkles have sprouted over the years. As I said before, fifty is right around the corner, and age happens. I've never been much for makeup, but I add a little foundation and some other junk, just to make me look at least somewhat attractive to Tim.

Heading back into the bedroom, I put on a pair of my best black undies and matching pushup bra. Then I look in the closet for a summer-weight dress that might be perfect for both church and an upstate Italian restaurant. And that's when I hear a truck pull up into the driveway.

"Holy crap," I say. "Is it that late?"

I gaze at my watch sitting on the dresser. Holy crap is right. It's already 4:10 p.m. Tim might be five minutes early, but I swear I thought it was only three thirty or so. I must have slept longer than I thought. Throwing on a white dress, I go to the window, open it, and stick my head out. Tim is just coming around the front from the driveway. He's got a large plastic Ferguson General Store bag in his hand.

"Hi, Tim," I say out the open window. "Running a tad behind on my end. Feel free to let yourself in. Anna should be inside or down on the dock."

He smiles at me.

"You got it, cutie," he says. Then, holding out his hand, palm up as if to catch the rain. "Don't forget your umbrella. It's gonna storm all night."

Cutie . . . love it . . . he's already cheering me up . . .

He's wearing cowboy boots, blue jeans, a clean button-down, and a dark blazer over that. Funny how he and Charlie have pretty much the same style. Maybe that's part of the attraction. I'm just happy Tim doesn't wear a bush jacket.

I find a pair of leather gladiator sandals in the closet, slip those on, put on my watch, a couple of silver bracelets and a matching silver angel necklace, and I am finally ready to go. Gazing into the mirror, I realize I've made myself more than just attractive. I'm looking pretty darn hot, if I don't say so myself.

"Hey, own it, honey," I whisper aloud.

Grabbing my cell phone and my leather bag, I head down the stairs, the bad memories and nightmares a thing of the past.

When I come to the landing, Tim is nowhere to be found. But I hear voices coming from out back. I go into the kitchen and spot the shopping bag set on the counter. Then, going to the back door, I can see that Anna is proudly showing Tim the job she did covering up the boat. He's clearly happy because he's patting her on the back, running his hand up and down her spine.

"You sure know how to take care of a boat," he says. "Looks like my instincts were right on, Anna."

I open the screen door.

"Tell Tim about our afternoon adventure out on the water, honey," I say.

He turns to me quick.

"Please don't tell me you went out on the lake today, Rose. There were severe weather alerts going off all day warning boaters not to venture out. Every year boaters die in storms like the ones we've been having. You guys need a radio."

"I'll look into it," I say.

But somehow, I'm thinking Tim will probably show up with one tomorrow. He turns to Anna.

"Hey, kiddo," he says, "you wanna see what I brought you to eat?"

"I'm starving," she says. "Let's see."

We all head into the kitchen. Tim pulls out not just a couple orders of what he describes as his sister's famous mac and cheese, but also two orders of spaghetti and meatballs, two orders of meatloaf and mashed potatoes, and two turkey dinners.

"Jeez, Tim," I say, "we'll be fat if we eat all that."

"I'll take the mac and cheese," Anna says.

She's already putting one of the orders in the microwave and heating it up.

"I figure you can freeze them and eat them when you don't feel like cooking," Tim goes on. Then gazing at his watch. "We'd better go if we're gonna get to church on time."

"Church?" Anna says. "My mom's like a total pagan."

"Bite your tongue, young lady," I say. "I'm still a believer."

She laughs. "Ha, I don't ever remember you going to church. Not even once."

"There's a first for everything, right, Tim?" I say. "And actually, I've been thinking a lot lately about making a return. Maybe Tim is an angel sent by God to help me make my decision."

Anna makes a gesture with her index finger like she's gagging herself.

"Wow," Tim says, "that's quite the compliment. But man, oh man, I'm most definitely no angel. Angels don't have nearly as much fun as devils."

He winks at me.

"Go have fun, you kids," Anna says. "I won't wait up."

"Actually, we'll be home no later than eight o'clock. If we're going to be later, I'll text you."

"You can stay out later," she says, as the microwave dings now that the heating cycle has ended. "I'm not a little kid, you know."

"But we're still strangers in a strange place, and I'd feel better if we make it an early night."

"Can't agree more, Rose," Tim says. "But I do believe Anna will be more than safe. This is Paradox, after all."

As reassuring as he sounds, I still don't like letting my guard down. I give Anna a kiss on the cheek. When Tim kisses her cheek, too, it kind of takes me by surprise. I guess he's just being sweet. As we exit the kitchen for the front door, I can't help but gaze at the cross hanging on the wall. I can't help but wonder if the Moores felt safe in Paradox on the day their daughter was abducted.

CHAPTER 32

WE'RE NOT ALL the way to the Paradox Lake Road when Tim slows the pickup truck and comes to a stop along the side of the road. Throwing the transmission into park, he leans into me and plants a long, hard kiss on me. He runs his hands through my hair and presses me into him, not like he lusts me, but like he's falling in love with me as fast and as hard as I am falling for him. What the hell is happening here? I'm beginning to think my decision to take a sabbatical on behalf of my art in Paradox was determined by fate.

Our tongues play and he shifts his hands to my breasts, gently squeezing them and, in the process, making me entirely damp. I lower my hand and press it against his hardness.

"Take me," I say. "Take me right here, right now."

He doesn't hesitate to unbuckle his belt and unbutton his jeans. He presses me back against the door. Placing his hand on my soft inner thigh, he slowly moves his fingers upwards until he's touching me outside my panties. When he slips the fingers inside, he feels the wetness and I feel an electric excitement rush throughout my entire body.

Outside the truck, the rain starts to fall again. Lightning strikes in the near distance. Pulling my panties down, Tim enters me slowly, thickly, and deep. A new round of thunder pounds and rocks the truck. He breathes heavily as he begins to thrust himself against me. I try and work with his rhythm, my cries and moans filling the truck along with the pounding rain. I can feel him swelling and filling, and I know he can feel my hot wetness. When we both release at the same time, I can't control my scream. He bites my shoulder and the pain is both deep and wonderful.

When we've caught our breath, he lifts himself up and begins to get dressed. I pull my panties up and inhale a deep breath.

"So that just happened," I say.

He looks at me with his very handsome smile.

"You realize what's happening here, don't you, Rose?"

"I do," I say. "I can't stop thinking about you, Tim."

He shifts himself back behind the wheel, starts the truck.

"What about Tony?" he says. "Your boyfriend."

"I need to tell him," I say. "He's coming up next Saturday. I'll tell him then."

He pulls back onto the gravel road in the direction of the two-track and then the Paradox Lake Road.

"Are you sure this is what you want?" he says. "I feel sort of bad about barging into your life and taking over."

"I'm a big girl," I say. "I knew what I was doing when you came into my life and I know what I'm doing now."

He reaches for my hand, squeezes it. It is as much a gesture of love as is his lovemaking.

"We'll make this work, Rose," he says. "You, me, and Anna."

I see my daughter in my head. She really likes Tim. I'm sure she can learn to love him too. She will always love Tony, but things change and it's time for us to move on. I will always consider him special, always have love for him for being there for us. But then why am I so afraid to tell him the truth? Why am I dreading his visit next Saturday?

Tim turns onto the main road. We sit in a happy, contented quiet until the town comes into view.

"We're gonna be a tad late for church," he says. "But I'm sure the good Lord will give us a break."

"I've been late for church going on ten years now," I say.

He laughs and pulls into the church parking lot. Finding a space towards the back, he kills the engine.

"We'll sneak in quietly and sit in the back," he says, taking hold of my hand, leading me to the front of the old, white, wood clap-board church.

When we come to the wood doors, he slowly opens them. We step inside to the booming voice of the short, balding, paunchy priest. The church is maybe half filled with local parishioners and, of course, we stick out like two sore thumbs when we enter ten full minutes late.

The priest looks up from the Bible passage he's reading aloud on the podium.

"Nice to see you can join us, Mr. Ferguson," the priest says.

The entire congregation turns and glares at us over their shoulders.

"Snagged," Tim says, under his breath. Then, "Glad to be here, Father O'Connor. Wouldn't miss it for the world."

Suddenly I feel like I'm living in a fishbowl. I see the all the curious faces staring at me, staring through me, and I see the portly priest eyeing me, and behind him, the crucified Jesus hang-ing on the far wall. They are all looking at us like they know Tim and I just had sex inside his truck. For a quick second, I feel like my dress is still hiked up over my chest. I actually touch my thighs just to make sure the hem is where it should be. I offer up a polite smile, but I can't help believe everyone thinks of me as the city woman who arrived in Paradox only this week with her daughter and who is already sleeping with the town's most eligible bachelor. Not that it's anyone's business. But you know how small towns can be.

We sit down in the wood pew and the priest continues with his reading. Now that everyone has refocused their attention on Father O'Conner, I can't help but take a casual look around. Mostly rural folk dressed in cheap Walmart clothing, their faces withdrawn and old despite their years. My eyes are suddenly drawn to the first pew. I feel a slight start in my heart when I see Tim's employee, Ed. The stocky, bald man is dressed like he always is, in his overalls and t-shirt, work boots no doubt on his feet. He slowly turns, as if he senses I'm staring at him. He locks onto my eyes and smiles, his brown crooked teeth pressed together.

I turn away from him, and stare down at my hands folded in my lap. Tim places his left hand on my thigh. It's not meant as a sexual gesture. It is, instead, something to calm me, since I'm sure by now he knows how uncomfortable I feel. In his right hand, he's holding a pair of red rosary beads. He's pressing each bead with his index finger and thumb while quietly whispering one Our Father after another. He's a remarkable man. A terrific lover, a terrific friend, the town's most successful businessman—at least as far as I know—and he's also deeply spiritual.

I decide then and there not to allow my nerves to get to me. In fact, I too start to whisper prayers in my head. I say the Lord's Prayer and then a Hail Mary. I pray for my daughters, both alive and departed. I pray for Charlie, and I even pray for Tony. I know he'll be trying to call and/or text me soon, and I'll have no choice but to ignore him. I pray the Lord forgive me and I pray the Lord my soul to keep.

The rain pours down while Father O'Connor offers up a short homily about everyone getting along, no matter what your politics, no matter what your religion. He makes a reference to his time as a prison chaplain, how his door was always open to all faiths and all persuasions. He reminds us how divided we've become as a nation and how we must rise above bigotry and become unified once more. Or else we'll find ourselves in a terrible civil war for which no one will escape unaffected. Strong words for a country priest who can't wait to hit up Bunny's Bar.

When it comes time to take Communion, I follow Tim up the center aisle to Father O'Connor. I almost find it entirely appropriate that lightning and an artillery-like thunderclap strikes the moment I take the Holy Communion in my hand and place it in my mouth. It's almost like the good Lord is trying to tell the priest that I don't deserve to take part in the sacred act.

Oh well, too late now . . .

But there is something about the way the priest looks into my eyes with his deep brown eyes. It's not like he's disappointed in me. How could he be? He has no idea who I am, after all. It's more like he's trying to tell me something, or relay something to me. Just what that something is, I have no idea. Or perhaps, I'm just over-imagining things as usual.

As we return to our pew, more lightning and thunder pounds Paradox. The noise reverberates inside the old church, makes the presence of God seem all the more real. We sit and we pray some more, Tim intently making sure he runs through his entire rosary. Father O'Connor asks us to stand one final time, and he gives us his blessing, tells us to go in peace and serve the Lord. Something I intend to do more of, going forward with Tim. That is, if it's our fate to go forward together.

Flanked by his bored-looking altar boys, Father O'Connor makes his way to the front of the church. We pile out and each member shakes his hand and tells him what a terrific homily he gave. When it comes time for Tim and me to greet him, Tim doesn't just shake his hand, but instead, gives him a hug.

"Father," he says, "I'd like to introduce you to Rose. She and her daughter, Anna, are staying at the old Moore house for a few months. Rose is a famous artist."

I shake the old priest's thick hand and smile politely.

"Well, I'm an art professor, too, Father," I clarify. "Tim is too kind because I only wish I were a famous artist."

Father O'Connor looks me in the eye.

"It's a pleasure to meet you, Rose," he says. "Perhaps one day I can pay a visit and meet Anna. You are both welcome at our church, of course."

His offer to pay a visit takes me a little by surprise. But that's the way priests are, I guess. Country priests.

"I would like that, Father," I say. "You can get in touch with me through my website. Rose Conley dot com."

"I'll look it up," he says. "Have a blessed evening."

We're about to turn and head back for the truck, when Creepy Ed approaches the priest. Tim can't help but notice him.

"Heading back to the store, Ed?" Tim inquires.

"Yes, boss," Ed says in his weird, boyish, high-pitched voice. "I'll be sure to lock up tonight."

"Good," Tim says. "I'll talk with you later."

"Yes, boss," Ed says. Then, to the priest. "That was a nice service, Father. Can we pray together again sometime?"

Father O'Connor nods. "You know you're always welcome in my church, Theodore."

"I like it when we pray together, Father. Just you, me, and Jesus."

"I like it, too, Theodore. Now do as Mr. Ferguson says, and get back to work."

"Yes, Father," Ed says. "I am going back to work right now."

Theodore...

We watch Ed shuffle across the parking lot in the steady rain to his truck. In my head, I can't help but picture him carrying that animal skin out the front door of his house and hanging it on that big wood rack around back. I can't help but see him toss a bloody chunk of raw red meat to his chained-up dog. The man truly gives me the creeps. If not for him and the persistent memory of Sarah Anne's murder, Paradox would be perfect.

"Ready?" Tim says, taking hold of my hand.

I'm suddenly broken out of my spell.

"Yes," I say.

"For a second there," Tim says, "you looked like you were seeing a ghost."

"Sorry," I say. "I was just remembering something."

Theodore... the man who killed Sarah... It's got to be a coincidence for sure...

"Hungry?" he asks.

"Famished," I lie.

As we make our way back to Tim's pickup, Ed's truck pulls out of the lot in the direction of the General Store. Eating. It's the last thing I feel like doing right now.

CHAPTER 33

THE ITALIAN RESTAURANT in Schroon overlooks the lake that bears the same name. Since the exterior patio is enclosed, we're able to sit outside even though it's still storming. The food is decent enough, but as I said, I'm not entirely hungry. I guess it must be a combination of seeing Creepy Ed and worrying about Anna. I'm also more than a little disturbed that Ed's real name is Theodore. How many Theodores are there in the world? A lot, I guess. But how many Theodores refer to themselves as Ed? A lot less, I'd wager. And how many Theodores who refer to themselves as Ed come from Paradox Lake? Perhaps just one?

Anna home alone . . .

I've checked my phone a dozen times already and she hasn't texted or called, so that's a good thing. Or is it? However, Tony has already texted twice and called three times.

What's going on? is the first text.

Why won't you answer your phone????!!!! is the second, rather emphatic one.

Even though I promised myself I wouldn't text or speak with him while I was out with Tim, I respond with this one short, overly simple text: *Out for dinner. Will call when I get home.*

Cryptic enough, but I think it gave him enough of a hint to stop serial calling me.

Tim and I share a bottle of red wine, while I mostly shuffle my spaghetti and meatballs around on my plate to at least give the impression that I'm enjoying my food.

"Something wrong, Rose?" Tim says after a time. "This is like the best Italian restaurant north of Albany."

He's already most of the way through his veal parmesan.

I smile. "I'm sorry. I guess I'm not as hungry as I thought. But everything's perfect."

He sips his wine, sets the glass back down.

"You're awfully quiet," he says.

"I guess I'm just worried about Anna," I say.

I might ask him about Ed. Or Theodore, that is. But something inside me tells me not to bring it up. I don't want to sound like I'm accusing him of hiring a child murderer.

"I get it," he says. "I know if I lost a child, I'd be super protective over the one I have left."

"That about sums it up," I say.

"But if you don't mind my saying so, I can bet dollars to do-nuts she's a young lady who can take care of herself. She's very smart, and she's developing into a very attractive woman. You should be proud."

His words are encouraging on one hand and a little unexpected on the other. Maybe some people might interpret his noticing Anna's development as creepy. But because it's Tim, I know he means what he's saying and that it comes from the bottom of his heart. At least, that's what I want to believe.

My phone vibrates and chimes inside my bag.

Not again, Tony . . .

"Excuse me," I say. "I'm sorry, but I need to get that."

"No worries," he says.

I look at the screen. I'll be damned if it isn't indeed another text from Tony. The man will just not let up. But then, who can blame him?

Getting up from the table.

"I'll be right back," I say. "I need to use the ladies' room."

"Take your time," Tim offers.

Grabbing my leather bag, I head into the restaurant, find the ladies' room, and enter into the empty stall. As I sit myself down, I stare at my phone and Tony's text.

I really feel like driving up there tonight. Something doesn't feel right Rose.

My stomach cramps.

Be patient T, I text. *We'll see you next Saturday.*

I quickly check to see if Anna has left any messages. Nothing. Returning the phone to my bag, I finish up my business and then wash my hands and give my face a glance in the mirror. I decide to freshen up the little bit of makeup I have on, then head back out to the table.

"You don't look too happy," Tim says, while wiping his mouth with a cloth napkin.

"Tony," I say, sitting back down.

I notice he's refilled my wineglass. Tim, the overly thoughtful.

"Oh no," he says.

"He wants to come up," I say, taking a deep drink of my wine. "Tonight."

"That might be a little awkward."

"Naturally, I told him to relax and wait till this weekend."

He looks at me a bit sheepishly. "When do you, ahhhh, plan on dropping the bomb?"

Now he smiles slyly. But I'm not much in the mood for smiling.

"I'm sorry," he goes on. "I don't mean to sound insensitive, Rose. And I certainly don't mean to press. If you need me to back off, I can."

Shaking my head.

"Oh no," I say, "you're fine. I guess I'm just having a bad case of the guilts."

He sips some more wine.

"If you were married and even if you lived with him, I'd say you should feel guilty. But the fact that you've decided to leave him for three months to start another chapter of your life in a new place tells me you were already finished with the relationship long before you met me. My two cents, of course."

His words are spot on.

"Maybe I'm having a tough time convincing myself of that, Tim," I say. "Like I told you, Tony has been there for us for a long time. I love him, but I'm not *in love* with him anymore."

He reaches across the table, takes my hand in his.

"And us?" he says.

"I'm in love with you, Tim," I say, my eyes filling with tears. "I am most definitely falling in love with you."

* * *

We box up our leftovers, and Tim pays the bill using the gift certificate he'd been talking about. As we exit the restaurant, I'm feeling a little tipsy. At one point, I trip on my way out the front door. If not for Tim grabbing hold of my arm, I would fall flat on my face. What a way to end our date, with a broken nose and my two front teeth knocked out.

"Easy, lady," he says. "I guess that wine did a job on you."

"Gee whiz." I say. "I recall only having two glasses."

"You had a teensy bit more than that, Rose," he says. "I counted four glasses."

"Okay," I say, "how about we call it three and a half?"

"Fair enough," he says. "Tell you what. How about some ice cream? The rain has stopped for now and we can walk around the town for a bit."

I'm not sure what's happening, but the more I walk, the dizzier I feel. It's almost like I've been drugged. Or perhaps I'm just exhausted from today's adventures out on the lake.

"If it's all the same to you, Tim," I say, "I'd like to get home to Anna. Why don't you hang out with us for a little while? Maybe we can watch some Netflix together."

"Sounds like a plan," he says. "Shall we stop for more wine?"

"If you'd like some," I say.

We arrive at the truck and he opens the passenger-side door for me. I'm suddenly so weak, I'm having trouble hopping up inside. He reaches over me with the doggy bag of food, sets it on the center console, then literally lifts me up and sets me on the seat.

"Why thank you, Sir Lancelot," I say, my words sounding not like they're coming from my mouth, but instead from someone else's. It's as if I'm caught up in a vivid dream.

"By all means, my lady," he says, buckling my seat belt for me.

Shutting the door, he comes around to the driver's side, opens the door, and gets in. Slipping the key in the ignition, he starts the motor and throws the transmission in reverse. I'm staring at his movements, but he's going in and out of focus. Before he backs out, he sets his hand on my bare thigh, and runs his fingers up my legs until they touch my sex. I'm not sure if he's trying to be sexy or not, but this is not exactly the time or the place for this. I want him to stop, but I don't have strength enough to stop him.

When I feel his fingers slip inside my underwear and enter me, I try to tell him to cut it out, but no words will come. A wave of ice-cold water feels like it's washing over me. I go to open the door, but . . .

BOOK II
THE STORM

CHAPTER 34

THE RAIN HAS stopped for now, but the clouds are only getting thicker, blacker, more purple. When the Big Bad Wolf stares directly up at the cloud cover, he can make out the jolts and bolts of electricity that are forming inside them.

What big dark eyes you have.

The better to see you in the dark.

He knows that soon the rains will begin again, and the storm that will accompany them will be so severe, it will frighten the entire town of Paradox. He gallops through the wet, rain-soaked forest like a hungry beast chasing down his prey.

What speed you have.

The easier to chase you down and eat you.

By the time he comes to the Paradox Lake trailhead he's breathing heavily, but he hardly notices it. He's drooling from hunger and his body is soaked with sweat. He's ripe for a kill and tonight is the Wolf's night. He scoots past the woodpile and along the brush-covered side of the old house until he comes to the Bilco doors. He opens the metal door and descends into the damp darkness, the spider webs sticking to his face and bare arms.

When a spider crawls down his face, he makes sure to open his mouth and allow the hairy black insect to enter into it. He then chomps down on the spider, its big belly popping and releasing its creamy mix of putrid, puss-covered baby spiders. He chews the spider and its children carefully, then swallows. It's his small revenge for the wolf spider that hatched a million little babies inside his skin.

The rains have started again, and by the sound of it, a wall of water is dropping from the sky. A bright flash of lightning lights up the night sky like it's midday, the white light leaking in from the still open Bilco door. The thunder crash that follows is so loud it makes his ear drums ache.

What big ears you have.

The better to listen to your pounding pulse.

Another series of electric lightning strikes, the thunder concussions that follow immediately after reverberating across the lake and against the mountains that surround Paradox. He senses something then. The new storm is so severe that it's likely tripped the house's power. For all he knows, maybe all of Paradox is without power now.

Just to make sure, he reaches out with his big hands and finds the long string that triggers the overhead light bulb. He pulls on the string, but no light ignites. He knows that, eventually, someone will come down into the basement to check on the breaker box. He knows that with Rose out on her date with his boss, the person who will descend those basement stairs will be Rose's daughter, Anna.

The Big Bad Wolf couldn't imagine a more perfect situation. He doesn't have to chase down the prey. The prey is about to come to him.

CHAPTER 35

THE RAIN IS coming down so hard it's amazing Tim can see even ten feet ahead of the truck's front grill. I'm going in and out of consciousness now as we speed along the storm-ravaged Paradox Lake Road. Quite suddenly, we come upon a tree that's fallen in the road and Tim has no choice but to swerve around it at the last second. I want to scream, but I can't. It's impossible for me to make any noise at all. Did the wine truly make me like this? Or did Tim or someone else slip something in my wine glass while I went to the bathroom? What do they call it in the detective novels? Slipping someone a mickey? I've heard of this kind of thing happening before. A man slipping his girl a date rape drug that makes her immobile and unable to move or even talk. Yet she is still somehow awake, even if only semi-conscious.

But Tim has no reason to slip me a drug just so he can take advantage of me. I've already told him I love him, already given myself over to him. Tim has been such a saint. He even prayed the rosary in church. He's been so kind and loving to me and Anna. How could he do something like this? Why would he do something like this?

He turns onto the two-track that will take us deeper into the forest and to the Moore house. It's not even seven thirty in the evening and yet the sky is black. Jagged streaks of lightning are striking everywhere like we're being attacked by aliens. The truck rocks from the thunder claps. I am so frightened I can hardly breathe. Still, I have no choice but to sit in this passenger seat at the mercy of Tim.

While he drives, he places his hand on my thigh. He squeezes the thigh and touches my sex.

"Don't be afraid, Rose," he says. "The night is young and we're just getting started. It's too bad you didn't eat all your dinner. You're going to need your strength later. Trust me."

What the hell is he saying? What's he doing? Who is this man? He's nothing like the Tim Ferguson I've gotten to know this past week. What does he have planned for me? Why will I need all my strength? And my God, what is happening with Anna? Has he somehow managed to do something bad to my daughter?

If only I could scream. If only I could grab my phone, dial 911, then dial Tony, tell him to get in his Jeep and drive up here immediately. I was so wrong to betray him, so wrong to be deceitful. He worried himself to death about us, and I just chose to ignore him.

Tim pulls the truck over to the side of the road. He doesn't shut off the motor, but instead, throws the transmission into park. He gazes at me with a smile that's no longer so nice, but instead, hungry, psychotic. He's the Dr. Jekyll who has suddenly turned into Mr. Hyde. With his wide eyes and clenched teeth, he looks like a rabid animal.

I can't move, can't say a word. He picks up the doggy bag, sets it on the floor. At the same time, he grabs hold of my legs, twists me around so that I face him. He hikes up my skirt past my breasts, grabs hold of my panties and tears them off. He yanks my bra off, too. If only I could scream.

He draws his pistol, sets it on the dash. He then unbuckles his belt, and unbuttons his jeans, pulls himself out. Grabbing hold of the gun, he presses the barrel hard against my right temple.

"This," he says, "this won't hurt a bit." Then he smacks me across the face with the pistol. "But I bet that hurt."

He laughs.

I begin to cry.

CHAPTER 36

FOOTSTEPS COMING FROM up inside the kitchen. Slow, tentative footsteps. More lightning flashes outside the house. More thunder. More driving rain. It's an unbelievable storm. A storm sent by God himself. It's perfect for a night like tonight. A night for hunting. For ravaging.

Coming from outside the house, the Big Bad Wolf makes out the distinct sound of a vehicle pulling up. Is it Tim? It's too early for Tim to arrive. It must be someone else. Maybe someone come to check on Rose and her sweet daughter, Anna, because of the severe weather. The Wolf chooses to ignore the vehicle since there's nothing he can do about it.

The basement door opens. The Wolf knows that Anna is about to make her way down here in the dark. He couldn't have planned it better if he tried. He inhales deeply, smells her body, sniffs her ripe sex.

What a big nose you have.

The better to smell your trembling body with.

She slowly descends the wood staircase, one step at a time, her breathing coming and going in shallow spurts. The Wolf waits patiently, his body perfectly still, perfectly silent. He is the beast hiding in the rough, readying himself to pounce on his prey . . . his Little Red Riding Hood.

He watches her shuffle across the packed dirt floor, her hands feeling along the wall for the breaker box. When she finally comes to it, she opens the metal panel cover, and feels for the switches. The basement is so dark, it's impossible for her to see anything. Why didn't she think to use the flashlight app on her cell phone? But when the lightning flashes, she spots him standing in the middle of the floor.

The Big Bad Wolf, with his thick hands by his side, his mouth opened wide, his sharp teeth exposed.

"Hello, Anna," he says. "Did you read *Little Red Riding Hood*? I left it for you on the front door."

The thunder crashes.

Anna screams.

The Wolf lunges at his prey.

CHAPTER 37

I WAKE UP with a start. At first, I'm overcome with confusion. I have no idea where I am. I smell burning embers and the room is entirely dark. Darker than dark, like the power is out. When lightning lights up the night sky, I see immediately that I'm down in the small living room of the Moore house. How the hell did I get here? When did I get here? Who put me here?

Bits and pieces begin to come back to me. I remember driving home in the raging rain with Tim. Not Tim, the kind, perfect man. But Tim the monster. I recall trees being struck by lightning. I recall Tim's hands on my body. I feel his fingers violating me.

My body is trembling. But at least I can move. I sit up and realize my dress is hiked up over my waist. Where are my panties? Where's my bra? I feel the side of my face. It's tender to the touch, like someone punched me on the jaw. Then, in my head, I see Tim slapping me with his pistol, not once but several times, the smile on his bearded face growing wider and wider with each pistol whipping.

Anna . . .

"Oh Christ, Anna," I whisper.

Standing, out of balance, I nearly fall backwards onto the couch.

"Anna!" I cry out in a dry, hoarse voice. "Anna!"

No answer.

I go to the staircase, climb. I'm still frail and feeble. I grip the wall-mounted bannister and use my arm strength to help pull myself up the stairs.

"Anna!" I call out again. But my voice is so weak, I can barely hear it.

Coming to the top of the stairs, I go to her room. I try the light switch, but there's no power. If only I had a flashlight or the flashlight app on my cell phone. Did I bring my cell phone back to the house with me? Did I bring my leather bag?

I go to the bed. My racing heart slows a bit when I see that she's buried under the covers. Set on the table beside the bed is another now empty carton of the cheese and macaroni Tim brought us. Her cell phone is also set on the table, it's power either purposely turned off or it needs a charge. Knowing Anna the way I do, the latter is more likely the case. I can't help but notice that her rare edition of *Little Red Riding Hood* has been placed on the pillow beside her. The book is open, both the front and back cover faceup, like she was saving her place without damaging the pages by dog-earing them.

I'm not entirely sure why I feel the need to do this, but I reach around her so I don't disturb her sleep—truth is, I don't dare wake her up and allow her to see me in this condition. Carefully, I pick the book up and gaze at the pages she was reading before she went to sleep, probably around the time the lights went out. The page illustration depicts the Big Bad Wolf. His black fur and sharp incisors aren't even remotely hidden by his granny getup. If I hold the book close to my face, I can make out some of the words.

The wolf said, "You know, my dear, it isn't safe for a little girl to walk through these woods alone."

I feel a chill when I read the words. Lightning flashes and the page suddenly lights up, the wolf's teeth appearing all the more ferocious. Thunder follows and the rainfall seems to intensify, if such a thing is possible. It's as if God is punishing us tonight. The wind blows through the open window. I close it, then set the book back down on the bed where I found it.

Tiptoeing out of the bedroom, I close the door, but not all the way. Then I head into the bathroom, to clean myself up.

*   *   *

I wash my face with cold water, feel the sting in my cheek. I'm glad the power is out, because I don't dare look at my face. I soak the towel in water from the tap, and run it across my sex. The cold water stings. I run it over my scratched thighs. Drying myself, I feel the tears building in my eyes.

My God, should I call the police? I've just been sexually assaulted by a man whom I was falling in love with. A man who is one of the most respected men in town. How could I have allowed this to happen?

I go to the bedroom, put on a pair of clean underwear and a pair of jeans and a t-shirt. I know I should be sleeping at this hour, but no way I'm sleeping tonight. Slipping into a pair of boots, I head back downstairs and look for my leather bag. I'm almost surprised to find it set on the floor by the couch. Picking it up, I bring it into the kitchen with me, and search for my cell phone. It's there. The power bar indicates twenty-five percent power. No way I'm able to charge it with the power out.

Someone has left me a series of texts. Could they be from Tony? When I press the text icon, I see that the texts are from Tim. My heart sinks and my stomach twists itself into knots. I almost don't want to open them. But of course I can't avoid it.

The first text is a picture that nearly causes me to faint on the spot. It's a photo of a girl. It doesn't show her face, but instead, the back of her head. Her arms look like they've been pulled tight around her back. She's wearing the red, extra large Lady Gaga t-shirt she uses as a nightgown.

"Oh, my sweet Jesus," I say aloud inside the empty kitchen.

Lightning flashes and the thunder echoes across the lake. I hardly even notice it. Next picture. This one is Anna's face. She is wide-eyed and looks frightened beyond frightened. Her face is pale and her eyes red, like she's been crying. She's wearing her silver cross. But there's another cross that hangs from the leather lanyard. It's the cross that hangs on the kitchen wall. Gazing up at the spot above the counter where it usually hangs, I see that it is missing.

My eyes fill with tears. I become so dizzy, I need to press my hand onto the counter just to stay upright. I press on to the next text. This one is words only.

Call the police and the Big Bad Wolf bites Anna's face off . . . I love you both so much.

I go to recent calls, find Tim's number, press redial. But an automated operator comes on the line telling me the number I've requested is either temporarily disconnected or out of service. I attempt to text him back.

Leave Anna alone you freak.

The system won't allow me to send texts either.

"Oh God no, please no."

I try to call Tony. Same message about a disconnect or a temporarily disabled line. I try 911. I get nothing. The phone is useless and now I'm down to twenty percent power. Should I shut the phone off to save on power? I can't risk being out of communication with my daughter even if her own cell phone is useless. Another lightning flash and more thunder. The rain spatters against the windows. The storm has got to be knocking out cell service.

I slap the phone onto the counter. At the same time, I ask myself the one painfully obvious question. If that's not Anna in her bed, then who is it?

CHAPTER 38

FIRST, I NEED a weapon. The most obvious choice is a knife. I find a long French knife in the drawer beside the sink, grip it tightly in my right hand. Pocketing my phone, I grab the flashlight off the counter, head out of the kitchen, through the living room, and back up the stairs. It seems to take me forever to climb the stairs, as if I'm not heading upstairs, but instead down into hell itself.

Heart pulsing against my ribs, my head buzzing with adrenaline, my entire body trembling, I head into Anna's room. The body in the bed now illuminated in the flashlight's dull glow, I slowly make my way over to it. Whatever or whoever is lying in the bed isn't making a move. It hasn't moved since I was up here minutes ago. Using the same hand I'm holding the flashlight in, I take hold of the end of the blanket and, with my heart now stuffed in my throat, peel it back.

I scream and thrust my back against the wall. The knife drops out of my hand, slaps against the wood floor. All of my wind is knocked out of me. The body in the bed hasn't moved because it's dead. Blood is everywhere. It has soaked into the mattress, sheets, and blankets like a giant sponge. The body is naked. No, that's not right. The body doesn't have any skin. It is instead raw, red and white flesh.

That the body belongs to a man, there is no doubt. A short, paunchy man, the body ghostly pale now that it's lost all its blood.

"Who are you?" I say through my tears.

But I have no way of knowing who this poor man is since his head is missing.

Throwing the blanket back over the body, I pick up the knife. I exit the room, close the door behind me. Lightning strikes close by. The thunder is immediate. Maybe I'm currently in a state of shock, because the horrible noise hardly registers. I'm trembling so badly, I grab onto the bannister with both hands as I rush back down the stairs.

Here's the strange thing: while I'm horrified with what I just witnessed in Anna's bed, a big part of me is so very happy that the body does not belong to her. But then, who does it belong to? And who could possibly commit such a horrible act?

Tim?

It's possible. But somehow, I don't even think he would be capable of that.

Ed?

If Ed is the same Theodore who killed Sarah Anne Moore, then it's possible he killed the man in Anna's bed.

When I get to the bottom of the stairs, I shine the light on the small living room. For the first time, I see the blood that stains the floor. It has to have come from the body upstairs. The trail of blood leads from the living room into the attached dining room. I find myself following it, even before I make the conscious decision to follow it. The trail runs the length of the narrow room, and all the way into my studio.

Raising the flashlight, I shine it into the room. The clay bust of Sarah Anne Moore no longer occupies the sculpting platform. Instead, it supports a human head that's been skinned of his face.

But I can tell precisely who the head belongs to by the eyes, the teeth, and the mouth. I can tell by the white clerical collar that's been placed at the base of the neck.

Father O'Connor.

*   *   *

What follows after that, I can't be entirely sure of. For certain I scream, and the floor seems to drop out from under me. All I know is I'm on my back, the knife having slipped once more from my hand along with the flashlight. When I come to, I pull my cell phone from out of my pocket and see that only ten percent of its power remains. How long was I out? One minute or ten minutes? I have no idea. All I know is I need to get away from the studio. That means getting back up on my feet and making my way into the kitchen where I can at least attempt to think things through.

Retrieving the knife and the flashlight, I pick myself up and go to the kitchen. Setting the knife and flashlight on the counter, I go to the refrigerator, pull out a beer, pop the top, and drink half of it down while standing there. This is no time for drinking, but I desperately require the calming effects of the alcohol right now. I swear, if I had heroin in front of me, I would swallow it. That's how rattled I am. My body is sweating, my t-shirt soaked. The sweat runs down my face. It runs into my eyes, burning them.

Another look at my phone. Eight percent charge. The storm seems to have lightened up a bit outside. Maybe if I check the breakers, I can turn the power back on. But that means heading back downstairs into the basement. Just the thought of going down there makes my skin crawl even worse than it already does. But what choice do I have? I must at least try, not for me, but for Anna.

But I do have another choice. I can grab my keys, head out to my car, and drive into town, head straight to the sheriff's office. I don't hesitate to give it another thought. Running into the living room, I grab my keys off the table beside the couch. Opening the door, I don't even bother to close it behind me. Instead, I make way down the porch steps, then cross over the lawn to the Mini Cooper.

Opening the driver's-side door, I plant myself behind the wheel, punch the key into the ignition, press my right foot on the gas, and turn the key. The engine doesn't start. All I get is a click-click-click.

"Come on, come on," I beg.

I turn the key again. I get the same click-click-click.

"Please," I say, louder this time, more desperate. "Please start."

Again, I turn the key. Click-click-click.

"Oh, please, God, make it start."

I don't even realize that I'm crying again, the tears running down my face and dripping off my chin.

One more try. Click-click-click.

"Fuck!" I slam my fist against the dash.

Getting out, I go around the front of the Cooper, pop the hood. What I see makes me weep all the harder. All the hoses and wires have been cut. The only explanation is that Tim knew I'd try to drive back into town or maybe even to Schroon to contact the sheriff or the state troopers. In my head I see him opening his pocket knife and systematically cutting each hose and every wire.

I close the hood. Jagged lightning strikes in the near distance. It takes a minute for the thunder to rumble and echo off the mountainsides. The rain is steadily soaking me, drowning me, combining with my tears. There's a dead man in my house. He's lying in Anna's bed . . . what used to be Sarah Anne Moore's bed. His head has been decapitated and now it rests on my sculpting platform. My daughter is missing and my phone is almost out of a charge.

Choices. I could walk into the town, but that would take more than an hour. In that time my phone would be dead. I can't allow that. Sure, I could maybe hope to flag down a passing car or truck, but on a night like tonight, almost no one will be on the road. No choice but to go back inside the house, try and flip the breakers down in the basement.

"God help me," I whisper, while wiping my eyes with the backs of my hands. "God grant me strength."

I head back into the house and into the kitchen. First, I chug the rest of the beer set out on the counter. Then, taking hold of the flashlight and the knife, I open the basement door, and take my first step down into the damp, spider-web-covered depths.

CHAPTER 39

THE WOLF STARES at his prey. He licks his chops and sniffs her sweet, delicate scent. He stands behind the chair to which she is presently duct-taped, and he runs his long, claw-like fingers over her smooth, naked thighs.

Saaaaaarrrrrrrrrrr! he shrieks. *Saaaaaaarrrrrrrrrrr!*

The sound of the cry pierces Anna's eardrums. All this time, she believed the noise was coming from a lonely loon when in fact it was coming from this creep. What's his name? Ed. Maybe some girls would be scared out of their wits right now, pleading for their lives. But not Anna. She's just angry as hell.

"It was you," she says. "You've been screaming that noise outside our house. Why?"

"*Saaarrrrrr,*" he repeats, not nearly as loud this time.

"What does that mean, creep?"

"*Saaarrrrrrr,*" he repeats, a smile painting his ruddy bulbous face. "*Saaaaaarrrrrraaaaaahhhhhh.* Understand now, sweet honey? Sarah. You are her. You, my Little Red Riding Hood, have returned to me. You are the same girl. You have returned to us. You have no idea how happy this makes us feel."

Anna swallows something cold and bitter. She tries desperately to break free from the thick tape that binds her, but it's impossible.

"Who is *us*?" she nervously asks.

"My boss and savior," he says.

Anna is confused for a moment. Until she realizes just who Ed's boss is. It's Tim. But Tim is a great guy. He could never have anything to do with Ed. Not like this anyway. If he gives Ed a job, it's because he feels sorry for him.

"Tim is a nice man," Anna says. "He would never do anything like this. When my mother finds out about it, she's gonna have you arrested, and they'll put you away forever, creep."

The Big Bad Wolf drops down onto all fours. He begins to snarl, spit, and chomp down on his lower jaws, like he's making a transition from human being to wolf.

"I want you to say something, Little Red Riding Hood."

"It's Anna, if it's all the same to you, creep."

"I want you to say, 'What big teeth you have.'"

"Are you serious?"

"Say it, Little Red Riding Hood. Say it now, or I will eat you up."

Anna stares into his eyes. She sees the muscles bulging out of his arms, shoulders, and neck. Somehow the freak looks more natural on all fours than he does standing up on two feet. His body is covered in thick black hair, and his teeth are unnaturally long and sharp. Even his ears are too long and pointy, like he carved them with a sharp knife. For the first time since she was snatched up from the basement, blindfolded with her wrists tied together behind her back with a rope, then dragged through the woods to an old house, she isn't feeling anger or rage, but fear. Not that she wasn't afraid before, but now the fear is becoming more palpable, as if it's growing like a tumor inside her belly.

Her mouth goes dry and her bowels turn to hot liquid.

"What big teeth you have," she swallows.

"The better to eat you up!"

His jaws wide open, the Big Bad Wolf attacks.

CHAPTER 40

IF ONLY I could just run away from this house and somehow seek out help. If only I could make my way into town, I could have Tim arrested and the sheriff would send out a search party for Anna. But that's just wishful thinking. The best bet is to get my phone charged up and pray for an outside connection. In the event that doesn't work either, I'll have no choice but to take a chance on driving the boat across the lake in this storm. We almost drowned this afternoon doing that very same thing, but it will be my only choice.

I make my way slowly down the basement steps, the flashlight gripped in my right hand, while my left holds the knife. Spider webs stick to my face. A spider scurries across my left hand. Instinctively I scream, drop the knife, and shake the spider off.

The knife has disappeared beneath the staircase. I'm entirely unarmed. Inhaling a breath of the damp, fungus-filled air, I continue down the stairs anyway, until I come to the bottom. Shining the light on the empty underground space, I go to the breaker board. Opening the panel, I see that the breakers have indeed been tripped. I don't hesitate to flip all four of them back into the on position.

Dull light coming from the ceiling-mounted fixture inside the kitchen spills down into the basement. I turn, grab the string that will turn on the basement's light bulb. I pull the string. The light comes on. I see Tim Ferguson standing only a few feet away from me, a long kitchen knife gripped in his left hand.

*   *   *

He's smiling. It's almost like he's happy to see me. I half expect him to say something sweet and corny like, "This has all been a big miscommunication, Rose. Let's start all over again."

But I know he's not about to say that. I start to slowly back-step towards the staircase.

"Now, Rose," he says, calmly. "Just where do you think you're going? There's nowhere to hide in Paradox."

I come to the stairs, nearly tripping over them and landing on my back. The flashlight still gripped in my hand, I look him in the eye.

"You stay away from me," I say. "You murdered that priest. You stole my daughter. Where is she? Is she alive, you twisted son of a bitch?"

His smile only grows wider as he begins to approach me.

"Rose, Rose, Rose," he says, "now why would you suggest such a thing? You know what a sweet, gentle man I am. We've made love. I've shown you how gentle and caring I can be with you."

"You raped me," I say. "You beat me with a pistol."

"Oh that," he says, with a carefree wave of his hand. "I was just testing the waters to see how kinky you might be. You know how many lady friends enjoy a little pain with their sex? I was just playing. It's perfectly normal."

He's coming closer, that long knife in hand. My heart pounds so hard, I'm finding it difficult to breathe. I turn quick and start running up the stairs, taking the treads two at a time. But Tim drops the knife and comes after me. He dives and grabs hold of my right ankle, pulling me backwards. I go down hard on my chest on the wood staircase and drop the flashlight. He yanks me back. I'm trying as hard as I can to fight him off, but he's too big, too strong.

"Easy, Rose," he spits. "Easy. Don't resist me. You can't resist."

I spin around and go after his face with my fingernails and manage to scratch his cheek. He begins to bleed and I can feel his skin under my fingernails.

"You bitch!" he barks, punching me hard in the side of the head. So hard, my world goes entirely dizzy. I begin to see double.

He takes hold of my hair then, drags me across the dirt floor to one of the vertical wood pilasters. He forces me to sit down with my back against the beam. Apparently, he's prepared himself for this moment, because he wraps a metal collar around my neck, and then runs a chain from it to the heavy wood pilaster. He secures the chain to the pilaster with a padlock, then stores the key in his jeans pocket.

Standing, he goes to the staircase, grabs the flashlight, which he shoves into his back pocket. Picking up an empty taping compound bucket, he carries it over to me, sets it beside me. I can't help but notice that a roll of toilet paper is stored inside the bucket.

Touching the bloody scratches on his face, he eyes me.

"Maybe I'll give you a few hours alone down here in the dark, with the spiders and snakes, to think about how badly you're acting, Rose. And to think we prayed together at church tonight. To think you participated in the Body of Christ. Just shameful."

"Where's my daughter?!" I scream. "Where's Anna?! What have you done with her?!"

"We'll talk later," he says, pulling on the string that kills the overhead bulb. "Enjoy the darkness."

He heads upstairs and slams the basement door shut.

CHAPTER 41

BIG TEARS FALL. I try and move around but I can't get five feet away from the pilaster without that chain choking me. I'm no different than Ed's dog. I'm a slave to my psycho master. I press my back against the pilaster and weep for me, for Anna.

"Please, God," I whisper, "let her be all right."

I sense something slithering near me. I reach out with my hand. I feel the scaly, cold-blooded snake as it slithers by. I slap it away and it makes a kind of splat against the stone wall. Not a minute goes by before I sense something crawling in my hair. I reach up quick and slap away a spider. It's not just any spider, but one of the big hairy ones that are so prevalent in the mountains.

"Oh Christ, get me out of here."

I yank on the chain, try my hardest to release it from the pilaster, but it's no use.

Charlie, what the hell do I do now?

Don't panic, Rose. Whatever you do, just don't panic.
Remember what my football coach used to always say.
Cool head win game.

Dad's right, Rosie. Cool head win game. Even I know that.

You're a fighter, Rose. We love you and so does Anna. She's depending on you to stay alive.

She's depending on you to save her, Rosie. Now get to work.

Easier said than done. First, I have to figure out where Tim could be hiding her. If she's not in the house, where the hell could she be? I sit in the dark and try to imagine what could have happened at the house tonight. For certain, Tim drugged me, then had his way with me after punching my lights out, coward that he's turned out to be. He then drove me back here, opened the door, and laid me out on the couch.

After that, he must have climbed the stairs and grabbed Anna right from her bed. But something must have happened while all this was going on. The priest—Father O'Connor—he must have showed up at the house unexpectedly. Maybe the priest even entered into the house without knocking. Or maybe the door had been left open. The house would have been dark because the power was out. I suppose it's possible the priest caught Tim in the act of abducting Anna.

Whatever happened, the end result was that Tim used Father O'Connor to his advantage. First, he made the priest head upstairs to Anna's bedroom, then he made him lie in the bed, and then Tim stabbed him to death. I'm no policewoman or FBI agent, but it's the only explanation. Otherwise, pools of blood would have gathered downstairs. Tim then cut off the priest's head, skinned the body, and pulled the covers over his torso. Downstairs, he replaced the bust of Sarah with Father O'Connor's head. He did it to scare the living daylights out of me. To show me he was in total control of the situation. That he was willing to go to any length, no matter how horrible, to prove he's in control.

But then, as horrible as he's turned out to be, is Tim capable of decapitating a man? Skinning a man? In my head I see the rack of skins outside Ed's house in the forest. It hits me then that Tim wasn't alone when he dropped me onto the living room couch. Ed must have already been inside the house. Ed would have been the one to kill the priest. Ed would have mutilated the body.

"Ed and Tim are working together as a team," I whisper aloud. "But where the hell have they taken my Anna?"

Little Red Riding Hood, Rosie.

What about it, Allison?

The book that was left open on Anna's pillow. Are you sure Anna left it there? Or maybe Tim or Ed left it there as a clue.

Why would they do that?

They want to make this a game for you. They're challenging you. If either Tim or Ed wanted you dead, they would have killed you already.

It never occurred to me that they want to play some kind of psychotic game.

Didn't Tim say you should have eaten your full dinner, Rosie? Didn't he tell you you're going to need your strength tonight?

He did, Allison.

With my eyes wide open in the dank basement darkness, I try my best to think clearly, without my red-hot emotions getting in the way. In my head I see the book, *Little Red Riding Hood*. I see the illustration of the Big Bad Wolf on the page, and the words beneath it.

The wolf said, "You know, my dear, it isn't safe for a little girl to walk through these woods alone."

Suddenly, I see the Paradox Lake Trail in my mind. I see the trail opening and I see the dark path that leads through the woods to the small, secluded beach where Sarah Anne was murdered back in 1986. I see my dreams of the past few nights. Vivid dreams of following a girl onto the Paradox Lake Trail. A girl who is both Sarah and Anna. Two girls who look so much alike it's frightening. Two girls who are the same age. I see myself standing on the hideaway beach, see the old, faded yellow crime scene ribbon we dug out of there, see the silver cross that once hung from Sarah's neck, until a monster who lived in these woods raped her and killed her.

I see Ed/Theodore. I see his horrid house in the woods. A house with the animal skins hanging off of a timber rack behind the house. I see the dog chained up to a post just like I'm chained up to this pilaster inside this pitch-dark dank basement. In my mind, I'm seeing the old 1986 newspaper photo of the man being led from the cop car to the jailhouse. A short, powerful-looking stocky man with thick scraggly long hair, his face partially hidden by a hoodie.

Theodore . . .

"Ed," I whisper.

Realization punches me in the gut.

For certain, Ed is the same Theodore who murdered Sarah Anne. He's not in prison after all. He works with Tim. He stole

Anna because she looks like Sarah. They both stole her, and there's not a damn thing I can do about it. My chest is so tight, I feel it might split down the center. My head is filled with enough adrenaline to make my brain explode. Mouth dry and stomach cramped. Reality washes over me like a cascading waterfall.

"She's in the woods," I whisper to myself.

I've got to get to her before they do something horrible to her. I've got to somehow break free of these chains.

Yell for Tim, Rose. Tell him you need him. That you want him. That you're sorry for doubting him. Tell him you love him. You can't live without him.

It makes me sick to even pretend, Charlie.

You have to do it, Rosie. For Anna. It's your only hope.

Listen to Allison, Rose. And when he's close to you, do everything in your power to see that you kill the son of a bitch, or at least injure him enough that you immobilize him. It's your and Anna's only hope.

My stomach grows even tighter, if such a thing is possible. My brain is spinning and the dirt floor under me feels like it's about to open up and swallow me whole.

"Get your shit together, girl," I whisper. "You can do this. You *must* do this."

Inhaling and exhaling a profound breath.

"Tim!" I yell. "Tim, are you there?!"

CHAPTER 42

I WAIT FOR a response. I get nothing. But I do hear something. Footsteps coming from directly above me in the kitchen. It's an encouraging sound. It tells me he's at least still inside the house. He hasn't left me alone. That's a good sign.

"I'm so sorry, Tim," I go on. "Will you believe me? I'm sorry I accused you of all those bad things. I don't know what I was thinking."

Again, I wait for a response and again I get nothing. Maybe I need to be more creative. I never finished my dinner. Maybe for some strange reason, hunger will somehow appeal to him. Wasn't he the one who suggested I eat all my dinner? That I would need my strength?

"Listen, Tim," I say, "if you're going to still be mad at me, can you at least bring me the rest of my dinner? I'm so, so starving, Tim. I know you want me to have energy for tonight. It's still early and the night is long. Can you at least bring me something to eat, Tim, honey?"

Outside the house, more rumblings of thunder. I can't be sure, but it sounds like the heavy rains have picked up again. I can't help but imagine my Anna being held outside in the elements.

Maybe that creep Ed has chained her up like a dog, just like I'm chained up.

"Tim," I say, "please, please bring me something to eat. Maybe you can bring me one of those delicious dinners you brought us from the general store. Please, Tim."

More footsteps overhead. He's doing something. Rummaging around the drawers. Maybe he's preparing me something to eat after all. More thunder. Louder this time. The storm is once again intensifying.

"Tim, please," I plead. "I love you, Tim. I love you so much. I need you. Don't keep me down here like a caged animal. Come release me and make love to me, Tim."

The basement door opens. The kitchen overhead lamp illuminates the staircase in a funnel of dull yellow lamplight. I make out footsteps descending the staircase, dead weight. I spot Tim's long legs and boots. He's got something in his hands. A tray with food on it. He makes it to the bottom of the stairs, and starts towards me, pulling the string on the overhead light. Harsh white light fills the square space. Insects scatter. Out the corner of my eye, I see the garden snake slither under the rock wall. A long centipede uses its hundreds of legs to search for the dark depths the single light bulb can't reach.

Tim isn't smiling, but the tray he holds with both hands contains the spaghetti and meatballs I didn't finish earlier. Looks like he's a true believer in not wasting your leftovers. Bending at the knees, he sets the tray down in front of me. Aside from the small bowl of food, there's a folded paper napkin and a metal fork resting on top of that. Immediately, I eye the fork, and my hand begins to gravitate towards it. But Tim is too quick, too smart. He takes hold of it.

"How about I feed you instead," he says. "Whaddaya say, Rose?"

I plant a false smile on my face while looking for his pistol. Maybe if I can somehow grab hold of the pistol, I can blow his brains out. But he's not carrying it. He must have left it in his pickup.

"Sure, Tim," I say with a heavy heart. "That's very thoughtful."

He twists some spaghetti onto the fork tongs, then stabs into a small bit of the meatball. He raises it up to my face.

"Open up wide, Rose," he says. "Here it comes."

Thunder roars outside the house. It's loud and forceful enough to rattle the place. I take the forkful of spaghetti into my mouth and chew.

"Now isn't that good?" he says, like he's speaking to a three-year-old seated in a high chair.

He digs into the spaghetti again, stabs some more meatball. He places it before my mouth.

"Here comes the spaghetti train," he says, in a playful voice. "Chew, chew, chew."

Is he freaking kidding?

More lightning and thunder. The crash is so loud and violent it steals my breath away. The lights inside the house flicker. Is the power about to go out again? I can only hope so. I take the spaghetti in my mouth, slowly chew.

"I'll have to keep one eye on the power," Tim says. "This storm keeps up, the whole town of Paradox will go dark. That would be a real problem, don't you agree, Rose, honey?"

"I do," I say. "I hope Anna is okay."

"Oh," he says, not without a little laugh. "She's being well cared for, believe you me. She's warm and dry where she is. I love you and Anna so very much."

I swallow. The food might taste good, but the last thing I am right now is hungry, and it is literally making me sick to my stomach. But still, no choice but to play the game. I need for Tim to trust me.

"Well, that makes me feel much better, Tim," I say. "You know how I worry about her."

"I can bet the Moores worried about Sarah Anne, too," he says, forking up more spaghetti and meatball. "Have you noticed yet how much Sarah and Anna look alike? They even share a similar name. Anne and Anna. And you, Rose, you look very much like Sarah's mom. It's really so very uncanny. It's like you have both come back to us from the dead. The second you walked into the general store, just last week, we thought we were seeing ghosts. It was a miracle happening before our eyes. We knew right then and there that we had to have you both."

I open my mouth and he shoves the food inside. Every chew takes a supreme effort, but I do my best with it.

"Who is *we*, Tim?"

He smiles and shoots me a quizzical look, like I should somehow know the answer to that question already.

"Why, I'm surprised at that question, Rose," he says. "You should know by now how close Ed and I are. We've known one another since grade school. Sure, he's a little slow and yes he grew up in poverty in a house in the woods with no electricity or running water." He laughs again. "Heck, I think his parents were also his cousins, or they were brother and sister or some bat shit craziness like that. You know how those backwoods people can be. I bet you've seen *Deliverance* on Turner Classic Movies." He giggles. "*You got a pertty mouth . . .*"

My heart, now racing in my throat. Nausea is building up inside me. The spaghetti is starting to come up. I can't help what's happening inside my body. My revulsion at Tim, at what he's telling me about the animal who is now surely holding my daughter captive while they both relive some sort of fantasy about Sarah Anne Moore and her mother.

More thunder. The storm is directly overhead. It's like a battle-ground outside the house. The lights flicker on and off. I need to get the hell out of these chains, even if it means killing Tim.

"Tim," I say, after the thunder subsides, "did you kill Father O'Connor?"

"Do I look like the kind of man who can skin a man from top to bottom in less than thirty seconds flat?"

"Ed," I whisper.

"Of course, Ed," he says. Then, with a sad shake of his head. "Why Father O'Connor decided to drive out here to make a check on you girls unannounced is beyond me. But then, that's the way he is. Or was, anyway."

"Did you kill Sarah?"

"Oh my gosh, no," he says, spinning up yet another forkful of spaghetti. "But I'll let you in on a little secret. Would you like to hear it, Rose?"

Of course he wants me to say yes. This is all a great big fantasy for him. It will get him off to know I want to hear all about his sick little secret.

"Yes," I say in a trembling voice.

The word makes the food come up on me all the more. He must see that my face has got to be turning pale with nausea. Or maybe he doesn't care. Maybe he's too wrapped up in his memories and his present-day fantasy. He shoves the spaghetti into my mouth.

"Chew it all up, yum," he insists.

I chew and do my best to swallow.

"Well, on the morning Sarah was killed, Ed wasn't alone. You see, I made it possible for him to find her. I was the one who used to stalk her day in and day out. But it wasn't up to me to touch her. That was for someone like Ed to accomplish while I watched. It was really something when he finally found her naked on that little piece of hidden beach. You should have heard her scream. It was so, so beautiful the way he forced himself on her. And when he started to bite her like he was the Big Bad Wolf, it was all I could do to control my excitement. And now, here you both are, back in our arms again." He smiles. "So to speak."

More lightning and thunder. This time two or three bolts that light up the entire Moore house. Three immediate blasts follow. The lights flicker. I vomit all over Tim.

"Jesus Christ!" he barks, dropping both the bowl and the fork. "Sarah's mom would never puke on me. You're not playing right, Rose."

I grab the fork, stab Tim in the face. The power goes out. The basement goes pitch dark.

CHAPTER 43

HE SCREAMS.

I stab him three or four times, then drop the fork and grab the chain, wrap it around his neck. I squeeze both ends of the chain with all my strength. Instead of fighting me, he's got both hands pressed against his bleeding face. I can only wonder if I stabbed him in the eyes. If I blinded the sick bastard.

I, too, am blind now that the basement has gone black. But when the lightning flashes again and the bright electric light spills in from the open basement door, I can see his bleeding face is turning red. He's gone from pressing both his hands against his stab wounds to trying desperately to loosen the grip on the chain wrapped around his neck. The light flashed for only an instant, but it was enough for me to make out his purple tongue protruding from his mouth and how the blood is pouring down his face from the eye I gouged out.

The rage in me is something I've never before experienced, never knew myself capable of. I never knew I had the strength. But then, have you ever seen a sculptor's hands and arms? We are built of tinsel strength, and I am using every ounce of it to kill this demented son of a bitch so that he never touches another woman again. Never rapes or kills another woman.

When he drops flat onto his face, I know I've done my job. I sit back against the pilaster and suck a deep breath. My heart is beating so fast and so hard, I swear it's about to explode right out of my chest. I need water. But most of all, I need to grab the key from his pocket so I can unlock myself and go after my daughter.

Reaching into his pocket, I search for the key. I find only some cash and small change. I toss it aside and go through his opposite pocket. The key is there. I immediately unlock the padlock, then pull the chain out of the metal shackle that surrounds my neck. I'm just about to place the shackle around his neck, when I feel the hand reach out and grab hold of my ankle.

Dropping onto my stomach, I kick at his face with my free foot. I do my best to plant the tip of my pointed boot in his bloody eye socket. He screams in pain, releases my leg. Standing, I use the chain like a whip and slap him hard on his back. He screams again.

"You bitch!" he shouts. "You bitch. You don't play right. I will get you for this."

I whip him again, then toss the chain and run for the stairs. But the place is pitch dark. I can't see where I'm going, and I run face-first into the staircase. I hear him getting up and coming after me. Using my hands to guide me, I come around to the foot of the stairs and start climbing.

"No, you don't!" Tim barks. "You don't leave me like this! Not when we're so in love."

I'm four steps up the staircase when again he grabs hold of my right ankle. I turn to look at him over my shoulder. Lightning flashes and I see his bloodied face and beard, and the gaping bloody hole of an eye socket. His teeth are stained with blood. He looks like he wants to sink his teeth into me.

I kick at him with my free leg and once more he falls back. I continue to crawl my way up the stairs, on all fours. The tears stream down my face. I'm screaming bloody murder. He grabs hold of my ankle again and this time he is able to grab hold of the other ankle. He starts pulling me back down the staircase, my chin slapping each tread as he yanks on me.

When I come to the bottom, he turns me around and tears my shirt. I punch him in the face but it seems to have no effect. He slaps me and pushes me back onto the stair treads. I have no defense at this point. No way to stop him. But that's when I remember I have my cell phone stored in my back pocket. Can it be used like a weapon? It has a glass screen. Maybe if I can crack the glass, I can somehow use it.

He starts unbuckling my belt. I pull out the phone, slap it against the tread. Lightning flashes, and for a split second, I see that the screen is shattered. I then slap the phone back down on the stair tread and I finger the now broken glass. Managing to locate a triangle of glass that's maybe four inches long, I jam it into his temple.

He rears back against the stone wall. His scream is not a scream at all, but more like the wail of a badly injured animal. A gut-shot animal. I don't hesitate to turn then and bound up the stairs, two at a time. Closing the door behind me, I quickly go to the kitchen table, grab hold of a chair. I also steal a steak knife from out of the drawer. I haven't yet returned to the basement door when I see it slowly opening.

"No!" I scream. "No you don't!"

White lightning fills the kitchen, and I see Tim's bloodstained hand slipping through the now open door. I thrust the blade into it. He screams again. I pull the knife out and stab it again and again. Shrieking, Tim pulls back his injured hand. That's when I open the door and push him backwards. He tumbles down the wood steps like a bearded rag doll. Closing the door again, I shove the chair back under the knob to secure it.

Turning, I press my back against the door panel, drop the knife to the floor, and weep.

CHAPTER 44

ANNA SITS IN the chair and faces the Wolf. He's stripped her of her t-shirt and now she's dressed only in her pink panties and a red-hooded robe that doesn't hide her bare breasts. She's both horrified and ashamed of her nakedness. But she feels something else too. She feels a rage building up inside her. It's an electric rage like no other.

"I want you to say something else," the Wolf says from down on all fours as he slowly circles his prey. "I want you to say, 'What big claws you have.'"

"Fuck you," Anna says through grinding teeth.

Her words take even her by surprise, because it's nothing she's ever imagined herself saying to another adult. How would her mother react? Perhaps her mother would be all for it considering she's being held captive in this basement by a madman who thinks he's the Big Bad Wolf and she's Little Red Riding Hood. She's never met Allison, her late older sister. But she suspects Allison wouldn't hesitate to curse this madman up one side and down the other.

"Play right," the Wolf says. "Play right or I will sink my fangs into you, I promise you that, Little Red Riding Hood . . . my Sarah Anne."

The storm rages outside the old farmhouse. The electric white light leaks in through the narrow windows located at the top of the basement's stone walls. Thunder rocks the forest and the nearby lake.

"Say it!" the Wolf screams. "Or I will make sure Tim chops your mother's head off and displays it in her studio."

Anna starts to cry. She doesn't want to cry because it shows weakness and fear. But she can't help it. She's desperate.

"What big claws you have," she whispers.

"Louder," the Wolf insists, circling her until he comes to a stop at her backside.

"What big fucking claws you have, you creep."

"The better to tear into you, my dear," he says, digging into her back with his filthy claw-like fingernails.

CHAPTER 45

MY PHONE IS dead and the power is out. But then, what difference does it make? My cell phone is entirely shattered now. I left it on the basement staircase. I can't go back downstairs. Not with Tim down there. He'll kill me on the spot. He could be dead, of course. But I can't take the chance that he might still be alive and kicking.

My mind spins while the wind blows and the rain spatters against the big picture window that overlooks the lake. It's coming down so heavy, and the night is so dark, all I see is blackness. But when the lightning shoots down from the sky in a frighteningly jagged bolt, I not only see the lake, I spot the angry white-capped swells that top it.

Anna is out there, somewhere...

As much as I hate to admit it, I know where she is.

The wolf said, "You know, my dear, it isn't safe for a little girl to walk through these woods alone."

Anna is in that old house in the middle of the woods.

Ed the Creep's house.

Picking the knife back up, I go upstairs to my bedroom, find a red windbreaker in the closet with an attached hood. I put on the windbreaker and place the hood over my head. It's not much, but at least it will provide some protection from the heavy rain.

Heading back downstairs, I make way across the living room floor, but pause at the basement door, press my ear against it. Nothing but silence. Is Tim knocked out? Is he dead? Or has he somehow found a way out of that basement? I've never entirely explored the space, so for all I know, there's a door that leads to the outside. It's entirely possible. But I can't think about that right now. All I need to focus on is rescuing the only daughter I have left.

The flashlight is resting on the counter. I press the latex-covered button. A round beam of white light shines against the wall. The batteries are still good. Let's hope they last awhile. The woods will be impossibly dark.

The steak knife in one hand and the flashlight in the other, I go to the kitchen door and open it. I step out into the angry Adirondack elements in search of Anna.

*   *   *

Crossing over the lawn, I enter onto the Paradox Lake trailhead. As the rain pours down on me and thunder rumbles in the distance, I swear I make out the sound of a car or truck door slamming shut. Is the sudden bright white light that shines through the narrow openings in the trees and brush a set of headlamps? Or just more lightning? I might pause to investigate, but I can't afford to waste more time. There's also the distinct possibility Tim has found his way out of the basement by having busted through the basement door and now he's back in his truck on his way to Anna. Who knows what he will do to her when he catches up to her. I gouged his eye out. I stabbed him multiple times in the hand. I pushed him down the stairs, knocked him out. He will want his revenge, and if he can't take it out on me, he will take it out on my

daughter. He and Ed will love every minute of it. Anna is the spit-
ting image of Sarah Anne, after all. She is their new Little Red
Riding Hood.

I head deeper into the woods.

I don't walk. Instead I jog, the branches and twigs slapping me
in the face, causing my eyes to tear. Between the tears and the rain,
I can't see three feet in front of me. But I keep going. Pulse pounds
in my temples. Breathing grows shallow. My entire body is soaked,
the clothing sticking to my skin. Lightning cracks overhead. It
strikes a tree. The tree breaks in half and crashes down only a few
feet from me. The thunderclap that accompanies it steals my
breath away. I stop, drop to my knees in a puddle of muddy water,
and try to catch my breath.

Shining the light on the downed tree, I can see that it's smoking
in the place where the lightning hit it.

"Dear Jesus," I say aloud, the rainwater and the tears dripping
into my mouth, "protect me on this night of nights. Protect Anna.
Protect my only little girl."

I get back up on my feet and climb over the big tree, then resume my jog through the thick forest. The round beam of flashlight aimed directly ahead, I make out the secluded beach on my
right-hand side. It's barely visible in the darkness. Moving on, I'm
determined to get to the house in the woods as fast as possible. If
I remember correctly, it should only take me maybe fifteen or
twenty minutes to get there. That is, if I can keep up my pace. I
have no choice but to keep up the pace. Every second counts.

*But what if Anna is already dead? What if she's already dead and
now they're waiting to spring a trap on me when I arrive at the house?*

"Oh God, don't let that happen. Promise me you won't let
that happen."

Don't think like that, Rose. Just use all your strength to get to Anna. She's alive. I can feel it.

I agree with Dad, Rosie. Anna is still alive. But she's hurting and she needs you. She's calling out for you right now, Rosie. Do not give up. You and Anna are survivors. Don't forget that.

"I am," I say through my short, labored breaths. "I swear to God I am. Give me strength, Charlie and Allison. I know you are with me. Send me the strength I need to save our Anna."

I see my family in my head and I feel their presence like I feel the rain on my face. They are that real. They are that alive. That's when something shoots out of the dark forest and tackles me so hard in the belly, the breath is knocked right out of me. My face buried in the mud, I turn quick onto my back, and try like hell to fill my stinging lungs with precious air. What the hell locomotive just ran me over? My knife and flashlight have dropped out of my hands. But I'm able to reach out for the flashlight. When I aim the beam up at whatever hit me, I see a raging bloody man who's missing his left eye.

CHAPTER 46

"SAAAARRRRRRAAAHHHHH!" SCREAMS THE Wolf as he digs his claws into Anna's red-robed back. "Saaaarrrrraaahhhhh!!!"

He wonders where Tim is. What is taking him so long? Anna's mother should be dead by now. He should be here, down in this basement, watching him feeding.

I can't wait much longer . . .

Anna screams, "Mama! Mama! Please save me!"

Tears stream down her pale face. She's never before felt this kind of pain. The Wolf props himself up onto his hind legs and removes his claws from her back.

"Now," he says, "I want you to say, 'What big teeth you have.'"

"No," Anna begs. "Don't make me. Don't make me say that."

"But that's how we play this game, Little Red Riding Hood. You have to say what I tell you to say."

"Mama! Please, Mama!"

She's weeping, crying the tears of a young girl who is now entirely convinced she's about to die.

"Say it, Little Red Riding Hood," the Wolf demands. "Say the words."

In her mind, she gives up. Duct-taped to that chair, half naked and covered in sweat and filth, with only an open red robe for clothing, she has no choice but to say the words and pray her death will be quick.

"What . . . big teeth . . . you have."

"The better to chomp away at your sweet flesh," says the Big Bad Wolf.

Aiming for her neck, the rabid animal opens its jaws wide.

CHAPTER 47

SLAPPING THE FLASHLIGHT from my hand, Tim grabs hold of me by my right arm, while I search desperately for the knife with my left hand. He drags my exhausted body over the newly felled tree and over the rain-soaked trail, in the opposite direction of the house in the forest.

"You thought I was dead, didn't you, Rose?" he says. "And after the nice date we had together. After everything I've done for you and sweet, luscious little Anna, this is the thanks I get."

He's yanking on my arm so hard, I fear it will dislocate. The pain is electric, and it shoots from my arm socket to my brain and back again. I still can't breathe. If only I could get enough air, I might get myself back up on my feet and run away from this madman. But I'm powerless.

We come to another, smaller path. He turns onto it, pulling me along, dragging me over roots and rocks. The sky lights up in brilliant white electric light, the thunder booms, and the rain soaks me to the bone. He drags me onto the patch of beach and releases me.

"This is where it happened," he says, not without a smile on his bloody face. "This is where I watched the Big Bad Wolf devour our precious Sarah. It was quite a thing to behold, let me tell you,

Rose. Now Sarah has come back. Now you, her mother, have come back to us. And now, we will send you both back to heaven so that you can return to us once more."

He bends down, picks something up. It's a rock. He's gripping the rock in his hand and he's approaching me with it. He's going to beat my brains in. It's the only logical explanation. I'm inhaling, my diaphragm finally allowing me to take a deep breath. I see his smiling, one-eyed face approaching me with the rock. When he reaches me, he drops to his knees and raises the rock high.

"Don't you see, Rose?" he says. "I'm going to kill you so that you will live forever. That's how the game is played. It's the perfect paradox."

"You are one sick fuck, you know that, Tim?"

His smile turns upside down.

"Sarah and her mother never used language like that," he says. "Now hold still and play right."

He's just about to smash my brains in with the rock, when I shove the knife into his crotch.

They say that sound travels fast over water. If that's indeed the case, then Tim Ferguson's agonized screams can be heard for miles and miles. I pull the knife out and dark, nearly black arterial blood spurts out. I've obviously hit an artery. He drops the rock and tries to stand, but he can't. He's in so much pain he's kneeling there stone-stiff. I raise myself onto my knees, and I feel the rage erupt in my stomach like the flames in a blast furnace. Using all my strength, I stab him in the face over and over again, until he is almost unrecognizable, his face turning into so much raw hamburger.

"Please . . . stop," he says, his words slurred and nearly incomprehensible. He's openly weeping now, like a child. "Please, for the love of God, stop hurting me."

I see the knife in my hand, the blade covered in blood, along with my entire hand. There's no way he's living through this. Standing, I clean the blade with the back of his rain-soaked shirt and then I wipe my hand. As I start making my way toward the path, he remains on his knees where he will no doubt die in a matter of minutes or even seconds. And I can honestly care less about it.

"Thanks for dinner," I say, before scooting back into the woods.

*　　*　　*

I no longer jog the trail.

I sprint.

There's so much adrenaline and rage flowing through my veins, I feel like I can sprint an entire marathon and still have energy enough to run a second one. The knife gripped in my hand, I soon come upon a white light along the trail bed. It's the flashlight I lost when Tim abducted me. I stop briefly to pick it up, and then I'm off again, the round circular beam of light illuminating my way.

Lightning strikes all around me and more trees are hit. One by one, they split and collapse to the forest floor. It's a like a war zone, but I'm no longer afraid. All fear has left my body while I focus on one single thing: saving my daughter from a second madman. When I start to smell smoke coming from a nearby wood fire, I know for certain I've come to the area where Ed's house is located. That's when I head off trail and into the thick woods. I plow through the brush like I'm a bull. Thorns stab at my face and arms, but I don't slow down for anything. When I come to the opening where the house is located, I stop at the tree line and take a minute to get my bearings.

The dog is still chained to the post, despite the heavy rain. It's a sad sight to see. The skins are still hung up on the rack. There's a light on inside the house, and for sure, a fire is going in the fire-place. I see no sign of Ed, but his beat-up pickup truck is parked in the two-track alongside the house. I know he's in there . . . in there with Anna.

My stomach cramps. It's like I've just been punched in the stom-ach. My body turns cold, like the rain that's falling on me is ice water. My God, what had been a rage-inspired determination is now turning into cold, crippling fear. It's a fear I need to overcome if I'm going to save my daughter.

Saaaaaarrrrrrrrrrr, cries the lonely loon.

But then, why does the noise sound like it's coming from the house and not the lake?

Sarrrrraaaaaaaahhhhh . . .

Saaaaaarrraaahhhh, I recite in my head.

"Sarah," I whisper.

That's not a loon's cry at all. It's Ed and he's crying for Sarah. Tim lied to me about the loon. He knew exactly who was making that sound the whole time. He must have known that Ed was mak-ing the noise. Ed was taunting us during the night. He was watch-ing us, stalking us. He's convinced that Sarah has returned, so he would come to the house every night and wail her name, like a wild animal. That wasn't a deer emerging from out of the Paradox Lake trailhead. It was Ed.

Creepy Ed . . . Theodore.

Now it's time to end this thing with Creepy Ed before he does something horrible to Anna. Something that resembles precisely what he did to Sarah Anne Moore way back in 1986.

CHAPTER 48

THE WOLF DOESN'T bury his fangs into Little Red Riding Hood's neck entirely. Not yet. He just wanted to get a taste of her. He's simply seeking an appetizer before he digs into his main course. He's hurt her, that much is for sure, and her tears are the proof. So are the little spots of red blood oozing out of the bite marks. She's also shivering, like she's cold. But he knows it's just a reaction to all the fear coursing through her veins. The shock.

He recalls that day when his first Little Red Riding Hood began to tremble with fear and shock. She had to know he was about to eat her up. Once more, he's acting just like a real wolf. The wolf doesn't kill right away. The wolf waits patiently. It baits its prey, teases it, stalks it. Until the prey is so exhausted and full of fear, it lies down and accepts its own death as inevitable.

The Big Bad Wolf enjoys the tasting and the teasing. Only now, he's about to do something else to his young prey. The same thing he did to Sarah before he feasted on her raw flesh. Before he ate her pretty face off her skull.

Coming around her, he kneels down and tears off her panties.

She screams. That's a good thing because the scream makes him all the more excited, all the more hard. He unbuckles his overalls, pulls them down, exposing his thick, crooked member. He knows he should be waiting for Tim to show up with Rose. But Tim is far too late, and he can't possibly wait any longer. Besides, maybe Tim is dead. Maybe Rose got lucky and killed him before he was able to kill her. The Wolf can't help but giggle at the idea of Tim dying at the hands of Little Red Riding Hood's mother.

"Now I want you to say, 'What a big cock you have.'"

"Please, mister," Sarah cries. "Please just let me go. Please."

"Play right, Little Red Riding Hood," he insists. "Say it, or I will eat your mother alive. I will cut her head off, skin her, and hang her hide up to dry."

Her tears flowing into her mouth, she whispers, "What . . . a big . . . cock you have."

"Louder!!!" he shouts.

"What a big cock you have!" she screams through her tears.

"The better to love you with," he says. Then, with a smile on his hairy face, "I love you, Little Red Riding Hood."

He's about to devour the face of his prey when, directly overhead, something heavy slams onto the kitchen floor.

CHAPTER 49

I ENTER THE house the easy way. Through the already open front door. The rain-soaked dog never once barked at me or paid attention to my presence, as though its prolonged exposure to the elements has sucked the life right out of it. I step inside the old house to a wall of stink that nearly makes me vomit a second time. I shine my flashlight at the bare walls. To my right is the fireplace with the fire dying inside it. Boxes of garbage and junk fill the floor spaces. The couch is so old, springs stick out of it. Beer bottles, pizza boxes, and plastic Ferguson General Store bags cover the coffee table. The wall behind the couch looks like it's covered in blood spatter.

To my left is the kitchen. To say the place smells like something died is putting it mildly. It smells entirely of death and rot. The counter is covered in chunks of raw meat, with flies buzzing all around it. What looks to be the torso of a deer is sitting in a slop sink in a bath of its own dark blood. My gag reflex kicks in. I'm trying my best to hold back the vomit. I can't get out of there fast enough. Turning quick, my arm knocks into a pot that's been set on the stove. It crashes to the wood floor, a bundle of pale human skin spilling onto the floor. The skin still has a face attached to it.

Just like I thought . . . Father O'Connor . . .

That's when I lose it entirely. Whatever is left inside me comes up and I puke all over the floor. Wiping my mouth with the back of my hand, I decide to breathe through my nose. It's the only answer. On my right is a wood door. In my gut, I know the door leads down into a basement. If my gut also serves me right, it's where I'll find my daughter and the psychotic murderer who's holding her captive.

Ed, or should I call him Theodore, or should I call him Satan?

* * *

Opening the door, I take a step down inside the dimly lit space. My body is shaking, my brain buzzing, the blood rapidly flowing through my veins and arteries.

"Anna," I say, like a question.

My mouth is so dry, I can barely speak her name. I still have the knife in one hand and the flashlight in the other, not that I need it any longer. But it feels good to have it since I might have to use it as a weapon. Take another step down, and another, then another. Coming to the dirt floor landing, I turn completely around.

That's when I see her.

Anna.

She's strapped to a chair and she's naked, other than a red robe that's been wrapped around her shoulders.

"Oh my God," I whisper.

Then I hear, "Are you Little Red Riding Hood's mama?"

I never feel the blow to the head.

* * *

When I come to, I'm on my back. He's on me, straddling me. He's torn my shirt off, and now he's trying to get at my bra. Only he can't because he's having trouble reaching around my back. Why he just doesn't rip it off of me I'll never know.

"Don't let him touch you, Mama!" Anna screams.

I'm not sure how long I was out, but it can't have been for very long. Creepy Ed is naked from the waist down, his grotesque sex staring me in the face. He has no idea that I still have a knife in my hand. Tim was right, after all. He is simple. A stupid, simple monster of a man. The knife gripped in my right hand, I thrust it into the wolf tattoo on his neck.

I pull out the blade, and he sits back onto the dirt floor. He gazes at me with wide, shocked eyes, like he can't believe I'm actually fighting back. He doesn't seem to be in the least bit of pain, while a thick stream of blood spurts out of his upper neck, like water from a suddenly punctured garden hose. Gathering up all my strength from whatever energy reserves I have leftover, I go to Anna and begin to cut her free.

Ed picks himself up off the floor, pulls up his overalls and buckles them. I manage to free one of Anna's wrists, then start on the other.

"Hurry, Mama," she pleads, "before he comes after us again."

Ed drops onto all fours.

"Sarrrrrraaaaahhhhhh!!!!" he wails in a voice that is most definitely not human.

He exposes teeth that look like long, sharp fangs. He's drooling a combination spit and blood. His eyes have gone wide and dark, and he's chomping down on his jaw. His fingernails are long and curved like claws. If I didn't know any better, I'd say he was transforming into the Big Bad Wolf right before our eyes. But I know better. He is just a man. A sick, mad man.

I manage to free Anna's second wrist. She stands. Pulling off my belt, I tell her to wrap it around her red-robed waist. She does exactly what I say. Then I tell her to step back.

"Step back against the wall," I insist, the knife poised out before me, at the ready.

"You can't fight him, Mama," Anna screams. "He's too strong."

"He might kill me, honey," I say. "But he's not getting near you ever again."

Ed growls. I see the thick muscles in his neck, arms, and shoulders flexing, like he's preparing himself for attacking me, just like a real wolf.

"What big teeth I have," he says, the blood flowing down his face. "I'm going to dig them into your neck."

His eyes wide, his mouth frothing, the wild animal lunges at me.

CHAPTER 50

IT'S LIKE I'VE been hit head-on by a Mack truck. I'm thrown onto my back, but not without burying the knife into his left shoulder. He's just about to pounce on me when something extraordinary happens. Something entirely miraculous. A man bounds down the basement steps, turns the corner, and jumps onto Ed's back. He pounds Ed in the face with his clenched fist, repeatedly. At first, I'm so dazed from the tackle Ed laid on me that I don't recognize the man. But when I'm finally able to focus, I make out the worn bush jacket, the blue jeans, and the cowboy boots. I see the round scruffy face and the receding hair.

"Jesus, Tony!" I yell.

"Tony!" Anna screams. "You go! Kill the monster!"

Ed shakes Tony off. But the knife is still buried in his shoulder and his neck is still leaking thick, dark blood.

"Nobody touches my girls!" Tony barks.

Ed reaches for the knife, and slowly pulls it out. It is a sickening sight to behold.

"Tony," I scream, "watch out!"

Ed goes for Tony with the knife, manages to cut his upper arm. But that doesn't stop Tony from pounding both his fists into Ed's face. That's when they both fight for control of the knife. Picking myself up, I make my way to them. Bending at the knees, I un-buckle Tony's leather belt buckle, yank the belt from his waist. I then wrap the belt around Ed's thick neck and squeeze both ends as hard as I possibly can. I put all my rage into it . . . all my sculptor's tinsel strength, just like I did to Tim. The monster's face begins to turn blue and purple, his black eyes wide.

He let's go of the knife while he desperately tries to loosen the belt with his thick fingers. But he can't. I'm too strong, too enraged, too determined. The knife drops to the floor. Tony immediately picks it up and thrusts it into the monster's barrel chest not once, but at least a half dozen times. The blood spatter is everywhere, and we're all screaming at the top of our lungs. Until Ed drops to his knees. The monster's body now covered in his own blood, he slowly glances over his shoulder at Anna.

"Saaaaarrrahhhh," he softly whispers.

He then face-plants onto the basement floor.

Tony looks me in the eyes. He's breathing so heavily I pray he doesn't suffer a heart attack.

"Let's get the hell out of here," he insists.

"You don't have to tell us twice," Anna says.

"I'll grab the flashlight," I say, bending at the knees and grabbing hold of it.

Like one big, happy, reunited family, we escape the horrible house in the woods.

CHAPTER 51

ONCE OUTSIDE, I can't help but eye the lonely, rain-drenched dog.

"One second," I say.

Making my way to the dog, I unclasp the chain.

Now realizing he is suddenly free, the dog bounds up and makes a run for it into the thick woods. I'm not sure where's he's going, but one thing is for sure, his days of being abused at the hands of a madman are over. Shining the light on the racks of animal skins, I feel a cold chill run up and down my backbone. While two of the skins are clearly deer skins, another contains no fur. The skin is smooth, like that of a human being.

"My dear God in heaven," I whisper.

Who knows what the police will soon discover in this nightmare of a house. Who knows how many missing persons will finally be discovered.

"Rose, we've got to go," Tony says.

We don't retrace our footsteps through the rain-soaked woods. We gather into Tony's Jeep and make our way to a two-tracked road that eventually leads to the Moore house.

As we pass by it, Tony doesn't slow down for even a New York second.

"Wait," I say. "I want to at least gather up my sculpture. It's important."

"I need my phone and my things," Anna says.

Tony rolls his eyes.

"You're kidding me, right?" he says. "We need to be going to the police."

"Listen," I say, "when that happens, they'll close the entire house off as evidence and I won't be able to get at my stuff. Come on, it'll just take a minute. Besides . . ."

"Besides what?" he says.

"The bad guys are dead."

*   *   *

He pulls up into the drive behind my now disabled Mini Cooper.

Opening the Jeep door. "I'll be right out."

"I'm not letting you go in there alone," Tony insists.

"I'm not staying out here alone," Anna adds.

Lighting the way with my flashlight, more thunder rumbles in the distance. Will this storm ever end? Christ, will this night ever end? The rain falls while we make our way up the porch. The door is unlocked because I never had the chance to lock it before I left the house earlier with Tim trapped in the basement.

Heading inside, Anna goes for the stairs.

"Wait," I say. "Tony, you go. Anna, you're not to go anywhere but right here, do you understand?" My eyes back on Tony. "You'll know what I mean when you go in there."

"But, Mom," Anna protests. "My clothes."

In my head, I see the skinned torso of Father O'Connor under the bed covers.

"But nothing," I say. "Tony, just grab her phone and her charger. You'll see them on the night table. We can always buy you new clothes, Anna."

She frowns and crosses her arms around her chest.

"You grab the phone, Tony, and I'll get what I need from my studio, and then we're back out this front door in less than one minute. Are we all clear on that?"

"Got it," Tony says.

Tony heads up the staircase while Anna stands with her back against the door. I turn, and swallowing a deep, bitter breath, follow the blood trail along the living room floor, into the studio.

It's like being caught up in a nightmare as I cross over the dining room, my eyes trying not to focus on the priest's severed head, but not able to avoid it at the same time. My stomach cramps and the nausea returns. Entering into the room, I try my best not to step in the puddle of blood that's accumulated on the floor around the sculpture stand. The bust of Sarah now resting on the worktable, I grab hold of it and cradle it under my left arm. I also tear the newspaper clippings of her abduction and murder off the wall. About-facing, I head back in the direction I came, happy as hell for the studio to be behind me.

I make out the sound of Tony coming back down the stairs. He's got the phone and charger in one hand, and in the other, the rare edition of *Little Red Riding Hood*. His face is noticeably pale even in the dark. I give him a look like, *Now you know why I didn't want Anna to go up there.* In return, he offers me a nod.

"Here you go, sweetheart," he says, a noticeable trembling in his voice.

She takes the phone and charger in hand.

"That book I never want to see again," she says.

Tony purses his lips and scrunches his brow like he should have known better. He crosses over the room, tosses the book in the fireplace. Too bad the fire isn't still going. In my head, I picture the cover and every page with the Big Bad Wolf illustrated on it burning up in the fires of hell.

"Let's go guys," I say. "Now."

Anna opens the door, and we step out onto the porch and down onto the path that leads to the driveway and the Jeep. In my head, I'm already making plans to have my Mini Cooper towed back to Albany once I make it safely back home and the state police are on the case. No doubt they'll want to use the car as evidence, at least for a while.

Lightning flashes and thunder follows. At this point, I hardly even notice it. The storms have been raging for more than a full day and we're lucky to be alive. I just want to get the hell away from this place, get back home, safe and sound with Anna and Tony. I hate myself for dragging her up here and I hate myself even more for drifting from Tony when I completely took his love for us for granted.

God forgive me . . .

Tony opens the passenger-side door of the red two-door Jeep Wrangler, pulls the passenger seat up so that Anna can get in. When she's safely planted in the back seat, he pushes the bucket seat back in place and I get it in. But before that, I take him in my arms, squeeze him, and kiss him on the cheek.

"What's that for?" he asks.

"For being there for us," I say. "For rescuing us. For being our hero."

He looks at me and smiles.

"I love you guys," he says. "What else did you expect?"

"Let's go home," I say.

He goes around to the passenger side, climbs in behind the wheel, and turns the key. The engine doesn't fire up. Instead, it goes, click-click-click.

"Oh no," I say, feeling my insides sinking to somewhere around my feet.

"Try again," Anna presses.

Tony pumps the gas and turns the key again.

Click-click-click.

"I don't know what's happening," he says. "It's never done this before."

Lightning flashes and I find myself glancing in the side-view mirror. The bloody face appears above the black printed words, "Objects in mirror are closer than they appear."

"Get out of the Jeep!" I scream.

Tony turns, spots Tim trying to open the passenger-side door. But I manage to lock it at the last second.

"Out my side!" Tony yells.

Anna climbs over the center console and follows Tony out. I follow. Tim comes around the front grill, but Tony tackles the taller man in the gut. Together they go to the ground. Tim screams like an animal and kicks Tony in the chest. Tony falls onto his back. I go to Tim and kick him repeatedly in the face until he passes out.

"What the hell do we do now, Mama?!" Anna cries.

My head is spinning. The lightning is exploding, the thunder crashing and the rain pouring down. The thunder reverberates off the lake. I see it in my head then. The boat.

"Head down to the dock," I say. "We'll take the boat across the lake and go straight to the state police."

"But the storm, Mom," Anna says. "You know what happened this afternoon."

I glance at Tim. How he's still alive is beyond me, but he's squirming. I know that in only a matter of seconds he will be up and coming after us once more. That's how much evil fills his veins.

"Your mother's right, Anna," Tony says. "Lead the way, ladies, and let's get the hell out of here once and for all."

We head back in the house. I grab the key to the boat on the end table. We make our way out the kitchen door and down onto the dock. We remove the cover from the boat, untie the lines, and hop in.

"I got this, Rose," Anna insists.

Tony gives me a look.

"Wait till you see her pilot this boat," I say.

She slips the key into the ignition, powers her up, and then turns on the running board lights.

"Hang on," she says, pushing the throttle forward, while depressing the button that lowers the engine screw further into the water. "Screw the rules, we're gonna give it all she's got now."

We pull away from the dock and head for the first buoy. I feel the wind and the cold rain slap my face. Somehow, it is the most wonderful feeling in the world. Are we really home free? It sure seems that way. Just to make sure, I turn around to eye the old Moore house. An old haunted house in the woods. A house that smells of death. I'm about to turn back around and face the white capped lake, when I see a second boat gaining on us.

The man standing in the cockpit is Tim Ferguson.

CHAPTER 52

TONY NOTICES THE expression on my face, even in the dark and the rain.

"What the hell is wrong?" he says.

"Anna!" I shout, above the wind and the heavy rain. "Whatever you do, don't stop!"

"What's happening?!" she says.

The boat is bumping and smacking against the heavy swells. I can feel the pounding in my knees and stomach. If Tony and I don't hold onto the center console windshield, we'd go down on our backs. Another glance over my shoulder reveals Tim's boat coming up on us fast. It's a bigger boat, its steering column located in the front. How he's managing to pilot his boat with his bloody injuries is a miracle. Or maybe, aside from the gouging out of his eye, his injuries are only superficial. Whatever the case, he's gaining on us fast.

Something else is happening at the same time. My feet are soaking. When the lightning bursts, I look down and see that there must be three inches of water already collected on the boat's floor. More water than would come from the rain.

Reaching around Anna, I tap Tony on the shoulder, point to the floor.

"We're taking on water," I say.

He glances at the floor, turns, and gazes at the oncoming boat.

"That's him, isn't it," he says like a question he already knows the answer to.

"No choice but to outrun him," I shout. Then, "Anna, can you make this thing go any faster?"

She shakes her head.

"It's going full throttle now," she says.

"He must have sabotaged the boat," I say. "It's the only explanation. He must have punched holes in the hull, the son of a bitch."

I turn to get a look at Tim again. He's only a few feet from our stern. A pair of oars are set against the port side of the boat. Emergency propulsion should the engine give out. I grab one oar, hand it to Tony. I take the other oar in both my hands. When Tim rams our bow, I nearly fall. If she isn't holding on to the wheel, Anna would fall too. Lightning strikes nearby, and I can make out Tim's blood-soaked beard and missing eye. I see the holes and gashes I cut into his face. His many wounds aren't slowing him down. He has the power of the devil in his soul.

"Jesus, he's trying to sink us!" Tony shouts.

"Next time he rams us," I say, "try and stick him with the oars. It's our only chance."

"Wait for it," Tony yells. "Here comes the bastard."

The bow of Tim's boat rams us again. That's when we both thrust the oars out and nail Tim in the chest. He flies onto his back, his boat making a hard-right turn and nearly capsizing. I shoot Tony a grin.

But then Tim stands tall. He rights the boat and begins gaining on us once more.

"Here he comes again," I say.

Our boat begins to slow down.

"What's happening, Anna?" I shout, over my shoulder.

"I don't know," she says. "I've got the throttle going full speed, but it's not getting the gas."

"Let me check," Tony says.

He goes to the stern, drops to his knees, and checks the black rubber hose that connects the red plastic gas tank to the outboard motor. Since it's nearly impossible to see in the dark and only the stern lamp offering any light whatsoever, he uses his fingers to feel the hose.

He stands, shaking his head.

"It's been cut," he says. "Unless somebody has some electrical tape on them, we're screwed."

Tim's boat is coming up on us fast. He rams us. Anna falls back onto the water-soaked floor and I do the same. Tony doesn't fall onto the floor. He goes over the side.

I bound back up.

"Anna, turn the boat around," I insist.

Tim is pulling up to our starboard side. I thrust the oar against his chest. I connect once and he falls back. But when he gets back up, he grabs hold of the oar and yanks it out of my hand.

"Help!" Tony screams while treading water. "Help me!"

The boat is now free floating. Anna is offering Tony her hand. He takes hold of it. I grab the second oar as Tim attempts to jump from his boat to ours. But that's not going to happen under my watch.

"Die, you son of a bitch!" I scream, sticking him in the face with the oar.

He screams and falls back. Dropping the oar, I assist Anna with pulling Tony back out of the water and into the boat. He's breathing heavily.

"Look," he says in between breaths, "I'll hold the hose together. You give it the gas, Anna. Before he gets up and comes after us again. But you gotta do it now—or all is lost."

Anna has one hand on the wheel, the other on the throttle. I'm standing beside her, while I'm hanging on with both hands to the center console windshield. She shoves the throttle all the way forward and we take off like a rocket. The boat's hull is colliding with the swells and the rain and the wind is once again slapping me in the face. Glancing over my shoulder, I see that Tony is desperately clinging with both hands to the hose. When more lightning flashes, I can see that we're actually putting some distance between us and Tim. If we can keep this up, he'll have no choice but to back off, and turn back for home, or else face the wrath of the Paradox county sheriff and the state police.

For the first time since we started out, I can make out the vague evidence of lamp lighting on the opposite side of the lake. It means that soon we'll be coming up on the town. It means we're almost home free. It means we're going to live. Releasing one hand from the windshield, I run it up and down my daughter's back. She shoots me a smile. She's clearly in control of her boat. She's grown up so much over the past week, it's incredible. Perhaps, in some small way, some real good has come out of this tragedy. It's forced Anna to grow up and it's forced me to let her go. I can't protect her for the rest of her life. She needs to learn to protect herself, and that's exactly what's happened at Paradox Lake.

Then, the boat begins to slow again.

Oh God no . . .

Hang in there, Rosie, you're doing fine.

Don't give up, Rose.

I'm trying. We're all trying. But our luck is running out.

Don't say that. You can beat this son of a bitch, Rose.

Thanks, Charlie. But we've tried everything.

Tony is a good man, Rosie. A creative dude. I can bet he comes up with something.

Jesus, let's hope so.

The swells are now pounding us instead of the other way around. I turn. Tim is once more gaining on us. The bow of his big boat is coming at us at full speed. If he smashes into us, he'll kill us all. I shift my focus to Tony. He's moving his hands up and down the black rubber line.

"The line is gone," Tony says, gazing up at me with a rain-soaked face.

Even in the darkness, I can see that gas is spurting out of the hose. Tim must have cut it in half a dozen places. He must have known we'd eventually have no choice but to escape by boat. He must have planned it this way. He wanted us to make it out onto the water where he could finish us off, then toss our bodies into Paradox Lake.

"It's not getting the gas," Anna barks.

Then, the boat stalls altogether.

"It just won't go," she cries, thrusting the throttle back and forth.

Tim is coming up on us fast.

"Tony!" I scream, "What the hell do we do now?!"

He stands, his clothing soaked and sticking to his muscular body. He's digging into his bush jacket pockets. He turns to me, looks me in the eyes. The look is a strange one because it contains both hope and desperation at the same time.

"I have an idea," he says. "But you're going to have to help me, Rose."

I don't hesitate to make my way to him in the stern. Pulling a blue kerchief from his back pocket, he then unscrews the cap to which the rubber hose is attached. He stuffs the kerchief inside the hole.

I gaze at Tim's boat. It can't be thirty feet away from us and gaining.

"Mama, do something!" Anna cries, her face a mask of panic and fright.

"We are, baby," I insist. "We're trying like hell."

"Okay, Rose," Tony says. "When I give you the word, we heave this gas tank overboard and into Tim's boat. You understand?"

For the first time, I see precisely what he's going for here. He's talking about turning the gas tank into a bomb—an oversized Molotov cocktail.

One eye on the incoming boat, the other on him. "You realize we could all be blown to bits, Tone?"

He digs out his Bic lighter, thumbs a flame, touches it to the kerchief. The now gas-soaked rag immediately lights up.

"Any better ideas, Rose?"

The boat coming closer, Tim's mangled but determined face lighting up in a brand new flash of lightning.

"Anna!" I shout over my shoulder. "Drop down onto your stomach."

"But, Mama . . ."

"Do it now!"

Eyes back on Tony.

"Wait for my command," he insists.

"Won't we still get rammed by his boat?"

"Chance we gotta take."

Tim's boat is now maybe fifteen feet away.

"Ready, Rose?"

"Ready, Tone."

We both pick up our separate ends of the half-full gas tank. The boat's bow is just about to ram us.

"Heave!" Tony shouts.

Together, we toss the gas tank into Tim's boat. Then comes the explosion and . . .

CHAPTER 53

I FEEL THE rain pelting my face and my body submerged in the cool lake water that's collected in the boat. I spring up fast.

"Anna," I say.

"I'm right here," she says, trying to stand. "I'm okay."

"Tony!"

He's on his knees, only inches from where the bow of Tim's boat rammed our stern, smashing it to bits so that we're now taking on water, big-time. I shake the cobwebs from my brain only to notice that Tony is glowing in firelight. That's when my eyes refocus onto Tim's boat. It's entirely engulfed in flames. Tim is standing in the middle of it, despite the rain, his body is going up like a piece of dry kindling. Entirely engulfed in red/orange flame, he's screaming a high-pitched cry that makes my stomach go tight and my mouth go dry. He's spinning around and around on the balls of his feet, like a top. He's hugging himself and trying to pat himself down when there's an entire lake at his disposal. Finally, he falls overboard and all I can make out is a loud hiss and a groan. His body sinks under the choppy surface. Just like that, the monster is gone.

For what seems like forever, all three of us just stare at the burning boat. Until Tony turns to me.

"So *that* just happened," he says while exhaling a long breath.

"He was a real bad man, Mom," Anna says.

"I sure know how to pick 'em," I say. Then, turning to Tony and placing my hand on his wet thigh, "That's supposed to be a joke."

He looks at me, reaches out and takes me in his arms. He squeezes until I can't breathe. That's when Anna crawls over to us and joins in on the group hug. We're sinking on Paradox Lake, but I never want to let go.

*   *   *

Tim's boat doesn't remain engulfed in flame for all that long what with the rain and the wind. But the light that's coming from the fire must be enough to alert the Paradox Lake authorities. Soon we can make out the sound of rotor blades cutting through the air along with a bright sodium search light that strafes the choppy lake surface. All three of us start waving our hands in the air as if on cue. It doesn't take the helicopter long before it's hovering over us and a basket is being dropped by a cable.

Anna goes first, of course, then me, then Tony. We sit inside the helicopter, buckled into our seats, the helmeted rescue team providing us with blankets. They don't ask us what happened out there on Paradox Lake nor who owned the boat that crashed into us. They don't ask us what happened in the Paradox forest or what went on in the basements of the two old houses. They don't ask us about the murdered priest. Their job is to save us. The many questions will come later.

I'm sitting in the middle, in between my daughter, and my boyfriend. I take hold of their hands and squeeze them as tightly as I can.

You did good, Rosie. Proud of you.

Thanks, Allison. I know you were there for me, for us, the entire way.

You're a survivor, Rose. The best wife and mother ever. I love you always.

I love you too, Charlie. The both of you.

We speed over the lake, faster than a speeding bullet, or so it seems, the dark sky lighting up in bursts of brilliant electric light. It's a wonderful sight to witness through my tears.

EPILOGUE

Three Months Later

THE ALBANY ART Gallery is kind enough to grant me a one person show. I'm not sure if this has anything to do with the quality of my new sculptures, or if it has everything to do with my new-found fame as the woman who, along with her daughter and fiancé, survived a harrowing ordeal on Paradox Lake. In any case, it's quite the affair with the local press showing up and even a few members of the national media. After all, who doesn't love a "We survived a psycho madman!" story? In this case, it was two psycho madmen, one of whom convinced himself he was the Big Bad Wolf from out of *Little Red Riding Hood*.

The show is one I'm especially proud of. Believing that simplicity is the best policy when it comes to art show titles, I'm calling it "Paradox Lake." Minimal, grounded geographically speaking, but thought provoking at the same time.

The busts are the best I've produced in my career thus far, but then I just might be slightly biased about that. Okay, very biased. The sculpted heads that make up the first portion of the show are, in no specific order, Charlie, Allison, and Anna. There's also one of myself—I guess you could call it a self-portrait—completing my original family. The faces are young, vibrant, and full of hope. Anna's face is based on the very first picture taken of her in the hospital maternity ward, moments after she was born without her father or big sister in attendance.

The gallery space that Part One takes place in is more like a big dark box. Everyone is asked to gather inside it and, at the appointed time, slides of my family, from the moment Charlie and I came together, are superimposed over their busts and against all four walls and even the ceiling. The sound that's pumped in through super-clear Boss speakers is part voice recordings, part music that we loved, part times of sadness, like a small recording of a distraught Charlie giving Allison's eulogy at her funeral. The presentation is intended as a visual feast for the senses, even if it does end on a sad, if not dramatic, note.

Part Two of the show is of Anna, myself, and Tony. It's the same deal. A second space has been prepared, and once Part One is over, the patrons are asked to gather into this second box. Again, a slide show that represents our lives in the form of slides, short videos, music, and voice-overs accompany the busts. It begins with mementoes of our lives after the deaths of Charlie and Allison, and around the time we met Tony, and continues all the way up until the day Anna and I left for Paradox Lake.

Part Three is the most shocking and, from what the critics have written thus far about the installation, has been the most controversial. The busts are not only of Anna, me, and Tony. They are also of Ed and Tim, not only as they looked alive, but as they appeared in death. In the case of the latter, I created a black, fire-consumed skull. Also added to the collection of busts is Sarah Anne Moore, both as she appeared when her seventh-grade yearbook photo was taken—the one that appeared in the newspaper back when she was abducted—and also her death face, which I was able to receive in photographic form from an old reporter who wrote about the case thirty years ago.

Also included is a bust of Sarah's mom, who, it turns out, was raped and strangled by a young Tim Ferguson, her body then dumped in the lake. Since the police department is still prohibited from sharing records of the case, the old reporter—who will go unnamed here now that he's enjoying a peaceful retirement in Florida—has provided a plethora of information. It was he who researched Tim's actions, and although there wasn't sufficient enough evidence for the Essex County DA to pin anything on Tim Ferguson at the time of Mrs. Moore's demise in 1991, the reporter knew better. When a diary was dug up at Tim's apartment above the general store after his death, which includes not only a confession of the rape and subsequent murder, but also locks of Mrs. Moore's hair and pubic hair, DNA tests were conducted and it was case closed for the county sheriff and the state police who were called in to investigate the entire ordeal posthumously.

The last two busts are the most shocking since they are reproductions not only of Father O'Connor when he was alive and preaching at the Roman Catholic Church in Paradox, but also the severed and skinned head that Tim or Ed placed on my sculpture platform. It is such a shockingly realistic reproduction that some visitors have gotten visibly ill and had no choice but to exit the space.

My humblest apologies if you are one of them.

The photos, video, Super-8 film, music, newspaper clippings, and music that are projected inside Space Three begin when Sarah was abducted in 1986 and continue right up until the present day, including crime scene photos that were made public of the Moore house after Theodore "Ed" Peasley skinned Father O'Connor's body as if it were a freshly killed deer. My gut instinct served me correctly when I surmised that the skins hanging on the rack behind Ed's house were not only those of the wild animals that lived in the Paradox forest—they also belonged to human beings, some of them men, women, and children who had gone missing ages ago and who were held captive in the monster's basement.

According to the old reporter, Ed and Tim's partnership probably worked something like this. Tim would spot a likely victim and manage to abduct him or her, either by sheer force, or as in mine and Anna's case, by seducing them with his charm. Once a trust was accomplished, Ed would be called in to do the dirty work, which Tim would observe with relish since, from a psychological point of view, it provided him with a perverse sexual pleasure. And that's putting it pretty mildly.

So what now?

Anna has been seeing a psychotherapist for PTSD, but she's getting along fine, or so it seems. Her physical injuries turned out to be nothing serious, although she did receive a series of tetanus shots due to Ed's filthy mouth, teeth, and fingernails. Her grades are good, and after a period of sleepless nights due to recurring nightmares about drowning and being chased in a dark forest, she's back to her old, sarcastic self. You know how resilient kids can be—how they can rebound so quickly, God bless them. She's even getting along great with Nicole and, get this, attending the eighth-grade Snow Ball with Jake Walls. I should note that he is still a head shorter than she is.

Tony is still Tony and I love him for it. Since his bush jacket pretty much got wrecked during that night when he saved our lives in Paradox, I gladly bought him a new one. He's planning a research trip to North Africa in order to, in his words, "break it in properly." In the meantime, he's been offered a small book deal by a true crime imprint that was just begging for the rights to our story.

In a move entirely unlike the Tony I've known and loved all these years—despite my taking that love for granted more recently—he kindly asked that Anna and I coauthor it with him.

"We can write it as a family," he said, not without a proud smile.

But we gladly declined since, even though we are two of the main characters, he's the real writer of the family and therefore the book is entirely his. We are to be married next September in a small ceremony that's to take place on a beach near Hyannis Port in Cape Cod. I can only hope the weather is good.

Charlie and Allison continue to talk to me and gift me with their advice. They are like my invisible family, but at the same time, so very real and so very much in my head at all times. I love them like no other and I know they will wait for me when it's my time to see them again in another place far away from here. And yes, they are very happy about my impending marriage to Tony. In Allison's words, "You just needed to figure out how much you really loved him, Rosie. Nothing wrong with that."

As for me, a strange thing happened to me just the other day. I received a package in the mail marked "Personal and Confidential." I opened the bubble-wrapped padded package having no clue what it could possibly be or who it was from, since there was no return address printed on the envelope. When I discovered that it was the rare edition of *Little Red Riding Hood*, and that it must have been rescued from the fireplace in the Moore house, I was more than a little taken aback. In fact, a cold chill ran down my spine.

Who could have sent this to me? Was it the local sheriff? Was it the new renters of the place now that it had been cleaned up of its blood, and once more listed on the Airbnb site? But digging further into the envelope, I discovered a short, handwritten note. Unfolding the note, I read,

Dear Rose,

I found this in the fireplace at the house you rented from me and my brother in Paradox some months back. It pains me to know you and your daughter will never come back here. It pains me more to know it's entirely my brother's fault. My brother and his partner, Ed, that is. When Tim and I purchased the Moore house almost 20 years ago now, I never could have dreamed something so terrible could happen there. Something so evil. I hope you believe me when I tell you I had no idea just who and what my brother really was. I spent decades feeling horrible about what happened to Sarah Anne, and when my brother and I purchased the house together, I was under the impression we could once more bring happiness to the precious little house on the lake. My God, how wrong I was. I'm not a psychologist, but I'd say he was waiting for the day Sarah and her mom would return. When you showed up, he and Ed got their wish. That said, I just wanted to apologize on behalf of my late brother, and I pray that one day, you will find enough forgiveness in your hearts for us and for Paradox Lake. I also pray that you and Anna will pay a visit—the cheese and macaroni will be on me.

Peace and love,
Kathy Ferguson

I read the note again and again, and the words never change. My stomach cramps and my mind recalls the events of that horrible night. They replay in my brain at lightning speed, like a video being fast-forwarded. From the moment Tim attacked me after drugging me in his pickup truck on the gravel road that led to the

Moore house, to the moment he burned up in his boat. That he and Ed were evil creatures, there is no doubt. That my heart aches for Kathy, there is also no doubt.

But I will never again visit Paradox Lake. Not in this life anyway. My guess is that Anna will never go back there either. We've put the entire ordeal behind us. Rather, we're trying to put it behind us. But I'd be a fool to think we're ever going to forget about it. It will forever occupy space in our heads. But life goes on, even when you're gone. Charlie and Allison are evidence of that. So is Sarah Anne Moore.

There comes an end to all things, or so they say. In this case, in the very end, it all comes down to good versus evil. One can either dive headfirst into the evil, or one can fight on the side of the good. What would become of us if not for the good?

I now surround myself with the good. My family is my rock, my foundation. They are my heart and my soul. I've sculpted them from the most delicate clay. They are all I have left in the world, but they are everything. All of them, alive or departed. They are forever.

I am a sculptor and I am a survivor, but I will be haunted by ghosts until the day I die.

PUBLISHER'S NOTE

We hope that you have enjoyed Vincent Zandri's *Paradox Lake*. As you know from the front pages of this book, Zandri has written over forty novels and novellas, won many awards, and frequently appears on best-seller lists. So, if you have not read his fiction, where to start?

We suggest *The Girl Who Wasn't There*, one of his more recent thrillers. Here the forces swirl around a missing young girl—good forces and extremely evil forces. Again, as in *Paradox Lake*, Zandri has captured the style and the mood and the desperation of another young girl, eleven-year-old Chloe in *The Girl Who Wasn't There* along the shores of beautiful Lake Placid in the midst of the Adirondack Mountains.

After that there are many more chilling-to-the-bone thrillers to read. They're listed up front in this novel just before the title page. You can also check them out on the author's website:

www.vinzandri.com

Warning: you may not be able to put them down and may lose sleep!

Oceanview Publishing